FLINTLOCK

A TIME FOR VULTURES

FLINTLOCK

A TIME FOR VULTURES

William W. Johnstone
with J. A. Johnstone

PINNACLE BOOKS
Kensington Publishing Corp.
www.kensingtonbooks.com

PINNACLE BOOKS are published by

Kensington Publishing Corp.
119 West 40th Street
New York, NY 10018

PUBLISHER'S NOTE
Following the death of William W. Johnstone, the Johnstone family is
working with a carefully selected writer to organize and complete Mr.
Johnstone's outlines and many unfinished manuscripts to create additional
novels in all of his series like The Last Gunfighter, Mountain Man, and
Eagles, among others. This novel was inspired by Mr. Johnstone's superb
storytelling.

All Kensington titles, imprints, and distributed lines are available at special quantity discounts for bulk purchases for sales promotions, premiums,
fund-raising, educational, or institutional use. Special book excerpts or
customized printings can also be created to fit specific needs. For details,
write or phone the office of the Kensington sales manager: Kensington
Publishing Corp., 119 West 40th Street, New York, NY 10018, attn: Sales
Department; phone 1-800-221-2647.

PINNACLE BOOKS, the Pinnacle logo, and the WWJ steer head logo are
Reg. U.S. Pat. & TM Off.

ISBN-13: 978-0-7860-3571-7
ISBN-10: 0-7860-3571-4

First printing: September 2016

10 9 8 7 6 5 4 3 2 1

Printed in the United States of America

First electronic edition: September 2016

ISBN-13: 978-0-7860-3572-4
ISBN-10: 0-7860-3572-2

CHAPTER ONE

"I don't like it, Sam," O'Hara said, his black eyes troubled. "Those women could be setting us up. Their wagon wheel looks just fine from here."

Sam Flintlock shook his head. "You know what I always tell folks about you, O'Hara?"

"No. What do you always tell folks about me?"

"That you let your Indian side win through. I mean every time. If you were looking at them gals with a white man's eyes you'd see what I see . . . four comely young ladies who badly need our help."

Now there were those who said some pretty bad things about Sam Flintlock. They called him out for a ruthless bounty hunter, gunman, outlaw when it suited him, and a wild man who chose never to live within the sound of church bells. At that, his critics more or less had him pegged, but to his credit, Flintlock never betrayed a friend or turned his back on a crying child, an abused dog, or a maiden in distress. And when the war talk was done and guns were drawn he never showed yellow.

Thus, when he saw four ladies and a dog crowded

around what looked to be a busted wagon wheel, he decided he must ride to their rescue like a knight in stained buckskins.

But his companion, the half-breed known only as O'Hara, prone to suspicion and mistrust of the doings of white people, drew rein on Sam's gallant instincts.

"Well, my Indian side is winning through again," O'Hara said. "It's telling me to stay away from those white women. Sam, it seems that when we interfere in the affairs of white folks we always end up in trouble." He stared hard at the wagon. "There's something wrong here. I have a strange feeling I can't pin down."

"You sound like the old lady who hears a rustle in every bush." Flintlock slid a beautiful Hawken from the boot under his left knee and settled the butt on his thigh. "This cannon always cuts a dash with the ladies and impresses the menfolk. Let's ride."

The four women gathered around the wagon wheel watched Flintlock and O'Hara ride toward them. They were young, not particularly pretty except by frontier standards, and looked travel-worn. Colorful boned corsets, laced and buckled, short skirts, and ankle boots revealed their profession, as did the hard planes of their faces. Devoid of powder and paint, exhausted by the rigors of the trail, the girls showed little interest in Flintlock and O'Hara as potential customers.

Flintlock touched his hat. "Can I be of assistance, ladies?"

A brunette with bold hazel eyes said, "Wheel's stuck, mister."

"I'll take a look," Flintlock said.

One time in Dallas he'd watched John Wesley

Hardin swing out of the saddle in one graceful motion and he hoped his dismount revealed the same panache. And it might have had not the large yellow dog decided to attack his ankle as soon as his foot touched the ground. The mutt clamped onto Flint-lock's booted ankle, shook its head, and growled as though it was killing a jackrabbit.

"Git the hell off me," Flintlock said, shaking his leg.

The little brunette grabbed the dog by the scruff of the neck and yelled, "Bruno! Leave the gent alone!"

But the animal seemed more determined than ever to bite through Flintlock's boot and maul his flesh. Bruno renewed his attack with much enthusiasm and considerable savagery.

All four women pounced on the dog and tried to drag the snarling, biting creature away while Flintlock continued to shake his leg and cuss up a storm. As the epic struggle with the belligerent Bruno became a cartwheeling, fur-flying free-for-all, O'Hara's voice cut through the racket of the melee.

"Sam! Riders!"

A moment later guns slammed and O'Hara reeled in the saddle. He snapped off a shot, bent over, and toppled onto the grass. His horse, its reins trailing, trotted away. Flintlock, dragging Bruno like a growl-ing ball and chain, stepped around the horse and looked toward the tree line. Four riders were charg-ing fast, firing as they came. Cursing himself for choosing fashion over common sense and leaving his Winchester in the boot, he threw the Hawken to his shoulder and triggered a shot. Boom! Through a cloud of gray smoke he watched a man throw up his hands, his revolver spinning away from him. The rider tumbled backwards off his horse and hit the ground hard, throwing up a cloud of dust. Flintlock dropped the Hawken and clawed for the Colt in his waistband.

Too late!

A big, bearded man drove his mount straight at Flintlock and the impact of horse and man sent Flintlock flying and convinced Bruno that he'd be a lot safer somewhere else.

Winded and sprawled on his back, Flintlock stayed where he was for a moment, then he sat up and looked around for his fallen Colt.

There! A few yards to his right.

He staggered to his feet and for his pains, the bearded man charged again. He swung his left foot from the stirrup and kicked Flintlock in the head, the boot heel crashing into his forehead. For a moment, it seemed that the world around him was exploding in blinding arcs of scarlet and yellow fire.

Flintlock's head tilted back and he caught a glimpse of the sky spinning wildly above him . . . and then his legs went out from under him and he saw nothing . . . nothing at all.

Sam Flintlock regained consciousness to a pounding headache and a sharp pricking in his throat. From far off, at the end of a long tunnel, he heard a woman's voice.

"What the hell are you doing, Buck?"

Buck Yarr stopped, his bowie knife poised. "Gonna cut that heathen thunderbird offen his throat, Biddy. Make me a tobaccy pouch, it will."

"Morg wants him alive," the woman said. "You know who he is?"

"Don't give a damn who he is," Yarr said.

"He's the outlaw Sam Flintlock," Biddy said. "Morg thinks maybe there's a price on his head, his head and the breed's."

Yarr said, "Morg didn't tell me that. I want the thunderbird. Now git the hell away from me lessen you aim to watch the cuttin'."

"I seen a cuttin' or two before and they didn't trouble me none," Biddy said. "One time down Forth Worth way I seen Doc Holliday cut a man, damn near gutted him. But Morg wants that Flintlock one alive."

"All I want is some skin, Biddy. He'll still be alive after I'm done."

"He'll be dead after you're done, Buck. Look, there's Morgan, ask him your own self," Biddy said.

Flintlock opened his eyes. He tried to move but his arms were tightly bound to one of the wagon wheels. A few feet away O'Hara, his bloody head bowed, was tied to another. Opposite Flintlock, a kneeling man in greasy buckskins held a wicked, broad-bladed knife, his mouth under a sweeping red mustache stretched in a grin. The man's hat—a tall, pearl gray topper, its high crown holed by a bullet—caught Flintlock's attention.

"Morg, the whore says I can't cut on this man," Yarr said. "What do you say?"

Morgan Davis was a tall, cadaverous man with black hair and penetrating black eyes. He affected the sober dress and measured speech of a country parson but the Colt in the shoulder holster under his left arm gave the lie to that image.

"Not now, Buck," Davis said. "I've heard of this ranny. His name is Sam Flintlock on account of the old smoke pole he carries and he makes his living as a bounty hunter and bank robber. There's some say he's real sudden on the draw-and-shoot and has killed a dozen men. Others say he's just plumb loco and talks to his dead kinfolk, but I ain't so sure about that. He looks like a mean one though, don't he?"

"He ain't so tough," Yarr said. "I want the big bird on his throat. Slice it offen him and make a pouch for myself."

"It will make a fine pouch, a crackerjack pouch, Buck," Davis said, patting the man on the shoulder. "But hold off on the cutting until we see if there's a price on his head. If he's wanted dead or alive, then he's all yours. But if the law wants him in one piece, then you can wait until after he's hung."

"Long wait." Yarr looked sulky.

Davis smiled. "Be of good cheer, Buck. There's a settlement close to Guadalupe Peak with a tough sheriff. We can take Flintlock and the breed there. If there's a dodger on them, once the lawman pays the reward I'm sure we can talk him into a quick hanging."

"What town? What sheriff?" Yarr said. "I steer clear of lawmen."

"Town's called Happyville and the sheriff's name is Barney Morrell," Davis said. "Me and Barney go back a ways, to the time me and him rode with the Taylor brothers and that hard crowd during their feud with the Suttons. Barney killed a couple men and then lit out for the New Mexico Territory ahead of a Sutton hanging posse. He married a gal by the name of Lorraine Day and for a spell prospered in the hardware business. But Barney never could settle down for long and he worked as a lawman in Fort Worth and Austin and then, the last I heard, became the sheriff of Happyville."

"He still there?" Yarr said.

"I haven't heard otherwise," Davis said.

"Then I guess I'll wait." Yarr slid his knife into its sheath. "But there's one thing I need to get straight, Morg."

"What's that?"

"I want to cut this man afore he's hung. Don't set right with me to go slicing a big bird offen a dead man's throat. It ain't proper."

Davis nodded. "I'm sure that can be arranged, Buck. Easy thing to cut a man before he gets hung."

"What about the sheriff? What's his name?"

"I'll take care of Barney. Kick back a share of the reward money and he'll cooperate."

Buck Yarr grinned, slapped off Flintlock's hat, grabbed him by the hair, and shook him. "Hear that, musket man? You'll get your throat cut afore a noose is tightened around it. I wonder how that will feel? Bad painful, I think. Real bad painful."

Flintlock's wrists were knotted to the wagon wheel at either side of his head. But to his joy his legs were untied. He measured the distance between the toe of his right boot and Buck Yarr's chin. Perfect! Gritting his teeth, he powered his leg upward, arching his back to increase the force of the kick.

The result was all he hoped it would be.

With a sickening thud, like a rifle butt hitting a log, the toe of his boot hit Yarr just under his chin. The man's head snapped back, his mouth spurting strings of blood and saliva. Kneeling on one knee and off balance, he fell heavily onto his right side.

"Never trust a wolf until it's been skun, idiot," Flint-lock said, staring at the groaning man with merciless eyes.

Yarr was hurting but he wasn't done.

Big and strong and snarling like a wounded animal, he got to his feet and charged Flintlock, his knife raised for a downward, killing thrust.

"Buck, no!" Davis yelled.

The enraged man ignored him, but the knife blow never came. Somewhere in Yarr's primitive, reptilian brain he decided that a stabbing was a much too merciful death. His eyes glittering, he switched his attention to the thunderbird on Flintlock's throat. Giggling, he concentrated on his task. The point of his knife pierced skin and drew a thin rivulet of blood and then slowly, carefully, like an eager bride cutting her wedding cake, he began to . . . saw.

"Buck, get the hell away from him!" Davis yelled.

Yarr ignored the man, intent on cutting out the skin of Flintlock's throat.

Blam!

Yarr's head exploded as Davis's bullet entered the man's right temple and exited an inch above his left ear, blowing out a gory fountain of brain and bone. For long moments Yarr remained where he was, per-fectly still, knife in hand, face expressionless. Then slowly . . . slowly . . . he opened his mouth wide, fell back, and lay still.

Davis kicked Flintlock hard in the ribs. "Now see what you done? You made me kill one of my boys and you already shot another." Davis shoved the hot muzzle of his Colt between Flintlock's eyes. "Mister, count yourself a lucky man. At the moment you're worth more to me than Buck. Well, maybe. If Barney Morrell tells me he's got no paper on you, I'll cut the bird off your throat myself."

Pain spiking at his ribs, Flintlock said, "Hell, you got our horses and traps. That's enough for any damned two-bit thief like you."

Davis shook his head. "No it ain't, not for me." He stared at Flintlock. "You got a big reputation, feller, but right now you sure as hell don't stack up to much."

"A lot of men have thought that," Flintlock said. "I killed most of them."

The man thumbed his chest. "Well, I ain't so easy to kill, feller. Name's Morgan Davis. That mean anything to you?"

"Seems to me I heard tell of a pimp by that name," Flintlock said. "They say he has a reputation for beating up on whores."

Davis smiled. "You're a funny man, Flintlock, a real knee-slapper, but there's something you should know." The man leaned closer and his voice dropped to a whisper. His breath smelled like rotten meat. "I was spawned in the lowest regions of hell and I've lived in a bottomless pit of depravity and violence since. Don't ever say something is funny again or I'll cut your tongue out."

Flintlock saw only hate, malevolence, and loathing in Davis's eyes, as though they were stricken with a foul disease. The pimp was a man to be reckoned with and Flintlock wisely kept his mouth shut.

After a final kick at Flintlock's unprotected ribs,

Davis stepped away. He stopped at O'Hara, got down on one knee, and buried his fingers in the breed's bloody hair. He jerked up O'Hara's head and stared into his face. "Hey Flintlock, your breed friend is dead."

Davis let O'Hara's head go and it lolled lifelessly onto O'Hara's chest. Sam Flintlock felt a devastating sense of loss . . . and then a spike of white-hot anger.

No matter what it took, how long it took, even with his last breath and final ounce of strength, he would kill Morgan Davis.

CHAPTER TWO

The man named O'Hara opened his eyes to darkness.

For a moment he thought his soul had traveled southwest to that cold, misty limbo where in the time after time he would become part of the spirit world. But as his eyes adjusted to the gloom, he saw the sky and the stars—the same sky, the same stars he had known in the physical realm. Was he alive or dead?

Then came pain . . . a pounding drumbeat in his head. There is no suffering after death, and in that moment of realization, O'Hara knew he remained in the land of the living.

Reluctant to rise, he stayed on his back, his eyes tight shut against the tom-tom beat of the pain in his head. He would lie where he was and sleep for a day, a week, whatever it took to restore him to health and strength . . . unless his ancestors came to take him away.

What was that?

He heard it again, a soft patter on the ground like the sound of falling leaves. The noise grew louder, more insistent, but O'Hara already knew what it was, the timid start of what would soon become an aggressive downpour. He stayed where he was, determined to sleep his pain away. But the rain fell harder and to the northwest thunder echoed among the canyons of the Guadalupe Mountains.

He was indignant.

What right had rain to interrupt a man's sleep? His head hurt even worse, an incessant thumping. Well, he'd soon put an end to this. Someone somewhere had to be responsible for such an outrage.

O'Hara rose to his feet and promptly fell down again. The rain-lashed darkness cartwheeled around him and the pounding in his head made him feel sick. It was only then that he noticed the rain running from his head onto his white shirt was the color of red rust. And he discovered why he'd fallen. He shared the noose looped around his ankles with a man lying beside him. Rivulets of rain streamed across the man's gray face, a dead white man with open, staring eyes, his mouth wide in a silent scream.

O'Hara stared at the man and then punched his beefy arm. "Are you to blame for this rain? Speak up now and state your intentions."

The dead man made no answer.

O'Hara kicked off the loop, stood, and dragged the body to its feet. "Answer me!" he yelled. "Why did you make the rain? Make it go away so I can sleep."

With unseeing staring eyes and a screaming mouth, the dead man made no answer. Lightning seared across the sky, shimmering on the cadaver's face, and thunder crashed.

In that hell-firing moment, as the blazing heavens conspired to destroy him, O'Hara realized what he had become . . . a raving madman.

O'Hara let go of the dead man and dropped to his hands and knees as the storm raged around him. He sank to the ground and plunged headlong into a bottomless pit.

CHAPTER THREE

O'Hara woke to a dreary dawn. The thunderstorm had passed, but the sky was a sullen iron gray as far as the eye could see. The sounds of the nighttime, the crash of thunder, and the rattle of the rain were gone, replaced by a solemn silence.

Slowly, warily, he rose to his feet. The left side of his head hurt and when he explored his scalp with his fingertips, they came away bloody. He looked around him at the ashen landscape. The vastness of the high plains stretched to the horizon in all directions, an enchanted vista, but one of aching loneliness.

"What am I doing here?" he said aloud. He knew that he was not in the spirit world, but in the all too real realm of the living.

The dead man at his feet, his mouth wide open, had been shot through the head at close range, the wound on his temple blackened by gunpowder.

O'Hara stared at the leaden sky, his face tense in thought. *Piece it together . . . piece it together. . . .*

It took a while, but his memories slid back in place, one by one, like the pieces of those jigsaw puzzles children loved so well. *Sam Flintlock . . . four women . . . the wagon . . . men riding out of the trees . . . a sledgehammer blow to the side of his head . . . and then waking up next to a corpse.*

But there was more . . . . a vague image of Sam Flintlock tied to a wagon wheel . . . and later, in the lightning-scorched night, his own mad dance of death with a screaming dead man.

The pain in his head and drizzling rain sharpened O'Hara's thinking.

Gradually his mind cleared of its fog and he recalled what had happened to him. He'd been shot, but the injury looked worse than it was, a grazing wound to the side of his head about two inches above his left ear. The looped rope at his feet told its own story. The outlaws had thought him dead, and he and the other man had been dragged from the wagon and left to rot on the plains.

But he wasn't dead and Flintlock needed him . . . if he was still alive.

A search of the dead man provided nothing of value. His guns and the knife he'd worn in the sheath on his belt were gone, as were his boots. In a drizzling rain, O'Hara scouted the ground and despite the downpour of the night, the drag tracks were still visible. The flattened long grass pointed due north and he followed the tracks.

Weak and dizzy from loss of blood, he stumbled and fell half a dozen times before the wagon came in sight. Next to it, a makeshift shelter with a canvas roof revealed a pair of blanket-wrapped forms too long and bulky to be women. He hoped they were men sleeping off last night's whiskey and slumbering soundly.

Sam Flintlock was still tied to the wagon wheel, his head lowered. He was hatless and his wet hair fell over his face.

To regain his strength, O'Hara lay flat on his belly deep in the long grass for a couple minutes and then got to his feet.

A woman in the wagon cried out in her sleep and he froze, hardly daring to breathe. The moment passed, the only sound the soft patter of the rain. He moved again and cast no shadow.

CHAPTER FOUR

The last thing O'Hara wanted was for Flintlock to wake up and cry out in either alarm or joy. He never could tell how a white man might react.

O'Hara kneeled beside Flintlock, grabbed him by the chin, and lifted his head. Flintlock's eyes flickered open and O'Hara held his forefinger to his lips.

"It's you," Flintlock whispered. "I must have died and gone to hell."

"Close. You're still in Texas."

Uncertain that he had the strength to untie the tight knots that bound Flintlock to the wheel, O'Hara said, "Barlow?"

"Right pocket."

"Hold still." O'Hara found the folding knife and in a matter of moments cut Flintlock free.

It was Flintlock's turn to indicate silence with a finger to the lips. He rubbed his raw wrists and on cat feet stepped to the far corner of the wagon, studying the two men asleep under the lean-to. He nodded to himself, smiled, and returned to O'Hara.

Under an ominous sky that darkened the morning,

he moved a few yards back and made a close survey of the wagon. After a while, he broke into a wide grin and rubbed his swollen hands together. "O'Hara, I've pulled off some good jokes in my time, but this is gonna be great."

The conveyance was a converted farm wagon with a narrow wheelbase. The upper structure was made of slatted timber boards and had been built high to accommodate the tiered bunks inside. The roof was V-shaped, covered in wood shingles, and as a result the wagon was top heavy, suited more to dirt roads than open country.

Flintlock, a man of medium height but stocky and big in the arms and shoulders, put his hands on the side of the wagon. His boots digging into the rain-softened ground for traction, he pushed with all his considerable strength.

The wagon moved, tilted, and teetered on two wheels for tense moments and then slowly . . . slowly . . . overbalanced and crashed to the ground. From inside, shrill female shrieks shattered the silence of the morning. Pinned under the wreck, men cursed in anger.

Flintlock stepped to the flattened lean-to. Just in time, he dragged out a black cartridge belt wrapped around a holstered Colt as a short, stocky man scrambled from under the tarp, rage on his face and a gun in his hand. He threw a vile curse at Flintlock and fired . . . but he hurried the shot and missed.

Flintlock didn't. Drawing fast from the black holster, he fired. His bullet hit the man in the chest at the V of his open undershirt, a killing wound that felled the shooter like a puppet that just had its strings cut.

The tarp bulged as the man under it crawled around like a blind mole in a tunnel.

Flintlock drew a bead but lowered the hammer as the trapped man yelled, "Don't shoot! For God's sake, can't you see I'm done here?"

"Git out from under there or I'll perforate you," Flintlock said.

The tarp moved again and Morgan Davis wormed out from under the canvas on his hands and knees.

"On your feet," Flintlock said over the barrage of outraged yells and cusses from the women trapped in the wagon.

Davis, looking mean, stood up. "Damn you, Flintlock. I should have plugged you." He glanced at the dead man. "You done fer good ol' Poke Murray."

"Yeah," Flintlock said. "He'll be sadly missed by all who knew and loved him. Now give me an excuse to kill you, Davis."

Ignoring that, the pimp looked at the overturned wagon and said, "You did that?"

"I surely did," Flintlock said, grinning. "At the time it seemed the right thing to do. Can you find it in your heart to forgive me?"

"The damned wagon fell on its door. Them women are trapped inside." Pushing that dire fact to the back of his mind, Davis looked at Flintlock and said, "Well, you got the drop on me. State your intentions but keep in mind that I saved your neck."

Flintlock nodded. "Literally."

"Huh?" Davis said.

"I made another good joke, but you didn't get it."

Davis nodded in the direction of the wagon. "That was a joke?"

"Yep. One of my better ones."

"All right, Flintlock, you've had your laughs. Now what?"

"I haven't made up my mind yet, Morg. Probably I'll just shoot you for the lowdown, dirty dog you are." He smiled. "We'll see."

O'Hara said, "Sam, we have to get those women out of there."

From inside the wagon a woman yelled, "Damn right you do, you rotten sons of bitches. We can't move in here and Biddy's got her foot in my face."

"We'll get you out," Flintlock said. "Once I figure how."

"This is Biddy. Are you Flintlock?"

"Sure am, lady."

"Then let Morg figure it out. He's a lot smarter than you are. Morg, make it fast. We're dying in here."

Nettled, Flintlock said, "You heard the lady, Davis. Figure it out."

The man, thin and ashen as a corpse, looked at Flintlock, shifted his gaze to the wagon and said, "It's too heavy for a straight lift."

"I may be stupid, but even I can see that," Flintlock said, still irritated. "We need the horses."

It took an hour of cussin' and discussin' and many false tries before the ropes held and Flintlock and the two other men, all mounted, finally righted the wagon and freed its bedraggled occupants.

The four women staggered around working kinks out of their backs and other places. Biddy sported a new black eye, the result of being hit by someone's head when the wagon fell. Hands on hips, the incensed ladies surrounded Flintlock and aired out their lungs, turning the air blue with their cusses as they assailed him for a barbarian, a brute, a thug, and a low person.

He decided to beat a hasty retreat and backed away . . . but in doing so, momentarily took his eyes off Davis. It was a bad mistake, giving the man all the time he needed to sprint to his horse, climb into the saddle, and light out at a gallop.

O'Hara aimed a revolver at the fleeing man and thumbed off three fast shots, but as far as Flintlock could tell, none took effect. Davis's mount kicked up a dust cloud as it stretched into a flat-out run and he was soon out of revolver range.

But Flintlock's horse was close.

He sprinted for the animal and tripped over Biddy's extended foot, landing flat on his face with a heavy thud. Before he could collect himself and force his winded body to rise, the four women jumped on him. In a flurry of white petticoats, they pounded and kicked, scratched and bit, all the time yelling like enraged banshees. Almost invisible in the dust, Flintlock was getting the worst of the free-for-all. O'Hara ran to Flintlock's defense and tried to pull the savage females off him, but it was like trying to stop a catfight with his bare hands. Just like Flintlock, O'Hara was clawed and bitten. Biddy landed a fair left hook to his nose, drawing blood.

Finally, the superior strength of the two men prevailed and they fought off the women. Flintlock managed to stagger to his feet. Like four harpies at bay, the ladies formed a line in front of his horse and dared him to mount. By then, Morgan Davis was long gone and Flintlock didn't make the attempt.

Battered and bruised, he was irritated beyond measure. He stooped, picked up the fallen Colt, and said, "I've never shot a woman before, but there's a first time for everything."

"Yes," Biddy said, "gun us down like you did Poke. Then see if the Rangers don't catch up with you and hang you from the nearest tree. There's a law in Texas against killing helpless women, you know."

O'Hara wiped blood from his nose with the back of his hand. "She has a point, Sam. Maybe now is not such a good time to gun them."

Flintlock grimaced. "Thanks for the advice, O'Hara."

The breed shook his head. "But I have to hand it to you, Sam. You sure got a way with women."

Biddy spat and said, "He plans to shoot us all right, Injun. He's a born killer if ever I seen one. You heard my name, but I'll tell you anyway. I'm Biddy Sales." She placed her hand on the shoulder of the plump young blonde next to her. "This here is Lizzie Doulan, as innocent a flower as ever lived. Maybe you'd like to shoot her first, Flintlock." She moved to the next woman, a hard-eyed redhead. "Meet Jane Feehan, but let her say her prayers before you gun her. And this is Margie Tott." Biddy laid her hands on the shoulders of a petite, hazel-eyed brunette. "She sends every penny she earns to her poor old mother in the Emerald Isle."

Biddy then stepped in front of Flintlock, belligerent and brassy. Her head tilted back and a great deal of firm cleavage showed above her corset as she said, "All right, we're ready. Open fire with your murderous revolver and be damned to ye! Let me be the first one to die."

O'Hara said, a hint of a smile on his lips, "Seems like you've got a decision to make, Sam."

"Damn it, O'Hara. Keep your opinion to yourself." Flintlock waved his Colt. "Right, you gals into the wagon. Now!"

Biddy again put her hands on her hips, her eyes blazing. "Make us."

"I won't tell you again," Flintlock said. The thought that he was entering into yet another losing battle was starting to nag at him.

She stood her ground. "And I said 'make us.'"

"Yeah, make us," Lizzie Doulan said.

All four took up the chorus, flouncing their skirts. "Make us! Make us! Make us!"

At a loss, Flintlock stood helplessly, his useless Colt hanging by his side.

Suddenly, the breed let out a loud, piercing shriek that abruptly stopped the female cries. He had Flintlock's Barlow knife in his right fist, the blade open, and he launched into an unrestrained tribal dance, his voice raised in a wild chant. "*Yi-hi-hi-hi-hi . . . yi-hi-hi-hi-hi-hi-hi . . .*"

Saved by O'Hara, Flintlock caught on quickly. "Oh my God!"

Biddy was alarmed. "What's the hell is he doing?"

"O'Hara is half Mescalero Apache," Flintlock said, suitable awe in his voice. "That's his scalp dance."

Lizzie Doulan said, "Whose scalp does he want?"

"Yours," Flintlock said. "And Biddy's and everybody's."

O'Hara's dance pace increased and his chanting rose in volume as he waved the knife above his head.

His face, bloodstained from his swollen nose, bore an expression of unrestrained fury.

The four ladies were bold, but not all that brave. Screeching, they beat a hasty retreat to the wagon and piled inside. Then came a loud *snick!* as the door bolt slammed into place.

Flintlock grinned. "All right, O'Hara, you can stop playacting now."

The breed stopped, waved the knife in Flintlock's face, and said, "Who was playacting, white man?"

CHAPTER FIVE

While the woman were locked inside the wagon, Flintlock dragged away Poke Murray's body and laid it in the brush beside the bushwhacker he'd killed in the first exchange of fire. The Hawken's .50 caliber ball had blown a fist-sized hole in the man's chest and Flintlock figured he'd died instantly.

"Admiring your handiwork, Sammy?"

Flintlock followed the sound of the voice and saw wicked old Barnabas, the old mountain man who'd raised him from a child, perched among the topmost branches of a wild oak.

"This is an unpleasant surprise. I thought I was finally rid of you," Flintlock said."

"Boy, you won't get shot of me until you find your ma in the Arizony Territory and she tells you your rightful name," Barnabas said. "I know you're an idiot, Sam, but try to wrap your mind around this fact. You can't spend the rest of your life called fer a rifle."

"I'll find her. Don't you worry about that," Flintlock said, irritated. He pointed to an object in the old man's hand. "What the hell is that thing you're holding?"

Barnabas held up the object that glinted in the sun. "This is an old-timey helmet, boy. See, you put it on your head like this." He lowered the helmet onto his head. His voice sounding hollow, he added, "Then you lift the visor." It was shaped like the bow of an iron steamship. He raised it and said, "There, now I can see you just fine."

"What are you doing with that thing?" Flintlock said.

"Polishing it up for a feller."

"What feller?"

"Not that it's any of your business, Sammy, but I'll tell you anyway. This here hat belongs to Baron Boris Von Baggenheim. Back, oh, four hundred years ago, ol' Boris made a career of galloping around the countryside slaughtering peasants and dragging maidens back to his castle to have his way with them." Barnabas sighed. "Boris sure misses them good old days."

"And that's why he's in hell?" Flintlock said.

Barnabas said, "Yeah, that and something to do with burning some holy man or other. But what you say is true, boy." He nodded and the helmet visor clanged shut. He opened it again. "Boris's corner of hell is reserved for them as You-know-who calls naughty noblemen, including that little puke the Marquis de Sade. Spends all his time talking about his female conquests, like anybody cares." Barnabas lifted the helmet off his head. "Damn, this thing is heavy and hot. Of course, in hell it's red hot, but Boris doesn't seem to mind."

"Barnabas, why are you here?" Flintlock said.

The old mountain man looked over his shoulder and then his voice dropped to a confidential whisper.

"You-know-who has advice for you about them uppity females. He says you should tip the wagon over again and then set it on fire. Burn them four harridans alive and you'll be rid of them."

"Yeah, that's the kind of advice he would give. Tell him it's not going to happen."

Barnabas polished the helmet with his buckskin sleeve. "Well, Sam'l, he's smart and you're a dunderhead, but suit yourself. Now I got to go. Hey, you ever hear of a bird they call a kingfisher?"

"Can't say as I have," Flintlock said.

"You will," Barnabas said.

He vanished in a puff of smoke that smelled of brimstone. Only the sound of his cackle lingered and then it too was gone.

CHAPTER SIX

"The women are still in the wagon," O'Hara said. "What took you so long?"

"Barnabas," Flintlock said.

"What did he want?"

"To tell me to burn the women alive and that I was an idiot."

"Sounds like Barnabas. His spirit is every bit as villainous as he was."

"Seems like." Flintlock looped his rope together and tied it to the saddle. "You ever heard of a bird called a kingfisher?"

"That's a strange question."

"Have you?"

O'Hara nodded. "The Sioux and Cheyenne respect the kingfisher because it is a mighty hunter."

"What does it hunt? Fish?" Flintlock said.

"With a name like kingfisher, it doesn't hunt rabbits."

"Barnabas said the bird is going to figure in my future."

"The old man is a prophet," O'Hara said, "but you

can't trust him. His spirit wanders between heaven and hell."

Flintlock fingered the thunderbird tattoo across his throat. "You think it has something to do with this?"

"I don't know. You should've asked Barnabas."

After several hours of waiting, someone banged on the inside of the wagon door and Biddy yelled, "Hey, you, Flintlock. Has that crazy Indian calmed down yet?"

"Yeah, you can come out now, but don't make him mad. He's a mean cuss when he goes on the warpath."

The wagon door opened a crack and then wider. Biddy stuck her head outside, her eyes, round as coins, going to O'Hara.

"Yip-yip!" O'Hara said.

The door slammed shut again.

Flintlock stepped to the wagon. "Come on out. O'Hara was making a joke."

"He's loco," Biddy said.

"Yeah, he is, but right now he's harmless," Flintlock said. "Come out. I'll make sure he doesn't do you any harm."

Long moments passed and the door again opened and four timid women stepped outside, all eyes on O'Hara.

The breed smiled and said softly, "Yip."

Flintlock stopped the stampede for the door, assuring Biddy and the others that O'Hara was no longer interested in scalps. "But he's hungry and a hungry Injun is an angry Injun."

Margie Tott, the little brunette, tightened the laces

of her red leather corset, and said, "Ain't we heading for Happyville, bird man? We got business there."

"You locked yourselves in the wagon for most of the damned day and now it's too late," Flintlock said. "We'll head out tomorrow at first light."

O'Hara, playing his role of wild man to the hilt, thumbed his chest and said, "Me hungry. Me getting angry."

"You women get a fire started," Biddy said. "We'd best feed the crazy man before he scalps us all in our sleep."

Sam Flintlock slept soundly in his blankets as the moon rose and silvered the grass and trees. As fragile as a bride's veil, a mist hung close to the ground and from somewhere close an inquisitive owl questioned the night. Deer, stepping high on graceful hooves, came down to the creek to drink, their eyes pools of darkness.

Flintlock slept on . . . dreaming of birds that hunted tiny silver fish . . . but O'Hara, a restless man, patrolled the night. Rifle in hand, he glided like a ghost through the gloom, his eyes searching for . . . he knew not what. His sleep had been troubled and the luminous night seemed to hold a thousand dangers lurking in the shadows.

The kingfisher had wakened him, pecking at his eyes.

O'Hara had sat upright in fear, remembering what the Ojibwa said of the kingfisher, that it was a bird of ill omen . . . a bearer of bad news.

On soundless feet, O'Hara stepped close to Flintlock

and stared at the slumbering man. Flintlock slept as white men sleep, deeply and unaware, hearing nothing. Yet it was he Barnabas had warned about the coming of the kingfisher. O'Hara squatted, his rifle across his thighs, and stared hard into Flintlock's face with its sharp, hard planes, shaggy eyebrows, and great dragoon mustache. It was a strong face, but then Flintlock was a strong man, brave without cruelty, caring sometimes, harsh, unforgiving and uncompromising at others. He was a man a certain kind of woman admired and little children did not fear. Sometimes a lawman, oft times an outlaw, he rode hard trails across a pitiless land and did what was needed to survive. He was a man of his time and place, and lived his life according to its dictates.

Why then the terrible dream about the kingfisher bird? What had Flintlock to fear? O'Hara had no answer to that question.

But this much he knew . . . for good or evil, the time of the kingfisher was coming.

CHAPTER SEVEN

After a quick breakfast, Flintlock and the others took to the trail for Happyville. Biddy Sales was at the reins of the wagon. By mutual agreement, she and Flintlock planned to sell the horses, saddles, and traps of the three dead men and split the proceeds.

"At least we'll make a profit out of this trip, huh?" Flintlock said to O'Hara as they rode ahead of the wagon across rolling grassland. But the breed, still disturbed by his dream about the kingfisher, made no comment.

"Hell, what's bothering you?" Flintlock said, his eyes on O'Hara's sour face.

"Forget selling the horses, Sam." The black hair that fell over O'Hara's shoulders was tangled and uncombed, unusual for the breed, who usually took great pains with his appearance. "We should leave the women and head for the Arizona Territory like we intended."

Flintlock glanced over his shoulder to make sure the swaying, jolting wagon was keeping up and then said, "All I want is one good meal and a soft bed to lie in. We'll stay in town tonight and ride out tomorrow morning. How does that set with you?"

O'Hara shook his head. "Sam, I got a bad feeling about this. Last night the kingfisher came to me in a dream. It was a bad omen."

"The bird? You mean the bird Barnabas talked about?"

"Yes, Sam. The kingfisher."

"O'Hara, being around all them condemned folk has made old Barnabas crazy as a loon, so pay no heed to a word he says. A little tweety bird isn't going to harm me . . . or you."

"I hope you're right, Sam," O'Hara said.

"Of course I'm right," Flintlock said. "Have you ever known me to be wrong?"

A day's ride south of the New Mexico border, the town of Happyville lay in a deep depression that looked as though it had been scooped out of the earth by the gigantic hands of God. A tall, tree-covered ridge rose to the west of town and then curved like a bent bow to the north. Unique among western cow towns, Happyville's single street was lined on both sides with carefully trimmed wild oak that provided the boardwalks with dappled shelter from the sun.

Flintlock and O'Hara sat their horses on slightly higher ground that overlooked the town. From that distance, it looked settled, peaceful, and prosperous . . . but O'Hara's sharp eyes noticed something that jarred him.

"Sam," he said, "take a looksee all the way to the end of the street."

From her perch on the wagon seat, shortsighted Biddy Sales said, "What do you see, Injun?"

"Sam?" O'Hara said.

Flintlock's eyes searched into distance. "Is that what I think it is?"

"What do you think it is?" O'Hara said.

"I think it's a gallows with a man hanging from a noose," Flintlock said.

O'Hara nodded. "I think you're right."

Biddy Sales shrieked. "Oh my God, it's not Morgan, is it?"

"I hope so," Flintlock said. "But I can't tell from here."

The three other women got out of the wagon and stared at the town.

"They've hung somebody," Jane Feehan said. "Is it Morgan?"

"We don't know," Biddy said, her face stricken. "It could be him. I just can't tell."

"Well there's one way to find out," Flintlock said. "We go down there and have a look."

"If it is Morgan, I'll miss the dear soul," O'Hara said.

Biddy glared at him, but the breed stared ahead of him as impassive as a cigar store Indian.

CHAPTER EIGHT

Flintlock led the way down the rise, rode through a stand of piñon, and then swung north, where he met up with the dirt road that led into town and provided easier going for the wagon. As he got closer, he saw something he'd missed because of the trees lining the street. A dozen or more tables covered with white cloths had been laid out alongside the boardwalks, groaning under the weight of food piled high in huge serving platters, bowls, and baskets.

O'Hara saw what Flintlock saw and grinned, "Fiesta."

Flintlock looked at Biddy and winked. "If they hung Morgan, they're making a day of it, huh?"

The woman bit her lip and said nothing.

Carried on the breeze came the smell of rot . . . and the sweet, carrion stench of dead things.

Flintlock drew rein and raised a hand to halt the wagon and the three jostling horses tethered to its rear.

Biddy Sales made a face. "What's that stink?"

"Maybe it's ol' Morg," Flintlock said. "I always had him pegged for a stinker."

She frowned. "Flintlock, I surely do hate you."

He grinned. "And I love you, Biddy."

"Of course you do," she said. "And so does your Injun."

"O'Hara? He's crazy about you, Biddy. Now we'll go say howdy to the hanging man and the good, well-fed folks of Happyville." Flintlock kicked his horse forward.

O'Hara rode straight to the gallows. The others stopped at the tables of food.

The buzzing drone of fat black flies provided a counterpoint to Biddy Sales's disgusted voice as she wrinkled her nose and said, "It's rotten. All the grub is rotten."

Every scrap of food in the bowls and on the platters—chicken, beef, potatoes, corn, cakes, and pies—was covered in a heaving black mass of carrion flies and the air was thick with a putrid, stomach-churning reek.

Talking from behind the hand that covered her pretty mouth, Margie Tott said, "Where are the people? There are no people."

Used to shouting above the din of dance halls and a few of the noisier brothels, Biddy yelled, "Hey! Where the hell are you? Where is everybody?"

There was no answer but the sigh of the rising wind . . . and something else.

Toward the end of the street in the direction of the hanged man, a player piano tinkled out the tune of "Home Sweet Home." It was a song regaining popularity after the Union had banned it during the

War Between the States for being too suggestive of hearth and home and likely to incite desertion, but its cloying sentimentality seemed tailor-made for a town named Happyville.

O'Hara returned and said, "You better come see this, Sam'l."

"Is it Morgan Davis?" Flintlock said.

"No. It's somebody else. I don't know who he is."

"Good," Flintlock said. "I aim to punch Morgan's ticket personally. Are there men in the saloon?"

"Like I said, you'd better come see." The breed's face was grim and Flintlock didn't push the question.

He kneed his horse forward but didn't follow O'Hara directly. He turned to his right, mounted the boardwalk and walked his horse slowly past the stores and offices. His bay's hooves thudding on timber, he rode as far as the saloon with the player piano and drew rein. He sat his saddle and looked over the batwings into the interior. The saloon looked like any other on the frontier, but was better than most. A substantial mahogany bar ran the length of the room and half a dozen tables with their attendant chairs were placed around the floor. One of the chairs was tipped on its back, suggesting that its occupant had left in a hurry. Above the bar hung a painting of a naked lady with fat thighs reclining on a sofa. Beside her, holding a salver that bore a champagne glass, stood a small black boy in a red turban who looked out from the canvas, his unsmiling face a study in boredom.

On the opposite wall, glaring at the nude in prim disapproval, was a portrait of the gallant Custer. It was draped in black crepe. Above the crown of his campaign hat were the Latin words *Maximo Heros Noster*.

The bar and tabletops were littered with glasses, some of them still holding beer and whiskey. The saloon was empty of people but "Home Sweet Home" continued to play on the piano against the far wall. The effect of deserted tavern and perpetual tune made Flintlock think of haunts and death and Judgment Day.

The face he turned to O'Hara was worried. "Nobody inside," he said. "Looks like they all got up and lit a shuck."

"Nobody anywhere," the breed said. "The town is deserted."

Flintlock frowned. "What the hell?"

"Seems like that's a question for old Barnabas, not me," O'Hara said. "Now come see the hanging man. He's a sight."

Sam Flintlock stared at the man hanging from the noose for long moments. Whoever he'd been, he looked tough. His duds and boots were of good quality, better than a puncher could afford.

After a while Flintlock said, "What's that stuff all over his face and his hands? What the hell is that?"

"I think it's smallpox," O'Hara said. "And if that's what it is, it can be deadly."

"What kind of pox?" The man who could be downright testy at times added, "That damned 'Home Sweet Home' is driving me crazy."

"Smallpox, Sam. One time I saw it wipe out an entire Apache village after they'd gotten their hands on infected blankets from a crooked Indian agent."

"It's catching?" Flintlock said.

"Only if you come close to somebody who has it. If

this man had breathed on you the chances are you'd get it." O'Hara read Flintlock's alarmed face and said, "Don't worry, Sam. He stopped breathing days ago."

"Is that why they hung him? Because he had smallpox?"

"Maybe, but I doubt it," O'Hara said. "My guess is they didn't know he had smallpox or they saw it on him and didn't realize what it was."

Flintlock said, "They planned to celebrate the hanging with a big feast but then somebody warned them there was smallpox in the town and they up and left."

"Or when folks started dying," O'Hara said.

"Hey, Flintlock! Get your ass the hell down here!" Biddy Sales stood on the boardwalk under a painted wooden sign that said SHERIFF.

"Now what?" Flintlock said to O'Hara.

The breed only shook his head in reply.

"What did you find, Biddy?" Flintlock yelled.

"Dead man," the woman said. "And he's wearing a lawman's star."

CHAPTER NINE

"His face is covered in sores, but I recognize him," Biddy said. "It's Sheriff Barney Morrell. Looks . . . smells . . . like he died two or three days ago."

"You didn't touch him, did you?" Flintlock said.

"Hell, no. I only touch men who pay me." Biddy frowned. "Why did you ask me that?"

"Because he probably died of smallpox and it's catching," Flintlock said. "I think the whole damned town lit out as soon as the dying started."

"Flintlock, this will come as a surprise, but I already lived through a smallpox plague," Biddy said. "I was in Deadwood during the epidemic of seventy-six when I was new to the whoring profession and but fourteen years old. When we caught the disease a gal by the name of Calamity Jane Canary—"

"Wild Bill's lady," Flintlock said. "I heard about her."

"She was never Bill's lady," Biddy said. "Jane was one for telling big windies. Are you listening to me?"

Flintlock nodded. "Go right ahead."

"Jane nursed me and eight of my regular clients.

She saved six, including me, and buried three, but them five that lived were never the same men again. I was lucky. I didn't get real sick and I didn't scar except in a place that nobody ever sees." She was quiet for a moment and then said, "Yeah, Flintlock, it was the smallpox that killed Barney Morrell and that's a natural fact."

"The sheriff would be in close contact with the prisoner he hung," Flintlock said. "It could be that he's the only one who died. I want everybody to scout around. We'll search the stores and the houses and see if there are more bodies. After that, we pull out of here in a hurry and report what we've seen."

"Report to who?" Biddy said.

"Hell, I don't know," Flintlock said. "There must be another town close."

"Don't count on it," Biddy said. "Up this way nothing is close."

"Well, we won't build houses on a bridge we haven't crossed yet," Flintlock said. "If there are bodies, stay well away from them. Don't touch anything. I don't know how this thing spreads."

"It's scaring the hell out of you, ain't it, hardcase?" Biddy said. "You can't shoot your way out of this fix—a damned town full of sickness and ghosts." Without waiting for Flintlock to comment, she added, "You heard the man, ladies. Search for stiffs. And listen up, especially you, Margie. Even if you see a ring on a finger that's covered in sores, leave it be. Same thing goes for necklaces and all other jewelry. Don't touch, savvy?"

Margie Tott argued. "But if the stuff ain't on a corpse, we can thieve it, right, Biddy?"

"Yeah, you can. The same goes for money." She glared at Flintlock. "You have any objection to that?"

"You want to rob the hurting dead that's up to you," Flintlock said. "It ain't something I'd do myself."

"No, you prefer to rob them while they're still alive. Ain't that so, pilgrim?" Biddy said.

The body count was eleven, including Sheriff Morrell and the hanged man. Flintlock and the others found the corpses of five men, three women, and a child. All were discovered in their beds as though too sick to flee. They'd lain down and waited for their inevitable end. By the evidence around them, the victims had died horribly and, like the sheriff, their skins had turned black.

Biddy said she'd seen a couple cases like that in Deadwood, caused by bleeding under the skin, a symptom of a deadly form of smallpox that was always fatal. "Them people were doomed from the first moment they felt poorly. After that, all they could do was lie down and let death happen."

Flintlock, O'Hara, and the women had gathered in the middle of a deserted street hung with red, white, and blue bunting. Above the partly brick-built city hall, the Stars and Stripes flapped and slapped in a growing wind that lifted veils of dust from the street and set any open doors to banging. The day had turned a strange amber color and the frame buildings creaked and groaned like arthritic old men. A long strip of bunting tore from the front of a hardware store and soared into the air where it coiled and writhed higher and higher like an escaping dragon until it vanished from sight.

Flintlock looked at O'Hara. Above the wild lamentation of the wind, he said, "Can we outrun it?"

"Not with the wagon," O'Hara said. "And maybe not without it."

It seemed as though the wind was trying to shred the clothes off the women and strip them naked for all to see. Their unbound hair tossed and writhed around their heads and made them look like four tawdry Medusas. The howling sandstorm and the nearness of death had transformed them. Hard-bitten whores with hearts of rock huddled together, all of a sudden becoming frightened and vulnerable young girls.

Biddy's scared, questioning eyes met Flintlock's.

He made up his mind. "You women get into the saloon. There are no dead inside. O'Hara, help me free the horses from the wagon and then we'll flap our chaps for the livery."

O'Hara swung out of the saddle and held onto the reins as his restless horse reared, frightened arcs of white flashing in its eyes. The nag in the traces decided right then was a prime moment to bolt and took off down the street at a shambling gallop, the three tethered horses stumbling after her. After only a score of yards, a wind gust hit the wagon and it crashed over on its side. The mare dragged the battered vehicle for a few feet, gave up the unequal struggle, and stopped, trembling. Frantic and terrified, the horses tied to the wagon plunged and reared and then broke free. Flintlock watched them run clear out of town, the broken ropes trailing behind. He barely had time to absorb that disaster when a shot rang out from the other end of the street. A moment later, a piercing shriek lanced through the turbulent day and it seemed that even the violent wind paused for an instant to hold its breath.

CHAPTER TEN

"The shot came from the direction of the livery," O'Hara yelled above the roar of the windstorm.

Flintlock gathered the reins of his horse and pulled the bay after him, heading for the livery. O'Hara, leading his own mount, followed. As Biddy and the other women ran for the saloon, Flintlock noticed that she had a Remington derringer in her hand.

A few yards from the stable's wide open doors, he stopped, dropped the reins, and slapped his horse's rump. The bay, eager to get out of the wind and stinging sand, trotted inside, and O'Hara's horse was glad to do the same. Flintlock pulled the Colt from his waistband and motioned to his left, where he wanted O'Hara to position himself. He stepped into the stable, his revolver up and ready, O'Hara at his side. Outside, the storm raved and butted at the stable walls, but inside, out of the wind, relative calm made it more serene, the air filled with the familiar musky odors of horse dung, wood shavings, leather, and hay.

The place was deserted—no horses, no humans, not even the usual rat-killing cat.

Flintlock climbed the ladder and checked the hayloft. It was empty. After a few moments, he lifted his great beak of a nose and sniffed. "Gun smoke. Somebody fired a gun in here."

O'Hara, Colt in hand, had already explored the stalls and now his attention was fixed on the open door at the back of the building. "Looks like somebody fired a single shot and then ran out the door."

"Hell, did he take a pot at us?" Flintlock said.

"And missed real bad? I don't think so," O'Hara said.

Flintlock stepped warily to the open door, his thumb on the hammer of his Colt. He glanced outside into a patch of scrubby waste ground where a few stunted mesquite tossed in the raking wind that rapidly set about erasing the man-sized boot tracks that led away from the door. There was no sign of the man himself, so Flintlock shoved his revolver back in the waistband. "He may still be close, but I'm sure as hell not going out there to look for him."

O'Hara's black eyes were troubled. "Sam, after this big wind blows itself out we got to get away from here. There's evil in this town. I can sense it."

"You'll get no argument from me, O'Hara. Take care of my bay and I'll unharness the mare from the wagon before the wind blows her away." Flintlock stared through the livery's open doors. "Damn storm is kicking up stronger. I can't see the end of the street. Looks like a wall of thick smoke down there."

O'Hara said, "If there's a road leading to the gates of hell, that's exactly what it looks like."

* * *

The women had taken a bottle from the bar and were huddled around a table drinking, except for the blonde, Lizzie Doulan, who sat and watched the others.

Flintlock and O'Hara walked inside and beat several layers of sand from their clothes. They looked as though they wore tan-colored masks, their faces thick with grit.

"All the horses are in the livery," Flintlock said. "Including three who made a run for it and then decided to come back. There's plenty of hay and I found a sack of oats."

"The old mare hasn't had oats in a long time," Biddy said.

"I guessed that," he said, looking at the newly formed sand dune at his feet.

It was O'Hara who first noticed the faded print on the far wall to the right of a large railroad clock. He stared at the picture for stunned moments before he said, "Sam. Look."

Flintlock followed O'Hara's gaze. The print showed a green bird with a long, dagger-like beak and bright black eyes. Written above the bird were the words *Gray & Sons Kingfisher Bourbon.*

"You boys look like you've seen a ghost," Biddy said. "Get yourselves a drink. It's on the house."

Flintlock tore his eyes from the bird and managed a smile. "I can't think of a better place to ride out a storm."

Beside him O'Hara, his gaze fixed on the garish print, whispered, "Kingfisher . . ."

Biddy sat back in the chair. "What's the matter with

your Indian, Flintlock?" She followed O'Hara's eyes. "He doesn't like birds?"

"The kingfisher is a bird of ill omen, a bringer of bad news," O'Hara said.

Biddy said, "Well, here's some bad news, redskin— we're stuck in this burg until the storm blows over, so make the best of it."

Flintlock stepped behind the bar, grabbed a bottle of rye and two glasses, dragged over a chair, and joined the women at the table. To the breed he said, "She's right, O'Hara. Come have a drink."

Ignoring that, he stood at the batwings and stared into the wind-ravaged street. His face set and determined, he held his Winchester across his chest like a devoted Pinkerton guarding a payroll.

"Suit yourself," Flintlock said. "But nobody's traveling on a day like this."

"Nobody honest, that is," Biddy said.

Lizzie Doulan's mist-gray eyes fixed on Flintlock. "'Something wicked this way comes,'" she said.

"Huh?" Flintlock said.

"Shakespeare. From his play *The Tragedy of Macbeth*," Lizzie said.

"I never saw that play," Flintlock said. "I never saw any play. I watched a Punch and Judy show in El Paso one time. I guess that's a kind of play, huh?"

The wind howled around the saloon like a hungry wolf and an errant breeze rattled the frame of the kingfisher print.

"'Something wicked this way comes,'" O'Hara said again, his face turned to Lizzie. "Do you know it comes?"

Lizzie nodded. "Yes, and it will be my death."

"Who was this Shakespeare feller?" Margie Tott said. "He's got no call to scare folks like that."

"A man who lived a long, long time ago," Lizzie said. "Like me."

Everybody smiled at that last except Biddy. She stared hard at Lizzie, her eyes troubled.

CHAPTER ELEVEN

Daybreak brought an end to the storm and an appalling discovery—the horses were gone from the livery stable, even the old mare.

"No tracks," O'Hara said. "If there were any, they've been covered up by the wind."

Sam Flintlock was irritated beyond measure. "Hell, six horses just don't vanish."

"Ours did," O'Hara said. "And so did the saddles and tack."

"All the saddles?"

"Every last one of them."

"Including the three—"

"Them too."

After he got all through cussing, Flintlock scouted the ground in front of the livery and saw, apart from boot prints left by him and O'Hara, there were no tracks, horse or human. Seething, he entered the stable again and walked to the back door. Gun in hand, he stepped outside and saw only what he'd seen before—a ten-acre wasteland of brush and mesquite. He searched more carefully, his eyes scanning every inch of ground. He was five minutes into his scout when he discovered the body, a man half-buried in sand. Only the right side of the corpse's head was visible and from where Flintlock stood it looked as though the man's gray hair was covered in molasses. Only when he stepped closer did he see that it was not molasses but dried blood. He took a knee beside the dead man and began to brush away layers of sand, revealing an old Confederate greatcoat and the man's right arm. A Griswold & Gunnison cap-and-ball Navy was clutched in the dead man's fist. Flintlock rose quickly in alarm when he saw blistering lesions on the skin.

"Smallpox," O'Hara said, his voice hollow like a judge passing a death sentence.

Flintlock turned and said, "Hell, you scared the hell out of me." He nodded in the direction of the dead man. "And so did he."

"Did you touch him?" O'Hara said.

"Yeah, I think so."

"We got to get out of here, Sam."

"How? Walk? Put the women in the wagon and pull it ourselves?"

"The women can walk," O'Hara said.

"This man fired the shot we heard," Flintlock said.

"Yes, he killed himself. Now his body is an unclean thing and his spirit is doomed to wander forever in darkness."

"Poor devil saw the pox marks and knew what was in store for him," Flintlock said.

O'Hara shook his head. "He didn't know what was in store for him, only the Great Spirit knows what awaits a man. He might have recovered from the disease, others have in the past, but he took the coward's way out and ended his life."

A faint smile touched Flintlock's lips. "He didn't make a good job of it, did he? Blew a chunk of his head off and had time to scream before he died."

"We will not speak of him any more," O'Hara said. "It is said that if you talk about a suicide, you will cause another suicide to happen."

"Hell, we don't want that." Flintlock stepped toward the door of the livery. "Now we'll go tell the ladies the bad news about the horses."

"Tell them the horses were spirited away by evil," O'Hara said. "Tell them that and you will be speaking the truth."

Flintlock shook his head. "O'Hara, you're a mighty strange Indian."

Slightly drunk, Biddy said, "Well, Flintlock, where do we go from here?"

"We? There's no we," Flintlock said. "There's me and O'Hara and there's you four women and we're going our separate ways."

"All right, then. Where are you headed, Flintlock?" Biddy said.

"The Arizona Territory. Me and O'Hara are going to find my ma. At least that's the plan."

"I'm sure she misses you," Biddy said. "How do you aim to get there?"

"I reckon another settlement must be close," Flintlock said. "Or even a ranch where we can buy a couple horses."

"And saddles and tack," Biddy said. "You got the money for all that?"

Flintlock and O'Hara exchanged glances.

Biddy smiled. "I thought so. You're both broke. The only way you'll get horses and saddles is to steal them."

"We'll find a way," Flintlock said.

"And end up getting hung for horse theft." She waited for Flintlock to say something and when he didn't, she said, "Show him, Jane."

Jane Feehan reached under the table, her long red hair falling over her face, and she came up with a money sack that clinked as she laid it on the table.

"Let him see, Jane," Biddy said.

The redhead opened the neck of the sack and tilted it toward Flintlock, revealing stacks of paper bills and some gold and silver coin.

"How much is in there?" Flintlock said, his eyes wide.

"A little over six thousand dollars," Biddy said. She stretched out a shapely leg, pulled her derringer from her garter, and laid the Remington on the table. "Don't get any ideas, Flintlock."

"Where did you get that money?" Flintlock said.

"It's Morgan Davis's money. But he ain't here, is he?" Biddy stared hard at Flintlock. "Is there still no *we*, big boy?"

Knowing he was caught flat-footed, Flintlock scratched his chest. "I reckon we're in this together, Biddy . . . me and O'Hara and you women."

She gave a short nod. "I thought you might say that."

CHAPTER TWELVE

"Taking the horses was easy but stealing women never is. Are you sure you saw gals?"

"Damn right, I did, Pa," Poter Stanton said. "I seen four of 'em, one fer each of us."

"We'll share, boy, just like you say. Share and share alike is the Stanton motto. Now, would you say them ladies was well shaped?" Pa Stanton said. "I can't abide a skinny female . . . or a fat one either."

"They was shaped in all the right places, Pa. I took 'em fer whores."

"Whores is the best," Pa said. "Knows what a man needs, does a whore." His eyes misted. "I ain't had a full-time woman since your ma died. Even afore that when she kept poorly all the time."

"Seen a redhead, Pa. Ma was a redhead."

"That she was, boy. And at one time ma was a whore, mind. And a good one if the truth be told."

"How much did you pay for her, Pa?" Ora Stanton said.

"A grade hoss an' a jug of drinkin' whiskey. Lookin' back, I think I could have probably got her for just the hoss, but I was feeling generous that day." Pa sighed and shrugged his thin shoulders. "Ah well, no use cryin' over spilt milk, boys. Too late to do anything about it now, huh? What about menfolk, Poter?"

"Seen two. One of 'em looked like an Injun. The other was a white man who didn't look like he stacked up to much."

"Hell, we can take them two," Skinner Stanton said.

Like his pa and brothers Skinner was a tall, skinny man with a full beard. Wolfers by profession, the four men were dressed in whatever duds they could find and they smelled of animal guts and ancient sweat. Each wore a holstered Colt and kept a Winchester close to hand. Collectively, the Stantons were rootless riffraff, the scum of the frontier. Rape, murder, and thievery was their way of life and they found no harm in that.

Ora, slightly more intelligent than his dull brethren, added a branch to the guttering campfire and said, "How come there's no folks in the town? Hell, I didn't even see a cur dog or a rootin' pig."

"I wondered that meself," Skinner said. "Pa, what do you reckon?"

"I don't know where all them people went an' I don't give a damn," Pa said. The green of his eyes looked like slime on a stagnant pond. "We ride in there, gun them two rubes, and take the women. And we grab anything else we find that will turn a dollar."

"Pa, there might be a bank," Poter said. "I couldn't see good because of the blowing sand, but I think there's a bank."

"If there is, we'll empty it," Pa said. "We're poor

folks and we deserve our fair allotment of rich people's money."

"That's what I say too, Pa," Skinner said. "Share and share alike, just like our motto says."

Pa grinned, revealing but few teeth and all of them rotten. "But that don't apply to the redhead. You can all have a taste, never fear, but she'll be my reg'lar belly warmer on account of how I'm right partial to her kind."

"That's as fair as ever was, Pa," Poter said. "Enough of them whores to go around, I say."

"Yup, share and share alike." Skinner grinned. "Hell, now all of a sudden I want a women real bad."

"All right, boys," Pa said, rising to his feet. "Let's go get 'em."

Earlier, under the cover of the sandstorm, the Stantons had stolen Sam Flintlock's horses with ease and it had led them to underestimate him as just another small-town hick with a head full of stump water. It was a serious mistake. A fatal mistake. Pa Stanton and his sons were destined to pay a high price for their arrogance. They were not fighting men. They were sure-thing murderers who killed from ambush and always at a distance. They'd gunned more than their share, but never before had they encountered the new breed of Texas draw fighters, embodied in men like Flintlock and O'Hara who were hell on the draw-and-shoot.

Confident in their numbers, the Stantons insolently rode down the middle of Happyville's main street, rifles still in the boots under their knees.

Previously, they had seen the town only through the murky prism of the sandstorm. As they rode, they gawked at the overturned tables and rotten food that littered the ground. Most of it was half-buried but still stinking. They stared at the hanged man, his face masked behind a thick coat of sand.

"Looks like we missed a hell of a hanging party," Skinner said. He grinned. "They were sure happy to string up this poor feller."

But Pa Stanton didn't like what he saw. "Something strange here, boys. Why did they hang this ranny, throw a big party, and then leave?"

"And why did nobody eat the grub?" Ora said.

Then Poter yelped, pointing. "Hey, lookee, Pa! There's our women."

"Follow me." Pa swung his horse around and headed for the boardwalk where Biddy and the others were gathered. He drew rein and said, "What happened here?"

"The smallpox happened, Methuselah," Biddy said. "Why are you here? State your intentions."

Stanton ignored that. "Where are your menfolk?"

"Around," Biddy said.

"Better for them if they stay away," Pa said, his face tight. "This is a death town. Do you have the pox?"

"Not so far," Biddy said. "Neither small nor any other kind."

Pa turned in the saddle. "Skinner, we passed the bank. Go clean it out."

"Sure, Pa." Skinner swung his horse and rode up the street.

Pa said, "You women are coming with us. Gather up your fixins an' get ready."

Biddy shook her head. "Not a chance, pops."

"Me and my boys need women. We aim to have you four, so there ain't any use in arguing."

"Is that your last word on the matter?" Biddy said.

"It is," Pa said. "Now get ready, or we'll horsewhip some damned sense into all of you."

"You ain't taking no for an answer, are you, Pops?" Biddy said.

Pa Stanton's face hardened and the lines at the corners of his eyes deepened. "Do as I say, woman. I won't tell you again."

Biddy nodded. "All right you horny old goat, you called it." She hiked up her skirt, pulled her derringer from the garter, and fired.

Several years before in New Orleans, Biddy had emptied an Allen & Thurber pepperpot revolver into a cheating gambler. At a range of ten paces, all six .30 caliber balls hit the man, rendering him hors de combat for several months.

The distance between Biddy and Pa Stanton was half that.

Her bullet hit the man just under his prominent Adam's apple. He reeled in the saddle, gasping, choking on his own blood, his eyes wild with pain and shock. For a moment, Poter and Ora were too stunned to react. When they finally pulled their guns, Biddy was already pushing the other women into the saloon.

Poter fired, aiming at Biddy. His bullet chipped splinters from the wall six inches above the woman's head. She returned fire, missed, scrambled through the batwings, and ran inside.

Cursing, Poter kicked his mustang into motion and charged for the saloon door. The horse charged the batwings, shattering them off their hinges. Poter ducked his head under the top of the doorframe as he hurtled inside, screaming his rage.

It was unfortunate that O'Hara, his black eyes glittering, waited for him on the other side with the saloon's Greener scattergun in his hands.

He cut loose with both barrels and blasted the crown of Poter's head into something that looked like a broken pot of Aunt Gertrude's prizewinning strawberry jam. Killed instantly, the man did not cry out. He was thrown from his terrified horse and hit the saloon floor with a crunching thud. The crazed animal kicked and reared and sent O'Hara and the women scrambling for cover behind the bar.

"Injun, shoot the damned thing before it kills somebody," Biddy yelled above the racket of the mustang's wrecking spree.

O'Hara drew his belt gun as a pistol shot shattered a bottle on the shelf above his head and he took refuge behind the bar again.

Biddy yelled, "One of them is inside!"

Poter's mustang was completely loco, rampaging back and forth across the saloon floor, smashing tables and chairs into matchwood in a frantic bid to escape, all the time ignoring the open doorway.

O'Hara stood, his gun up and ready as he searched for a target, the bucking, rearing horse obscuring his view. He caught a glimpse of Ora Stanton, plastered to the far wall out of the way of the frantic animal. O'Hara fired and his bullet slammed into the wall close to Stanton's head. The man shot back and smashed another booze bottle on the shelf. It seemed that a close-range gunfight complicated by the presence of a panicked horse did not appeal to him. He thumbed off a couple shots in O'Hara's general direction and dashed for the door.

Unfortunately, the mustang had the same idea as it finally entered his dim brain that the door was a way out. Ora reached the doorway a split second before the horse. The charging animal hit him hard and the man crashed to the boardwalk. Dazed, he took a few moments to collect himself. He'd lost his Colt and was out of the fight. He looked up, saw O'Hara eying him with little compassion, and got to his feet.

Ora held his arms away from his sides and said, "I'm done, breed."

"No you ain't," O'Hara said, his toleration of white men an uncertain thing that always teetered on a razor edge. He emptied his revolver into Ora's chest and watched the man fall. "Now you're done."

As death rattled in Ora's throat, O'Hara's eyes lifted to the end of the street where Flintlock had gone after Skinner Stanton.

In the street, Flintlock had his gun pointed at Skinner standing on the boardwalk outside the bank with his arms raised. Clutched in his left hand were some banknotes that amounted to only a few dollars. Flintlock waved his Colt and Stanton walked along the boardwalk, his arms still raised. Flintlock kept pace with him in the street, looking tense and ready, as though he hoped the man would make a run for it.

Skinner stared at his pa's body and then acted like a man who'd lost his mind. He threw himself on his father's body and shrieked in anguish. "Pa," he wailed. "Who done this to you?"

"He done it to himself," Flintlock said. "Man comes into a respectable town looking for women and plunder, he should expect to be met with lead."

Skinner raised his head. His father's blood had turned his face into a horrific scarlet mask. "Who shot him down in the street like a dog?"

O'Hara was about to claim responsibility for Pa Stanton's death, but to his surprise Biddy Sales stepped out of the saloon and said, "I did. The piece of filth you call your pa came hunting for a bitch in heat. Well, he found me instead."

Skinner bellowed in fury. "I'll kill you, slut!" He'd had to drop his gun, but his hand dropped to the Green River knife in his boot. He jumped to his feet and lunged at Biddy. Skinner Stanton was good with the blade, but he'd gambled on a grandstand play that came to nothing.

Flintlock and O'Hara fired at the same time and Skinner fell with two bullets in him. He landed with his chest on the boardwalk and Biddy took a quick step back as he swung the knife. Having followed Biddy out of the saloon, Lizzie Doulan stamped violently on the man's knife hand with her high-heeled ankle boot. Skinner Stanton stared at the blonde in impotent wrath and opened his mouth to speak, but death drained all the life that was in him and forever robbed his tongue of speech.

A moment later, Lizzie looked at the sky as a roaring rush of wind flattened her skirt against her legs. The gust lasted for only a few seconds and then was gone as suddenly as it had come.

She smiled and said, "The Valkyries don't want

these men. They were rapists and murderers, not warriors."

O'Hara stared at the woman for long moments and then heard Flintlock say, "Woman, what are you talking about?"

Biddy said, "Nothing. She's just making a good joke, is all."

But Lizzie ignored that. "The Valkyries are winged female warriors who decide who will die in battle. In ages past they carried dead Vikings to the Hall of the Slain where they would fight a great battle every single day and then, the battle dead brought to life again, the warriors would feast on the flesh of the resurrected beast Saehrimnir. This is how the Vikings spend eternity. It's a good way."

Her pretty eyes as round as silver dollars, Margie Tott said, "Lizzie I wish you'd stop saying stuff like that. We've all been scared enough today."

Lizzie shook her head. "Margie, one day you will meet the Archangel Michael, the Christian Valkyrie. He is a mighty warrior, the sworn enemy of Satan, and God's soul-gatherer. In heaven, the spirits of the dead are weighed on Michael's scales, so perfectly balanced that a single mortal sin can tip them."

Flintlock grinned. "Hell, my sins will tip them scales like an anvil."

"Mine too," Biddy said.

O'Hara did not smile. To Lizzie he said, "Are you the kingfisher?"

The woman shook her head again. "No. But I sense that the kingfisher is near."

CHAPTER THIRTEEN

Flintlock and O'Hara dragged the Stantons into the brush away from a town that already hosted enough dead. At first light, they'd use the mustangs to backtrack their way to the Stanton camp and recover their horses.

That night, the men bedded down on the saloon floor and Biddy and the other women slept in a room at the back where cots had been set up for travelers and those too drunk to make it home. The railroad clock on the wall, wound up by Margie Tott, who said she couldn't abide a stopped timepiece of any kind, woke Flintlock when it chimed midnight. He lay awake, his eyes open, listening into the hushed night. Footsteps, light as thistledown, sounded on the boardwalk outside. A woman, Flintlock guessed, pacing up and down outside the saloon, perhaps courting sleep.

He rose from his blankets and padded silently across the floor in sock feet, picked his way around the debris of the shattered batwings and stepped outside.

Biddy, an amber glass in her hand, stopped when she saw Flintlock and said, "Speak thou, apparition."

"I heard footsteps," Flintlock said.

"And you walked outside without a gun to investigate?"

"O'Hara is close. You can bet he's awake and listening. Besides, I knew they were a woman's footsteps."

"Why do you have a bird on your throat?" Biddy said.

"It's a long story. Is that why you can't sleep, wondering about the bird?"

"No, buckskin man, I wasn't thinking about you."

"Worrying about the smallpox maybe?"

"That neither."

"All right. I give up. You going to tell me?"

Biddy stared at Flintlock, his face shadowed by darkness, his mustache a black bar across his face. "Why do you give a damn?"

He shrugged. "Maybe I don't."

"Then why are you out here?"

"Like I said, I heard your footsteps. Made me think of haunts and spooks an' sich."

Biddy came at Flintlock from an angle he didn't expect. "What do you think of Lizzie Doulan?"

Flintlock considered that for a moment and said, "Well, she's quite pretty and she's got really big—"

"Big tits. Yes, I know. Do you think she's mad? Is she a madwoman?"

"I haven't studied on it, but no, I don't reckon so."

"All us, we're whores. Did you know that?"

"I guess I did. I took Morgan Davis for a pimp."

"And you were right."

"You should go inside and get some sleep," Flintlock said.

"Lizzie constantly degrades herself," Biddy said as

though she hadn't heard. "The filthier the man, be he smell rank, be he flea-ridden or diseased, she sells herself to him. She lies with such men to degrade herself, to make herself suffer."

Flintlock suddenly found himself tongue-tied and said nothing.

"Do you know why?" Biddy said.

"She hates being a whore, I guess," Flintlock said.

"That's not the reason."

From the direction of the livery a barn owl hooted and a pair of yipping coyotes hunted close. The moon was almost full and hung high in the sky but shed no light. In the darkness, the town looked like a collection of moored prison hulks crowded into a small harbor.

"I'll tell you something, Flintlock," Biddy said. "And in return you will tell me whether or not Lizzie is mad."

"I talk to my dead grandfather." He smiled. "Am I one to judge madness in others?"

"Right now, standing out here, you're all I've got," Biddy said.

"Then tell me what you need to say."

The woman took a deep breath as though steeling herself for what was to come. "Do you remember in the New Testament that the Roman governor Pontius Pilate condemned the Lord Christ to be crucified?"

"Yeah, I recollect that," Flintlock said. A man who'd rarely read the Bible, he all at once felt uncomfortable in his skin.

"Lizzie says she was there," Biddy said. "She said she was a young, rich Roman lady named Liviana who was visiting Jerusalem because Pilate was her uncle. When our Savior was dragged away to the cross, she laughed at his suffering."

Flintlock said, "Quite a story."

"There's more. Lizzie says she will not be allowed to die until she makes amends for her terrible sin."

"You should talk to O'Hara. He's half-Indian and likes all that strange spiritual stuff. Maybe he can make up some kind of potion that will help make Lizzie normal again."

"You do think she's crazy, don't you?" Biddy said, her eyes searching Flintlock's face.

"Hell, yeah. The little lady's biscuits ain't golden brown, lay to that."

"Then I'll take care of her," Biddy said. "For the rest of her life if need be."

"Maybe you should find her another line of work," Flintlock said. "The profession she's in sure don't fit her pistol." He saw Biddy shiver. "You'd better get inside out of the night chill."

The woman nodded and stepped into the saloon. Flintlock looked around. Satisfied that the street was empty, he followed her.

In the darkness of the narrow alley between the saloon and a shoe store, O'Hara stood with his back to a wall, his dark face troubled. Was there a sin so heinous, so wicked that it could never be forgiven? He remembered the monks at the mission where he'd been raised and wished he could ask them that question. He looked up at the sky but saw no answer there, only the distant, uncaring stars as expressionless as holes in a tin roof.

CHAPTER FOURTEEN

Riding over the flattened buffalo grass that marked the trail the Stantons had taken to Happyville, Flintlock and O'Hara followed the loops toward the timberline in the distance. The sun was low on the horizon, rising into a flaming sky streaked with jade and amber. The morning was cool and the breeze hinted at the coming fall. The fair land had banished the night shadows and was ready to welcome the new aborning day.

"Flintlock, you really didn't need me to read this trail," O'Hara said. "It's as plain as the nose on your face, if you don't mind me saying so."

"I needed an Injun to help me wrangle the horses," Flintlock said. "And I'd be grateful if you'd keep my nose out of any further discussions."

"It troubles you, huh?"

"If it was yours, wouldn't it trouble you?"

"Not in the least," O'Hara said. "That there is a beak, a proboscis, a snout, a honker, a hooter, and a schnozzle, better yet, a schnozzola. Man should be proud of a nozzle like that. Yes sir."

"Let me ask you a question, O'Hara. Do you mind?"

"Ask away, Sammy."

"How would you like me to pull my gun and shoot you right off the back of that pony?"

"A bit grouchy this morning, are we?"

"I'm always grouchy when people discuss my nose. They are usually impolite and lowdown."

"Sorry Sam. I won't mention your smeller again." O'Hara shook his head. "But I never noticed until I saw the morning light shine on it just how big it really is."

"Injun, you're playing with fire," Flintlock said. He kneed his horse into a canter.

O'Hara followed, grinning.

The Stantons had staked out the stolen horses on a patch of rocky ground where the grass was thin. Flintlock and O'Hara released the hungry animals and let them graze. To the joy of both men, a full pot of coffee stood among the dead coals of the campfire. O'Hara soon had a fire going with the pot in the middle of it.

As they drank the coffee, O'Hara stared at Flintlock for long moments before he said, "I heard you talking to Biddy Sales last night."

"Hell, I didn't see you."

"I know. I'm half Injun, remember."

Flintlock fished something out of his coffee. "Did you hear me say that Lizzie Doulan should talk to you?"

"Yeah, I did."

"She's a crazy lady."

"She believes she can never die," O'Hara said.

Flintlock nodded. "Wild Bill Hickok believed that as well and look what happened to him."

"I'll talk to her," O'Hara said. "Pontius Pilate."

"Huh?"

"Lizzie says she was visiting Pontius Pilate, the man who condemned Christ."

"By the time you talk to her, O'Hara, she'll probably believe she was Pontius Pilate himself. Crazy folks have all kinds of notions. I mind one time up in the Montana Bitterroot Mountains country an English feller thought he could fly."

"And could he?"

"Well, he jumped off Trapper Peak and flapped his arms all the way down. He must have dropped ten thousand feet before he hit ground." Flintlock shook his head. "There wasn't much left of him to bury, so they planted him in an Arbuckle coffee sack." His face creased in thought. "Yeah, now I recollect that his name was Professor Ezra Shoredish and he was as crazy as a loon."

"He'd have to be to jump off a mountain," O'Hara said.

"O'Hara, when you talk with the crazy lady tell her to steer clear of mountains. She might just take a notion to jump."

"Suppose Lizzie is telling the truth?" O'Hara said.

"If you think that, you're as nuts as she is," Flintlock said.

CHAPTER FIFTEEN

"Where are the people?" Biddy said.

Flintlock had just gotten through forking some of the rapidly dwindling supply of hay to the horses and he straightened his back. "That's a big mystery. How do you expect me to answer your question?"

"You were out in the flat but didn't see a living soul," she said. "If the citizens of Happyville ran away from the plague, some of them must surely have headed farther west into the long grass."

"I reckon they put a lot of git between them and the town and are scattered to hell and gone. We could only see as far as the horizon, and they're likely well beyond that by now."

"I still think it's strange that they vanished without a trace," Biddy said. "While you were gone, me and Margie counted up the houses and the shacks and reckoned that Happyville had at least five hundred people who called this place home. Five hundred men, women, and children don't vanish off the face of the earth without a trace. Do they?"

"I don't know and to tell you the truth, I really

don't much care," he said. "We're pulling out of here tomorrow and I hope we don't carry smallpox with us."

"Flintlock, I want to find Morgan Davis first," Biddy said. "I owe him that much."

"He's a damned pimp. You owe him nothing."

"Morg saved my life in Fort Worth. Shot a man in a Hell's Half Acre bawdy house who was about to cut me up real bad. I told him then that I owed him. That was two years ago and I've done nothing since to return the favor. If I can find Morg and give him back his money, I'll consider us even."

"You're on your own, Biddy," Flintlock said. "You want to find Davis. I want to find my mother, so we'll go our separate ways. What do the other women plan to do?"

"Lizzie will stay with me. I don't know what Jane Feehan and Margie Tott have decided."

"I'll ask them." He walked to the door of the barn.

Biddy followed. She had shadows under her eyes and curled tendrils of hair tumbled onto her forehead. The woman looked tired, the kind of soul-numbing tiredness that comes from the wear and tear of living and not lack of sleep. She sniffed and said, "The smell of this town is getting unbearable. I can scarcely stand it any longer."

Flintlock nodded. "Bodies are rotting. It will get worse before it gets better. Come tomorrow, we'll be well gone from this hellhole."

"I hope you find your ma, Flintlock. You're a rootless man and the wind blows you. Maybe when you find her, you'll settle."

"Maybe so. What about you?"

"I thought whoring would be my life and then I'd grow old. Men wouldn't want me any longer and I'd take to laudanum and gin and then die. But I think I've found a purpose in my life."

"You mean taking care of the crazy lady," Flintlock said.

"Yes, watching over Lizzie. But she's not crazy. She honestly believes she's been alive since the time of Christ."

He shook his head and initially said nothing. But after a few moments he found words enough to say, "The lady is sick in the head, Biddy. She needs help."

"And I'll see she gets it. Maybe we'll head east and I'll see if I can find one of them doctors that treat Lizzie's kind of sickness."

"It's a thought," Flintlock said.

Biddy looked at him as though she expected him to say more, but when he remained silent, she said, "Margie has a skillet of canned beef and beans cooking on the saloon stove. You and the Indian are welcome to come eat, if the stink hasn't taken away your appetite."

"It hasn't," Flintlock said. "And thank you for the invite. We'll be over in a few minutes."

She grinned. "Don't forget to bring candy and flowers, big boy."

In the echoing emptiness of the saloon, Flintlock and O'Hara ate beef and beans with the four women. It was not yet dark, but to keep out the stench of rot and decay Biddy had closed the storm doors behind the batwings and shuttered the windows. The place was lit by oil lamps that smoked badly and cast shadows that brought furtive life to the walls, so many dancing phantoms seeking partners for a devilish cotillion. She had liberally sprinkled lavender water around the saloon floor to cut the odor from outside, but the smell still leaked into the building like a poisonous gas.

Marge Tott laid down her fork and said, "Am I the only one who hears that?"

"Hears what?" Flintlock made an effort to appear relaxed, but the fact that he'd charged his Hawken with powder and ball and kept it close gave the lie to that. In times of trouble the trusted old rifle was both wife and child to him.

"That strange noise," Margie said.

"I don't hear it," Flintlock said. "Maybe it's the wind."

O'Hara said, "There is no wind." Then to Margie, "You have good ears, woman."

"You hear it?" the woman said.

"Yes, for the past hour or so. It surges like waves on a shore."

"Then what is it?" Margie said.

O'Hara shook his head. "I don't know."

Flintlock pushed his plate away, sighed, and leaned back in his chair. "You make good beef and beans, Margie." He rose to his feet and picked up the Hawken. "I reckon I'll take a stroll outside, look at the stars for a spell."

"And listen to the strange sound," Margie said.

Flintlock nodded, grinning. "Yeah, I'll be sure to do that."

CHAPTER SIXTEEN

The strange sound worried the hell out of Sam Flintlock.

A dull, pulsing roar, it came from east of town somewhere out in the flat. *Is it a steam locomotive? No, impossible.* Happyville was miles from the nearest railroad. More important, did whatever caused the damned noise pose a danger?

He stared at the sky. A halo surrounded the horned moon. *Is that a bad omen?* He remembered a line he'd read. *Here there be dragons.* Where had he read that? He couldn't remember. In a storybook probably, maybe one about King Arthur and his Knights of the Round Table. Them old boys were forever rescuing maidens from fiery dragons.

All kind of varmints lived in West Texas, but no dragons, fiery or otherwise, so the noise was being made by something else.

Well, there was one way to find out. Flintlock stepped into the livery and threw the saddle on his horse.

"Going somewhere, boy?"

Flintlock tightened the cinch and said, "Looks like it, don't it, Barnabas?"

"You're an idiot, Sammy. I should've left you in the Louisiana swamp with them man-eating Injuns."

"As I recall, you didn't do much to help me get out of there." Flintlock turned and saw old Barnabas standing in an unoccupied stall.

He wore a smock and some kind of strange floppy hat. He'd set up an artist's easel and dabbed at a canvas with the thin paintbrush in his right hand. In the other, he had his thumb through a palette. Even in the dark, Flintlock saw that the predominant colors were scarlet, orange, and black.

"What are you doing, you crazy old coot, and what's that thing on your head?" he said.

"What should be obvious, even to you, is that I'm painting a picture," Barnabas said. "And my chapeau is called a beret. It's French. You-know-who says that the great Henri Rousseau wore one just like mine. He badly wanted Henri as his guest, him and Vincent van Gogh, but they slipped through his claws. Fingers. I meant, slipped through his *fingers.*"

"Let me see the picture," Flintlock said.

Barnabas shook his gray head. "Boy, this is a painting of the lowest level of hell. One glance would drive you insane, and you're already crazy enough." He gathered up his easel, brushes, and paints and said, "When are you heading for the Arizona Territory to hunt for your ma?"

"I'm pulling out of here at first light," Flintlock said.

"The kingfisher has other ideas about that," Barnabas said.

Suddenly Flintlock was alarmed. "What do you mean?"

"You'll find out." Barnabas slowly dissolved into mist, but his voice remained like an owl hooting in distant darkness. "Barnabas, you raised an idiot."

The familiar odor of sulfur remained after the old mountain man vanished, but Flintlock dismissed him from his mind. He leaned the Hawken against a wall. The old rifle could reach out, but its blinding flash was not suited for night work. He'd rely on his booted Winchester. He mounted and rode out of the barn.

In the distance, the mysterious noise still throbbed and he was determined to identify it. If the sound posed any danger, he'd deal with it. Suddenly, an unsettling thought struck him. *Does it have anything to do with the kingfisher?* Flintlock's brain told him no, but his gut instinct warned him that the noise had *everything* to do with the kingfisher.

CHAPTER SEVENTEEN

Sam Flintlock rode east through a tunnel of darkness, allowing his horse to pick its way. The breeze that had been still all day rose again and rustled among the buffalo grass where the scurrying, squeaking creatures lived. The moon climbed high, spreading a blurred light among the dim stars.

The noise grew louder, a rumble like far-off thunder . . . or the voice of divine retribution.

After an hour, he saw lights in the distance. Scattered across the prairie to the north, they were dull red in color like the burned-out cinders of fallen stars. He drew rein and his gaze probed the murk. He nodded, his eyes confirming his suspicion that he was seeing campfires, at least two score of them. Since the Apaches were long gone from that part of Texas, the fires had been built by a much different tribe . . . the lost citizens of Happyville.

Flintlock's horse tossed its head, the bit chiming. It pranced a little, eager to get back on the trail, but he held his mount in check and listened into the night.

He heard no sound from the camp, nothing he could identify as the cadenced rumble he'd been following. The noise was still to his east, somewhere out there in the blackness.

After a last lingering look at the encampment, he kneed his mount into motion. He was strangely uneasy, like a man opening the door to a darkened room, distrustful of what lies within.

Flintlock had ridden less than a dozen yards when his horse suddenly reared and he found himself flat on his back. A moment later, a fanged, snarling wolf sprang on top of him, its slavering jaws lunging for the thunderbird tattoo on his throat. Flintlock desperately held off the animal with his left hand while his right probed for the Colt in his waistband. It was gone, lost when he fell. He used both hands to battle the wolf, trying to throttle it, but he knew he fought a losing battle. The wolf was immensely strong and unspeakably savage. Strands of saliva from the animal's jaws dripped onto Flintlock's face and its snapping teeth were only inches from tearing him apart.

Suddenly, he heard the clanking of a heavy chain and the wolf was gone.

"Stay right where you're at or I'll turn him loose on you again." It was a man's voice, but strangely high-pitched, almost childlike.

During the wolf's initial attack, its fangs had raked Flintlock's forehead and when he wiped his face with the back of his hand it came away bloody. He raised his head and his eyes opened wide in surprise.

Facing him stood a tiny man and a gray wolf, the wolf almost as tall as the man. The dwarf grasped a chain that circled the animal's neck and in his other hand he held a Colt, the hammer back. The man's head was of normal size and well formed. His face was quite handsome, but his body was terribly stunted, the arms and legs very short and stumpy. Flintlock had seen dwarfs before at a circus, but this was the first time he'd ever met one up close, and it would probably be the last. The little man seemed to have every intention of shooting him.

"Why are you here?" The dwarf wore a fine gray top hat with a pair of goggles parked above the brim. A thick gold watch chain crossed the front of his brocade vest.

The wolf attack had shaken Flintlock and it took him some time to collect his thoughts.

"I won't ask you the same question a second time," the little man said.

Flintlock shook his head, clearing his fogged brain. "I was following the sound."

"What sound?"

"The roar. Can't you hear it?"

The wolf growled a threat at Flintlock and the little man had to pull it back, a feat of considerable strength since the huge animal must have weighed at least a hundred and twenty pounds.

"Easy, Quicksilver," the dwarf said. "It is I who will decide this man's fate, not you." He stared hard at Flintlock. "The noise you hear is the engine of Helrun the Black Howler warming up for her journey tomorrow."

"Who is she? Or what is she? Is she a locomotive?"

"You'll find out," the dwarf said. "She shakes the

earth and sets the night afire. That's all you need to know."

Flintlock decided to cut his losses. "Ah, so it is. Well, I'll be on my way as soon as I round up my horse."

"No, you will come with me." The little man's wolf was a fearsome weapon, but the Colt in his hand was just as lethal. He pointed the revolver at Flintlock and said, "Are you one of the folks camped on the flat?"

Flintlock shook his head. "They're from a town west of here."

"I know that," the dwarf said.

"It's a smallpox town."

"I know that as well. Mister, there ain't much I don't know. Pick up your gun and then catch your hoss. We got some traveling to do."

Flintlock smiled. "You trust me with my gun?"

The little man was scornful. "Who the hell is scared of you?"

Annoyed, Flintlock said, "My handle is Samuel Flintlock. You may have heard that name."

"Sure I heard it," the dwarf said. "You're the loco bounty hunter who talks to dead people."

Flintlock said, "I'm not loco and I only talk to one dead people." Aware of how truly crazy that sounded, he added, "Or so folks say."

"Hell, mister, I don't care how many dead people you talk to," the little man said. "Now do as I told you or I'll let Quicksilver do my telling for me."

Irritation niggled at Flintlock, but he let it go. He decided to stay on the trail and see where it led. After all, that's why he was there.

* * *

Flintlock's stud was uneasy at the close proximity of the wolf and to make matters worse, he'd come up lame. Surprised by how rapidly the dwarf moved on his short legs, Flintlock led his restive horse eastward, following the dwarf across rocky, broken ground until they met up with flat grassland again.

Half an hour later, the little man swung north with no break in his stride, the wolf loping at his side.

Flintlock, wearing new boots made on a narrow Texas last, had been hobbling in pain for the last twenty-five minutes, and he vented his spleen on the dwarf. "Hey, Shorty, hold up there," he yelled. "I need to rest a while."

The little man turned and stepped closer to Flintlock, his hand on the growling wolf's chain. "Not far now. You will come now."

"The hell I will, runt," Flintlock said, angry now. "We do as I say and rest for a spell."

The little man thought that over and then said something to the wolf, a series of growls and guttural whispers that Flintlock didn't understand.

"What did you just say to that skillet licker?" Flintlock said. "I don't speak wolf."

"He will not harm you," the little man said. Then he moved with lightning speed, stepped into Flintlock, and effortlessly threw him over his shoulder.

Outraged, Flintlock yelled, "Hey! What the hell are you doing?"

"I will carry you," the little man said.

"The hell you will." Flintlock's head dangled over the dwarf's shoulder and he'd lost his hat. "Let me down, you little runt."

"Will you walk?"

"I'll walk."

The dwarf threw off Flintlock, who landed heavily flat on his back. Infuriated, he said, "Damn you. I ought to put a bullet in you."

"If you do, a second later the wolf will tear you apart." The little man bent from the waist until his face with glittering black eyes was close to Flintlock's and he whispered, "In the fairy stories, there is always an evil dwarf, is there not? Well, I am he."

Flintlock nodded. "I've been inclining to that way of thinking." He drew from the waistband and shoved the muzzle of his Colt into the little man's face. "I also have a notion to blow your head off and take my chances with the lobo."

"It's best you keep me alive," the dwarf said. "A time is coming when you may need a friend."

"You're not my friend," Flintlock said. "Now where are we going? No, don't move. Stay right where you are with my gun barrel up your nostril."

"To the camp of the king," the dwarf said.

"King? What king?"

"King Fisher," the little man said.

CHAPTER EIGHTEEN

"We are very close now," the dwarf said.

"The noise has stopped," Flintlock said. They'd walked for another half hour and his feet ached.

"Yes, and the camp lies in darkness. But our coming will wake everyone."

Flintlock grinned. "Including the king?"

"Most especially King Fisher."

"Well, lead on, runt," Flintlock said. "I could sure use a cup of coffee."

"Before we go farther, my name is not runt," the dwarf said. "I am called Grofrec Horntoe. To call me anything else in the presence of King Fisher could result in your immediate execution."

"Gro . . . Gro . . . what the hell?" Flintlock said.

"Grofrec Horntoe."

"Did your mama name you that?"

"Did yours name you Sam Flintlock?"

Flintlock remained silent.

"King Fisher named me and if you are lucky, he will welcome you and give you a new name. If he chooses to do otherwise, he will kill you." The little man glanced at the sky. "The moon still rides high and will light our path as we traverse the grove of skulls." He saw the baffled look on Flintlock's face and said, "Anyone who wishes to visit the camp of King Fisher must enter by the grove of skulls."

"Hey, hold on a minute," Flintlock said. "I wondered where I'd heard the name before. Are you talking about King Fisher out of Collin County, Texas, built himself a gun rep down in the border country and then ran with Ben Thompson and that hard crowd?"

"No, the man you speak of is not he," Horntoe said.

"You sure, Hornytoad?"

"The King Fisher you knew is dead. And my name is Horntoe."

"I didn't hear that King was dead," Flintlock said.

"He and Ben Thompson were shot to death three years ago in the Vaudeville Variety Theater in San Antonio. The King Fisher you speak of was shot thirteen times and is dead, dead, dead. This is the new King Fisher."

Flintlock rubbed his stubbly chin. "Well, if that don't beat all. I met King a time or two and he was all right when he was sober. He was mighty fast with the iron and that's a natural fact."

"Now we must go," the dwarf said.

"I hope it ain't far. My boots are punishing me."

"The grove is very near." He glanced at the wolf next to him—gray as a ghost in the pale moonlight, its eyes glowing with green fire—and grabbed the lobo's chain. "Follow me, Flintlock . . . and be brave."

* * *

There was no grove of trees leading to King Fisher's encampment. Rather a shallow dry wash was lined by two parallel rows of three stakes, each about five feet high. The objects spiked on the stakes startled Flintlock and chilled him to the bone.

Each bore a grinning skull painted in the Mexican Day of the Dead style with red, white, and black flowers intertwined with green plant tendrils. The resemblance ended there. Each eye socket was filled with a rusty gearwheel, and large springs held the jawbones in place. The crowns were made of thin brass, plated by a skin of gold leaf and adorned with bits and pieces of machinery and small gauges from steam engines so that the skulls looked inhuman. The gearwheel eyes, their centers complete with irises of colored glass, gave the skulls the appearance of life. It was as though each stared at Sam Flintlock and wondered at his identity.

By inclination, Flintlock was not a religious man, but he immediately invoked the deity with considerable passion. "My God in heaven!" he yelled. "What abomination is this?"

Grofrec Horntoe said, "There is no abomination here. These are the skulls of the first men King Fisher killed in fair fight after his transformation. He has killed many men since, but to these six he does great honor."

It had taken a while, but it finally dawned on Flintlock that he'd made a great mistake going there to identify the sound. The skulls grinned at him, warning him that he would be lucky to get out alive.

As though reading his mind, Horntoe said, "Unless you adjust your thinking, Flintlock, you won't be alive come sunup. It's too late to consider and escape on a lame horse. King Fisher would soon hunt you down and kill you."

"Yeah, if he can get past my Colt," Flintlock said, testy as he realized that he'd run out of room on the dance floor and had nothing to offer but idle boast.

Horntoe shook his head. "Don't be so damned foolish, Flintlock. No man on earth can shade King Fisher, though many have tried. Part of his gun arm was forged in iron and bronze. He is the wonder of our modern age and invincible."

CHAPTER NINETEEN

The dwarf and his wolf abruptly walked into the surrounding darkness and Sam Flintlock found himself left alone on the middle of a tent encampment where several fires burned. A few women moved around like shadows in the gloom and paid no heed to him or his horse.

Deciding that it was not a time for shyness, he led his mount to a horse line that was situated back a ways near a stand of pine. He unsaddled the bay, tethered him to the rope, and then tossed him an armful of hay from a nearby stack. No one questioned his actions or even glanced in his direction.

Following his nose, he stepped to a fire where coffee simmered on the coals. A stack of tin cups stood nearby and he poured himself a cup. The coffee was black and bitter the way he liked it and after the first few sips he felt his weariness begin to slide off his shoulders like a damp cloak. Squatting by the fire, he built and lit a cigarette and looked around. For a moment, he was distracted by a pretty young woman who threw a few sticks onto the fire then stepped away without even a glance in his direction.

The girl's mode of dress intrigued him almost as much as her slim, shapely body. She wore a dark brown skirt with a buckled corset and blouse of the same color. Her skirt was short, reaching to the middle of her thighs, and her calf-length boots were laced up the front. A pair of goggles was pushed high on her forehead and her right cheek was smudged with what could have been soot.

Flintlock thought the girl looked like a locomotive engineer, but she was a fair piece away from any railroad. He followed her with his eyes until she faded into darkness at the far southern edge of the encampment. A couple minutes passed, then a strange green light glowed where he'd last seen the girl. This was followed by a low hum, like the buzz of a score of beehives.

He drained his cup, tossed the butt of his cigarette into the fire, and rose to his feet. Ignored as he was and having nothing better to do, he thought it was a mystery worth investigating.

Flintlock strolled to where he'd seen the light. As his eyes became accustomed to the darkness, a massive black shape emerged from the gloom. The coach, for that's what he initially took it to be, was shaped like a gigantic egg, looking as though it had been laid on the prairie by a roc, the legendary bird of prey the Sioux and Cheyenne believed was capable of seizing and devouring a full-grown bull buffalo.

But no egg was made out of riveted boilerplate with a row of round windows like a ship's portholes. Where the coach driver would sit was a glass-enclosed cabin, the likes of which Flintlock had never seen before. The girl who dressed like an engineer sat inside. Her goggles were over her eyes, the lenses tinted green as though a shaded lantern shone on them.

Moving closer, he saw that the coach had six immense wheels, four at the rear and two at the front. As tall as a man, their steel rims were spiked with sharp, piercing skewers set a few inches apart. A brass Gatling gun was mounted in an open turret on top of the iron egg, its action covered by an oilskin tarp.

Flintlock had seen enough to convince him that it was not a coach designed for comfortable travel over rough terrain, but a dreadful weapon of war. His opinion was reinforced when he stepped to the rear of the vehicle and discovered it was powered by a mighty steam engine that looked as though it had been taken from a naval ironclad. The boiler was lit and the engine emitted a steady *thrum . . . thrum . . . thrum . . .* as it turned over. Steam escaped, hissing like angry baby dragons from the joints of its brass and bronze pipes.

"Hey, you. Git the hell away from there!"

Flintlock turned and saw the outline of a man standing in the shadow of a tall tent, a rifle cradled across his chest. He also wore a belt gun.

"What is this thing?" Flintlock said.

"None of your business, that's what it is." The man stepped out of darkness into moonlight and the eerie light from the machine's cabin. "You'll find out soon enough."

The man who talked with his dead grandfather was not much given to surprises, but the sentry's appearance made Flintlock's words jam tight in his throat.

The rifleman wore black pants and boots, a dark shirt with full sleeves, and an old, battered, black plug hat. His bright scarlet vest added drama to his getup, as did the polished brass studs that decorated his gun belt and holster, but what caught and held Flintlock's attention was the finely wrought bronze plate that emerged from the collar of the man's shirt and was shaped to cover the entire right side of his face like a mask. The plate was beautifully engraved around its border in what was known as the Celtic style and its gold inlays of strange beasts suggested long man-hours and considerable skill. Where his right eye should have been was a large, round lens that looked as though it had been taken from a pair of army field glasses. Stranger still, the man's right leg was encased in what at first glance appeared to be medieval armor, except that the cuisse, poleyn, and greave were made of brass, covered in a tangled network of pipes, valves, and exquisitely designed cogwheels. Flintlock watched the man walk a short distance. The artificial leg— swung forward by a motion of his hip when he wished to take a step—seemed efficient, an engineering masterpiece of the new Steam Age.

"I thought I recognized you," the man said suddenly. "There ain't two men in the west with thunderbirds on their throats. You're Sam Flintlock. Am I right or am I wrong?"

"You called it."

"Last I heard, you were running with Jesse James and them in the train robbing line of work."

"I did for a spell, but I never did take to it. Me and Frank couldn't get along, so Jesse wasn't real broken up when I left."

"And then?"

"I took up the bounty-hunting profession," Flint-lock said. "It's good work if a man's got a flair for it and can keep his nerve."

"Still got the old Hawken?"

Flintlock was surprised. "How did you know about the Hawken?"

"I'm Clem Jardine. Remember me? Our paths crossed a time or two up in the Red River country that time. The newspapers called it the Harper-Mclean range war. I called it a waste of time."

"I recollect," Flintlock said. "I never drew a day's gun wage after Mose Harper and Drew Mclean patched up their differences."

"A pair of no-good lowlifes. Took the bread right out of our mouths with all that damned peace talk."

A night bird raised a ruckus in a nearby piñon and then fell silent.

Flintlock said, "Clem, I heard you was dead. Got all shot to pieces by a bunch of bronco Apaches down Eagle Pass way."

"You heard right about me getting all shot to pieces, but some newspaper reporter from back east made up that story about Apaches," Jardine said. "The truth is I got shot up by a posse of sodbusters and store-keepers after me and some others who robbed their town bank. Loco Lawson—remember him? He got shot in the mouth, blew the back of his head clean off. Snake River Bob Styles was killed by the first volley."

"Sorry to hear that," Flintlock said. "He was a rum one was ol' Bob, but he could sing them Irish songs."

"He could that," Jardine said. "Uriah Hanbury got cut in half by a scattergun, Broady Wells was wounded and then got beaten to death by rifle butts, and Hiram Anstruther—"

"The older feller. Was a monk at one time," Flintlock said.

"Yeah, that was him. Hiram got scared, fell off his horse, and died after his ticker suddenly gave out on him." The metal half of Jardine's face glinted as he shook his head. "We were bushwhacked at a place south of the pass called Dead Horse Creek. It wasn't a creek, not that day. It was a dry wash and hot and dusty as hell. We had eight men dead on the ground and me all shot to pieces and left for the buzzards. Then Doctor Obadiah le Strange happened by."

How did the doctor save you? Why did he spare your lives? Did he turn you and King Fisher into clockwork men? What the hell is going on here? Those questions sprang into Flintlock's mind but went unasked.

A tent flap opened and a tall, slender woman stepped outside. "Clem, come to bed. It's very late."

"Blanche, first come over here and meet a friend of mine," Jardine said. "Sam Flintlock, meet my wife Blanche."

The woman extended her hand. "Pleased to meet you, I'm sure."

Flintlock gaped at the woman and stuttered some kind of reply. His gaze was fixed on Blanche's face. It was not a human face. It was the still, expressionless face of a porcelain doll.

A cream-colored ceramic mask covered her features and extended lower, molded over her breasts. Her face mask was decorated with elaborate and vivid paintings of rolling dice and the clubs, hearts, diamonds, and spades of a deck of playing cards. The arcs of the areolae that showed above the woman's tightly laced corset were tinted a delicate pink in contrast to the bright colors of the porcelain mask.

"Before I met her, Blanche was a faro dealer in Denver." Jardine slipped his arm around the woman's slim waist and held her close. "As you can see, Doctor le Strange also helped her." He saw the question on Flintlock's face and said only one word. "Acid."

"I hope the morning brings you life and not death, Mr. Flintlock," Blanche said. "We will see."

Jardine touched his hat. "Good seeing you again, Sam." He and Blanche turned to walk back to the tent, his artificial leg making slight clanking sounds.

Flintlock still had a question, something that had been puzzling him since he'd met Grofrec Horntoe. Talking to the man's retreating back, he said, "Clem, you know I'm fast with the iron. Why did no one take my gun?"

Jardine's answer was to turn with blinding speed, throw his Winchester to his shoulder, and lever off six shots in the space of a single heartbeat. The bullets sang and whined on each side of Flintlock's head, missing his ears by fractions of an inch.

"That's why, Sam." Jardine held up his right arm. "Dr. le Strange did some work on my gun hand, too."

Blanche laughed, a sound so melodious and delicate it could have come, not from her vocal cords, but from the strings of a Stradivarius violin.

Flintlock stood rooted to the spot for long moments. He'd never seen gun-handling so fast, and he'd been around some of the best. If he'd braced Clem Jardine and gone for the Colt in his waistband, the man would have killed him before his fingers touched the handle. No human being could lever off six shots at that speed, taking only a split second to get his work in.

But someone with a repaired and surgically improved gun hand could.

Suddenly Flintlock felt emotions strange to him and he put a name to each of them . . . *fear, dread,* and *terror of the unknown.*

Something was at play here, something appalling that he could not understand. He recalled Clem Jardine's words. *We had eight men dead on the ground and me all shot to pieces and left for the buzzards . . .*

Flintlock shivered.

Did the dead walk again in this place?

He looked around him. No one had come to investigate the rifle fire shooting . . . yet another mystery.

Sam Flintlock lay beside the fire and dreamed of dead men who rose from their graves and danced in the cobwebbed moonlight with painted porcelain dolls who smiled painted smiles.

He woke to someone calling his name.

CHAPTER TWENTY

"Flintlock! Sam Flintlock! Get the hell up. Somebody wants to meet you."

Groggily, Flintlock rose to a sitting position. "King Fisher?"

"Maybe," Clem Jardine said. In the dawn light the uncovered half of his face was ashen, his pale lips bloodless. "Get yourself some coffee. You got time yet. You look like hell."

"When bullets have made a man's hat look like a colander, he tends to look a tad peaked."

"Hat? Hell, I was aiming for your ears."

"You're a funny man, Clem," Flintlock said, rising to his feet. "That was a real knee-slapper."

"Coffee's on the coals and there's biscuits and bacon in the pan." Jardine's voice was weak, as though the man was all used up. "I'll come back for you."

Before Flintlock could say anything Jardine turned and slowly walked away. He seemed weary and his strange brass leg dragged, clinking with every faltering step.

Alone by the fading fire, Flintlock ate his third

biscuit and then refilled his coffee cup for the second time. He had begun to build a cigarette when he heard a man shriek in torment.

Flintlock rose to his feet and his hand instinctively dropped to his waistband for his Colt.

"There's no need for violence," a female voice said. The woman who dressed like a locomotive engineer walked toward Flintlock.

In the light of dawn he saw that she had green eyes that glowed like a cat's and thick auburn hair that cascaded over her shoulders in glossy waves. She had undone the row of straps and buckles that closed her red leather corset and her goggles hung around her slender neck. She was exceptionally beautiful.

Flintlock smiled. "You startled me."

"I fear you're easily startled," the woman said. Her mouth was wide, full-lipped, and eminently kissable. "Is the coffee still hot?

"Sure is, and there's biscuits and bacon," Flintlock said.

"Bread and grease. I can think of no finer breakfast. My name is Doctor Sarah Ann Castle."

"Right pleased to make your acquaintance, ma'am," Flintlock said, touching his hat. "Mine is—"

"I know what your name is." She poured herself coffee.

"Are you a sawbones?" Flintlock said, prepared to be sociable.

"I'm a physician, yes."

"I bet you're a good one."

"How would you know?"

"Just by looking at you."

"What does a competent doctor look like? What does an incompetent doctor look like?"

Flintlock floundered, trying to grab words that were as elusive as butterflies. The fact that he didn't know what the hell *competent* meant didn't help. Finally he managed, "Seems that everybody I've met here is made of brass or pottery." He smiled. "Except you."

"Really?" She pulled her corset wide, revealing firm, coral-tipped breasts. But between them from the top of her chest to the bottom of her rib cage ran a wide, scarlet scar, raw and angry, as though a ferocious animal had recently clawed her.

Dr. Castle's smile was remarkable for its beauty. "The metal is inside me." She read Flintlock's bewildered expression and said, "I have a heart valve made of brass."

"A what?" Flintlock said, amazed that the woman's voice was so matter of fact.

"A valve, basically just a little tube. Two years ago when I was one of Dr. Obadiah le Strange's medical assistants my heart began to give out, and other doctors told me it was only a matter of time until it stopped altogether. We were in London at the time when Dr. le Strange was called in by Scotland Yard to consult on the Jack the Ripper case."

Flintlock nodded. "One time I read about that Ripper feller in the *Refined Ladies' Home Companion* magazine."

"You read women's periodicals, Mr. Flintlock? How very modern of you."

"I picked up the paper in a dentist's office while I was waiting to get a chipped tooth fixed," Flintlock said on the defensive. "I have no truck with women's fixins."

"Then you disappoint me," Dr. Castle said.

"Well maybe not, because I've got a notion on who that Ripper gent could be," Flintlock said. "You can tell old Queen Vic next time you see her."

"I'd be interested to hear what you have to say since Scotland Yard's brightest and best never identified him."

"Here's the way of it, Doc. Down Galveston way I met a seafaring man by the name of Jake Roper, a petticoat chaser and whoremonger. Chances are he dropped anchor in London town for a spell and then did all that cuttin'. Name *Jack the Ripper* is only a holler and a half away from the name *Jake Roper*, and that's a natural fact."

The woman pulled her corset closed and refilled her coffee cup. When she looked at Flintlock again, she said, "His name was . . . is . . . Professor Christian Prescott Tynan, a world-renowned research scientist."

"Who?" Flintlock said.

"Your man Jack the Ripper."

"If you know his name—"

"The British government knew his name. And I assure you so did Queen Victoria."

"Then how come he didn't get hung?" Flintlock said.

"He was too valuable to the Royal Navy and the defense of the realm. The professor was working on a turbine steam engine that would power the new breed of dreadnaught battleships. The engine was so efficient the Admiralty believed it could reduce a warship's coal consumption by half while increasing its speed by at least five knots." Doctor Castle's coffee steamed in the morning cool. "The politicians and the admirals were prepared to tolerate Christian's little hobby for as long as it took to get the steam turbine into production."

"And you knew all this while you and Dr. le Strange were working for Scotland Yard?" Flintlock said, intrigued.

"Of course. Christian and I were lovers for a year. I could hardly betray him." She smiled. "Contrary to what you might expect, he was a gentle lover, very tender and considerate. The trashy magazine you read, what is it? The *Refined Ladies' Home Companion*—"

"I don't—"

"Would describe Christian Tynan as being all hearts and flowers."

"Except when he was gutting whores," Flintlock said, intentionally trying to be brutal.

Dr. Castle nodded, a coiled tendril of hair falling over her forehead. "Yes, I must say that was the least attractive of all his little peccadillos."

"Where is he now?" Flintlock said.

The camp was stirring and a woman wearing a beautiful pearl gray top hat, an almost-there skirt and knee-high red leather boots, stepped to the fire. She picked up the fry pan and said to Flintlock, "Hey, cowboy, you finished breakfast?"

"No. Leave the grub there by the fire."

"I'd rather feed you for a week than a month," the woman said. She clumsily tossed the pan beside the coals. It was only then Flintlock noticed that both her hands were made of brass, the articulated fingers of some white metal, probably silver.

When the woman left, Dr. Castle said, "As soon as the turbine engine passed its sea trials, Christian was taken to a hospital for the criminally insane. His six-foot-by-six-foot cell is guarded night and day by marines and he'll die there. Soon, if he's lucky. Twice a week the queen sends him a bottle of wine from her own cellar, and the admirals supply fresh fish for his dinner. I'm told Christian's mind is gone and he raves constantly about fallen women and how he is the instrument of divine justice sent to destroy them and cut them open to release their souls to hell. But I don't know if all that is true or not. The British authorities are terrible liars." She tossed out the dregs of her coffee. "I have to be going. King Fisher will call for you soon."

"Wait," Flintlock said. "This Dr. le Strange, what did he think of Jack the Ripper?"

Dr. Castle shrugged, her wide, shapely shoulders moving under her blouse. "He considered Christian a valued colleague in the field of steam engineering research. Nothing more. Of course, he knew Christian and I were lovers, but he was fine with that."

"Lucky for you or he wouldn't have fixed you up with a steam heart," Flintlock said.

"No, he was eager to do it. To Obadiah I was just another engineering experiment. The heart, after all, is merely a pump. It's not powered by steam, though, but electricity, the elemental power of the universe. Before God, there was electricity, and He employed it for His own creation."

"How long will it last? Your heart, I mean."

Dr. Castle smiled. "If the valve doesn't get clogged and the micro generator—"

"What's a micro?" Flintlock said.

Dr. Castle smiled. "Micro means small, very teensy. If the generator . . . if the battery doesn't wear out, my heart will still be beating at the end of time."

Flintlock grinned. "I'm glad to hear that. You're way too pretty to die young."

"Good-bye, Mr. Flintlock," Dr. Castle said.

He watched the woman go, her hips moving under her canvas skirt. It was only then, in the brightening light of the morning, that he saw the name painted on the egg-shaped machine that the doctor had just entered through a top hatch.

HELRUN
The Black Howler

"What the hell?" Flintlock whispered.

"Turn around, you damned blockhead," a man's voice said behind him. "It's me again."

As he turned, Flintlock said, "Go away, Barnabas."

"Lookee here." The old mountain sat on the grass beside a birdcage made from copper wire. Inside, perched on a stick, was a tiny yellow bird. "Watch this." Barnabas pushed something at the back of the cage and the bird immediately flapped its wings and began to sing a tinny *cheep, cheep, cheep.* "It ain't real."

"I could tell that," Flintlock said. "Where did you get it?"

Barnabas blinked. "Found it." He held up a small brass key. "It's clockwork. A clockwork bird is what it is. But it ain't a kingfisher. No sir, this here is one of them canary birds."

"Why are you here, Barnabas?" Flintlock said. "To show me a bird?"

"To tell you that you're an idiot."

"You tell me that every time I see you."

"And every time I see you I know it's true." Barnabas lifted the cage and stared at the bird. He made a clicking sound with his tongue and then said, "You need wound up again, little chicken." He set the cage down, put his key in and cranked the mechanism. The bird cheeped again and flapped its wings. "You ever hear tell of Huggy Brampton up Kansas way?"

Flintlock frowned. "Can't say as I have."

"He wasn't too smart, kinda like you, Sammy. One time a feller sold him a bird dog an' Huggy killed it when he threw it up in the air to see how high it could fly." Barnabas stared at Flintlock. "He was an idiot."

Irritated, Flintlock opened his mouth to speak, but the old mountain man held up a silencing hand. "Listen and learn, boy. Everybody in this camp should be dead. Most of them, including the pretty lady who showed you her tits, were dead, at least for a spell. They got no right to be casting a shadow on the ground. Both men and women, they all belong in the graveyard. They shouldn't be here among the living."

Flintlock frowned again. "The dead should stay dead, including you, Barnabas. I don't even know how those folks are still breathing. Maybe this is all a nightmare and pretty soon I'll wake up"—he smiled—"or could be they got a good doctor."

"You mean le Strange? He ain't any kind of doctor, sonny, he's an engineer. He created monsters." Barnabas shook his head, rose to his feet, and picked up the birdcage. "You're in a heap of trouble, Sam, and there's not a damned thing I can do to help you."

"Barnabas, I don't need—"

"Talking to yourself again, Flintlock?"

Flintlock turned and saw Clem Jardine standing behind him, a smile on his patched-up face.

"King wants to see you now." He inclined his head. "I thought I heard a bird around here."

"Like you said, I was talking to myself."

"And singing like a bird?"

"A man who's been on as many high lonesome as I have does some mighty peculiar things by times." Quickly changing the subject, Flintlock said, "A few minutes ago I thought I heard a man cry out in pain."

"Is that so?" Jardine said. "Maybe you did."

CHAPTER TWENTY-ONE

As the crow flies, twenty-five miles southeast of the King Fisher encampment Captain Gregory Holden Usher and his five-man patrol breakfasted on salt pork, hard biscuits, and gritty coffee. His troopers were in a foul mood, dirty, tired, sullen, and angry at tracking a will-o-the-wisp over endless grassland with no end to the chase in sight. Most of all, they resented this detail and the man who commanded it, a fifty-three-year-old, alcoholic officer who would never recover from the disgrace of fleeing the field of battle and leaving thirteen men to die in his stead. The charge of cowardice in the face of the enemy had been dismissed at Usher's court-martial, but the stigma remained.

Sergeant Rollo Martin, whose younger brother had been killed in the massacre, studied Usher, despising him with a passion. With hate in his black eyes, Martin again silently vowed that he'd execute the captain for cowardice when he had the opportunity to make it look good . . . probably when he was surrounded by men who detested Captain Usher as much as he did.

"Scout coming in," a trooper said, looking to the north. "Seems like he's carrying something in a sack."

Usher's scout was an unwashed, buckskinned creature named Luke Gamble, a former Barbary Coast enforcer who smelled like a gut wagon and was said to have killed seven white men and twice that many Indians and Mexicans. Gamble had recently strangled a brothel madam for the fifty dollars in her purse. That murder had forced him to flee San Francisco and sign on as an army scout.

He squatted by the fire, laid the bulging sack beside him, and used his knife to spear a chunk of pork. He had the manners of a pig.

Captain Usher looked at the man with bleary-eyed distaste. "What do you have in your poke, Mr. Gamble?"

The scout stared at Usher, chewing, grease running into his wispy, yellow beard. Finally he said, "Came on a dead Mex about five miles north of here. I couldn't find a wound on him, but I brung this." Gamble dipped into the sack and withdrew a human head. Expressionless, the features were placid as though the man had fallen asleep and died. Gamble tossed the head onto the grass, where it rolled against Sergeant Martin's boot.

Angrily, the big man kicked the head away and cursed at the scout.

Gamble smiled, then looked at Usher. "Notice something strange about the face, Cap'n?"

Disgusted, Usher said no. He was already half-drunk.

"Look how pale it is," Gamble said. "A Mex should

never look that white. His whole damned body was the same way, white as a fish's belly. Kinda like Sergeant Martin when he takes his blue shirt off."

Martin growled, his teeth showing under his mustache. "Gamble, I'll put a bullet in you one day."

"Sergeant Martin, that is enough," Usher said. "We don't bandy words with civilians. Mr. Gamble, throw the head away. I don't know why he's so pale under his skin color. Sheer fright perhaps."

"When I used this"—Gamble took a steel trade tomahawk from his belt—"to top the Mex, there was hardly any blood. Strange that."

Usher said, "Get rid of the head, Mr. Gamble. Sergeant Martin, load up the pack mule. We will renew the pursuit of King Fisher. How far ahead of us, Mr. Gamble?"

"The paymaster wagon is slowing them down, and they're hauling another wagon, something with big wheels . . . maybe like a brewer's dray."

"How far, Mr. Gamble?"

"I reckon we'll catch up with them tonight or at first light tomorrow morning."

"I'll plan on a dawn attack," Usher said. "I have no stomach for a night action."

Gamble stared at the officer, his eyes hard. *Mister, you got no stomach for any action. You proved that much at Dead Tree Pass.* "They say King Fisher is a gun. I heard he was dead, but I guess that was just a big story."

Usher slapped the holstered Colt on his right side. "We're all guns, Mr. Gamble."

* * *

Eighteen-year-old Private Seth Proud, a Louisiana swamp boy, paused in roping the pack to the mule's back. "Sarge, how much money did them fellers get in the payroll robbery?"

Rollo Martin turned his black eyes on the boy. "More than you'll see in your lifetime, Private Proud. Enough to keep a careful man in whiskey and whores for a hundred years. As for the rest of us, we'd be worn out and used up long before the money was spent."

Proud whistled between his prominent front teeth. "Man, I could sure use some of that."

"Dream on, boy," Martin said. Then, smiling, he added, "Though who knows? Sometimes dreams come true."

CHAPTER TWENTY-TWO

As Private Proud dreamed of a hundred years of whiskey and whores, Clem Jardine led Sam Flintlock to a large tent at the edge of the encampment. The flap lifted and two men carried out an unconscious elderly white man, his face ashen.

A voice from inside the tent said, "Max, see he gets plenty of red wine."

"I reckon he'll be a goner soon, King," said the man called Max.

Disinterested, the voice from inside said, "Hell, try it anyway."

"Whatever you say, boss," Max said.

As the old man was carried past him, Flintlock said to Jardine, "What's ailing him?"

"He's old and I guess he doesn't have enough blood in him," Jardine said. "It happens to old-timers, or so I've been told."

Flintlock hesitated and watched the two men carrying the comatose oldster. "Here, ain't that Max Eades and Jasper Aston, guns for hire from down Laredo way? I recollect Max killed Dan Polk in Beaumont that time, and for a spell Jasper was top gun in the Colfax County War up New Mexico way. Come to think of it, I believe there are dead-or-alive dodgers on both them boys."

"Flintlock, forget it," Jardine said. "Max and Jasper work for Mr. Fisher, and he sets store by them. He'd take it hard if a bounty hunter tried to collect on them."

"I have other things on my mind," Flintlock said. "I have no interest in those boys. For the time being, anyway."

From inside the tent came the call. "Git the hell in here, Sam Flintlock. You're not so damned tough."

CHAPTER TWENTY-THREE

Clem Jardine grinned as he opened the flap and Flintlock stooped and stepped inside. After the brightness of the morning, the tent was gloomy and shadowed, but it was the smell, not the dim light that caught his attention. It was not a bad odor, but strange, like how the air smells before a thunderstorm. That and a vague tang of gun oil.

The smell was a little unsettling, but then Flintlock saw King Fisher . . . or what was left of him . . . and thought he was losing his mind. This was not the robust Fisher he'd known. The man was painfully thin, his face ashen, like someone recovering from a long and serious illness. Unlike Clem Jardine, there was no metal on Fisher's face, but his right eye was peculiar. As though made of colored glass, it glowed with the same green light Flintlock had seen in the cabin of the Helrun.

King Fisher held a small, bloodstained towel to the inside of his left arm as he turned to Flintlock. "Been a while, Sam. Hell, man, you look like you've seen a ghost."

Flintlock's words came slowly, choking as thought he was coughing up walnuts. "I heard you was dead, King. All shot to pieces along o' Ben Thompson in San Antone."

"Ben is dead," Fisher said. "A couple balls to the head destroyed his brain and he couldn't be saved. I was luckier, if you can call it that. More dead than alive, I was carried to the Holy Redeemer church and Dr. le Strange found me there." His right hand had been covered with the towel and now he showed it . . . a hand and wrist of flesh and blood but overlaid by a delicate tracery of thin steel and brass rods and wires of the same materials that vanished into scar tissue.

"He saved my gun hand, Sam," Fisher said. "It's better—stronger and faster than it ever was before."

"Did I just hear my name?"

The tent flap opened and a tall, slender man stepped inside. He wore a hooded black cape, the cowl pulled over his head, and a floppy, wide-brimmed hat of the same color. His face was not visible, covered by a mask made to look like the beak and round eyes of a large crow. About a foot long, the beak gave off an odor of sweet herbs and spices. Behind the mask, the doctor's breath hissed.

King Fisher, his face strangely immobile as though it was frozen into its bland, neutral expression, said, "Obadiah, I think you're scaring our guest."

"He's right, boogeyman," Flintlock said. "And when I'm scared, I get nervous and when I get nervous, bad things tend to happen."

"No need for violence, Mr. Flintlock," le Strange

said. He removed his hat, pushed back his hood, and removed the mask, revealing the smiling, handsome face of a man in his mid-forties.

"You had me worried there for a spell, Obadiah," Fisher said. "A narrow tent is a bad place for a gunfight on account of how all the parties involved usually end up dead." His stiff face showed no emotion, but there was a smile in his voice. He turned his attention to Flintlock. "Dr. le Strange is testing a plague mask that he says was first used during the Black Death back in the olden days. The place I'm planning to, ah . . . farm . . . is stricken by smallpox, or so we believe."

"You mean Happyville," Flintlock said. "I just came from there and it's a ghost town. Them as didn't die of the smallpox have all lit a shuck."

"Where are they?" King Fisher said, his voice registering alarm.

"I don't know," Flintlock said, wary of giving the location of the townspeople's encampment to this man. "They're still around, somewhere."

Fisher looked at le Strange. "Obadiah, we must find them."

"We'll find them, King," the doctor said. "I didn't save your life only to have you die on me."

"How did you save his life?" Flintlock said. "You turned King Fisher into some kind of tin man. Who has a mitt like that? Hell, I talked to a woman who has a mechanical heart and I saw another with silver hands. How did you do that, huh? It don't seem right to me."

"It seems right to King, I assure you," le Strange said.

"Obadiah says Sarah Castle will live to be ninety with her repaired heart and I'll live just as long with my artificial eye and mechanical hand," King Fisher said. "A word of warning, Sam. I'm still considering what to do with you, so don't make my decision too easy."

Flintlock could be pushed, but not far. He would not be railroaded now. "King, I wasn't scared of you when you were alive. I'm sure as hell not scared of you now."

"Ah, Mr. Flintlock, be not so hasty," le Strange said. "You should be afraid. I engineered King Fisher to be the deadliest human fighting machine that ever lived. The Spartan hoplite, the Roman legionary, the medieval knight pale in comparison, and in our own time so do the likes of Hickok and Wes Hardin. There is not a man alive today who can draw faster or shoot straighter than Mr. Fisher." He laid a hand on Fisher's shoulder and his voice rose. "And should his fast new gun hand be damaged, it can be repaired."

"My God . . ." Flintlock said.

"God has nothing to do with it," le Strange said. "Modern engineering, the forge, the furnace, the steam engine and electricity . . . those are the new gods that will soon replace the old and give mankind what their impotent god could not—power. And perhaps eventually, immortality."

"Hell, man, what kind of sawbones are you?" Flintlock said.

Le Strange smiled. "My doctorate is in engineering, Mr. Flintlock."

"But how . . . I mean Sarah Castle's heart, the woman with the silver hands—"

"And many more," le Strange said. "But the woman you mention and King Fisher are my masterpieces. A good engineer can be as delicate as a surgeon when he has to be."

"Damn right," Fisher said. Worked up as he was, his mechanical forearm vibrated.

Le Strange made an adjustment to a tiny valve near the elbow and the barely perceptible oscillation stopped.

"As you can see, Mr. Flintlock, I still have to perfect my creations, but I will in time. Like King's arm and Dr. Castle's constant palpitations, they are inconvenient but not permanently damaging."

"Sarah Castle says you worked with a murderer in London called Jack the Ripper," Flintlock said. "Is what she says true?"

Le Strange winced. "That is coarse and vulgar, the sort of boorish question I had not expected from any gentleman with the slightest claim to refinement."

"Mind your manners, Sam," Fisher said. "Remember that I set store by Dr. le Strange."

"It's quite all right, King." Le Strange looked directly at Flintlock. "We were once colleagues, the man you call the Ripper, Professor Christian Prescott Tynan. He worked on steam turbine engines for the Royal Navy but dabbled in anatomy on the side. Chris taught me much about the workings of the female body, the reason I was so successful with Dr. Castle."

As the sun rose higher and heated up the tent, Flintlock felt the canvas walls close in. It began to dawn on him that he was trapped in an asylum where everyone was stark, raving mad. "Tynan murdered women, slashed them to pieces. Damn you. He was Jack the Ripper!"

"Easy, Sam," King Fisher said. "Mind your deportment. I won't warn you again." He was on his feet and his automated hand with its beautifully articulated metal fingers was close to his gun.

"No harm done. Mr. Flintlock speaks the same sentimental ignorance of the great unwashed," le Strange said. "Allow me to enlighten him. Mr. Flintlock, Professor Tynan contributed vastly to the sum of man's knowledge in steam engineering and the advancement of anatomy and surgery. If it were not for him, Dr. Castle, a fine physician, would not be alive today. And at what cost? The lives of a few whores who sold their diseased bodies for a couple pennies. They were hardly a great loss to humanity. Those worthless women redeemed themselves in the end by dying for science."

"I know some women back in Happyville who would disagree with that," Flintlock said.

"Whores?"

"Of a sort."

La Strange turned to King Fisher. "Good news."

Fisher nodded. "It's a start."

Le Strange nodded in Flintlock's direction. "What about him?"

King Fisher said. "I have a decision to make. Do I spare this man for old times' sake or am I being a sentimental fool? We'll see."

"See what?" Flintlock said.

"You'll find out, Sam. Maybe later, if I decide I can trust you, I will let you in on my plans." Fisher nodded. "Big plans, Sam. The foundation of an empire."

Flintlock was on edge. The thought occurred to him that in King Fisher he faced an abomination. The creature in the tent with the artificial eye and mechanical shooting hand was barely human, a far cry from the tall Texan he'd known, the bronco buster, cowboy, rancher, rustler, saloon owner, sometime law officer and above all, a shootist of considerable skill, daring, and courage.

Fisher's uncanny skill as a gunman was revealed in all its hell-firing glory back in the spring of 1874 on his Pendencia ranch near Eagle Pass. Four Mexican vaqueros had mocked King's usual gaudy duds, a fringed buckskin shirt, scarlet sash, pearl-handle Colts, and jinglebob spurs. King was always on a short fuse. An exchange of words led to King's fast draw and when the smoke cleared all four Mexicans lay dead on the ground, among them Juan Santos, the Nogales Wildcat, who some said had killed eleven white men in gunfights.

That was then, and the dashing King Fisher of 1874 no longer existed, replaced by this . . . madman who spoke of building empires.

Le Strange was talking again. "You don't like me much, do you, Mr. Flintlock?"

"No, not much," Flintlock said.

"Pity. I'm a good person to know. A man in your line of work needs a friend like me, someone who can repair him if he gets shot trying to apprehend a fugitive."

"How come you were in San Antone the night Ben and King were . . . killed?" Flintlock said, hesitating over the final word.

Le Strange smiled as though the question pleased him. "I was attending a lecture at Trinity University on the writer and visionary Jules Verne. His vision of a world turned into a utopia by steam power and engineering thrilled me, especially since the lecturer had actually met and talked with the great man. When the lecture ended and I left the university, I heard that two notorious gunman had been shot to death at the Vaudeville Variety Theater, a place frequented by persons of the lowest sort."

"That's what I was, Obadiah? A person of the lowest sort?" Fisher said, savoring the words.

"You were, my dear, until I exalted you and raised you up to the heights of perfection where now you stand like a warrior god."

"He's sitting," Flintlock said. "So you headed for the theater and grabbed King's body, huh? Or what was left of it."

"That is an approximation but close enough," le Strange said. "On my return from London, being of independent means due to a generous legacy left me by my late father, I had taken a suite of rooms in the Brackenridge Park district of San Antonio and had set up a modest machine shop and laboratory."

"But you'd already given Dr. Castle her heart valve," Fisher said.

"Yes, in London, assisted by Professor Tynan, a most caring colleague and friend . . . and a meticulous engineer. You seem surprised, Mr. Flintlock, but what is the heart but a simple electrical pump? Professor Tynan had studied the beating heart, though fleetingly, of several woman, and its mysteries no longer baffled him. Between us, we made the doctor's heart valve out of scrap metal and electrical wire and by the Lord Harry, sir, it works. Mr. Flintlock, there is no limit to what the engineer can do. Given enough time and money, I could build a steam-powered vessel that would take us to the moon and back. That is, if I can convince those dolts back in Washington that it can be done. It seems nowadays all they talk about is iron-clads and dreadnoughts and building more of them than the combined fleets of Europe and Japan. Fools. One day I can give them immortality."

Morning thunder growled hollow in the distance and from close by a woman sang "O'er the Sea" in a sweet soprano voice. King Fisher's right arm made a soft, ticking noise.

"As for King, I made what emergency repairs to his limbs and chest as I could and stabilized him," le Strange said. "I brought him back from the brink."

"From the brink of hell," Fisher said.

Flintlock felt a shiver run down his back. He'd thought King Fisher half-human. Was he in fact half-demon? The man's strange green eyes might explain much.

Le Strange said, "You were still alive, King, I assure you. Perhaps you flickered between life and death, but at no point were you all the way gone. Mind you, it took me the best part of a year to reengineer you and restore your eye and hand. The human body is not an efficient machine, and I had much to improve on, had I not?"

"I saw hell," Fisher said. His face showed no emotion. "And I heard how the damned scream."

Le Strange smiled. "Stuff and nonsense, King. Gammon and spinach, as Professor Tynan was wont to say in his jollier moods. In our modern machine age, there is no room for medieval superstition. Steam is our new god, and if there is indeed a hell, well, it's in the foundries where our steel is made, the scarlet and black infernos where the ignorant, sweating masses toil."

"Who lies in King's grave in Uvalde?" Flintlock said.

"Not who, what," le Strange said. "Just rocks in a three-dollar coffin."

Horrified, Flintlock said, "Then, what about the rest of the people around here? The woman with the doll face, the one with the silver hands?"

"And there are others, mostly charity cases," le Strange said. "Burn victims, some of them. Others suffered gunshot wounds and one poor fellow was hanged. Along with Dr. Castle, who understands the finer points of anatomy, we made all of them functional again."

Flintlock said, "King, do you recollect the Scarlet Garter cathouse in San Antone? Remember Fifi la France, the blond gal who was so tall we called her High Timber?"

Fisher nodded. "I remember her."

"Could you still do her, King?" Flintlock said.

"What a disgusting thing to say," le Strange said, wrinkling his nose. "Have you no manners of any kind?"

Flintlock ignored that. "King, could you still do her?"

Le Strange opened his mouth to speak, but Fisher held up his natural hand in a silencing gesture. "No, Sam, I couldn't. My body has not recovered all of its functions, at least not yet."

"It will, King," le Strange said. "Trust me. One day it will."

Ignoring that, too, Flintlock said, "Could you drink champagne out of her slipper like you and Ben used to?"

"No, Sam, I couldn't. I couldn't eat Russian caviar off her belly like I used to either. I have trouble digesting food."

"I will repair that function, as well one day," le Strange said.

Flintlock said, more prolonged sigh than statement, "King, I'm saying this for old times' sake . . . this man gave you back life, but you're no longer a human being. You're some kind of machine." His fingers strayed to the Colt in his waistband. "Say the word and I'll send you back where you belong . . . with the dead." He expected a bad reaction from Fisher, a draw-and-shoot within the close confines of the tent where there would be no winner, only losers, but King surprised him.

His face impassive, incapable of revealing emotion, King said, "Women, champagne, and caviar were the childish things I once pursued and cherished. Now my interests are very different, Sam. I want power, vast power. I mean the power of a United States president and later the ruler of the world."

Fisher read the shock and surprise on Flintlock's face and said, "I'm in no hurry. I have nothing but time. Sam, when we are both dead and buried, my shadow will still fall on the earth. A hundred, two hundred years from now people will talk of my time of unlimited authority and how I used it to change the world for the better. Those are the things I now cherish. I am done with all carnal desires."

"It's in the blood, King," Obadiah le Strange said, smiling. "Your power lies in the blood."

"King, I think you'd be better off sticking with High Timber," Flintlock said.

"Sam, I grow weary of you." Fisher's mechanical hand streaked out with the speed of a striking rattler and plucked the Colt from Flintlock's waistband. He held up the big revolver. "This is for your own good, Sam. I don't want to be forced to kill you before I decide if you have any role to play in my future."

"Find yourself another boy, King," Flintlock said. "You're mad and so is— I was going to say your doctor, but he's an engineer, isn't he?"

"Don't say anything further that you may later regret, Sam," Fisher said. "Now get out of here."

"Aren't you scared I'll run away?" Flintlock said.

"You won't get far on a lame horse. Go have yourself some coffee and stay close. We're moving out in an hour."

Flintlock lifted the flap of the tent, but stopped as Fisher said, "I've been told you're on a hunt for your rightful name, Sam. Behave yourself and I just might give you one."

Flintlock nodded. "I already have one for you, King. It's son of a bitch."

"I'll very much keep that in mind."

CHAPTER TWENTY-FOUR

"Damn it all, Sergeant Martin. They've flown the coop," Captain Gregory Usher said. "Letting the mule escape cost us time and the element of surprise." The officer unscrewed the top of his hip flask and took a swig. Then, as he always did, he glanced at the Usher crest engraved into the flask's silver side before he put it away again. The Usher arms dated all the way back to medieval times and in hundreds of years of existence had never been known disgrace . . . until Dead Tree Pass.

"We'll run 'em down, Cap'n," Martin said. "They're only hours ahead of us."

Black arcs of sweat stained the armpits of Usher's shirt as the heat of the new day intensified. His protruding, pale blue eyes were bloodshot, his mouth tasted as though it was full of cotton dipped in cat piss, and he badly wanted this detail to end.

Take the money and run.

"Huh?" Rollo Martin said.

Usher knew a moment of panic, thinking he'd spoken his thoughts aloud. But Martin stared over his shoulder into the distance. "It's Luke Gamble coming in, Cap'n. Maybe them outlaws are in sight."

"Is he carrying a head?" Usher said.

"Only the one on his shoulders," Martin said.

Gamble drew rein, hawked up phlegm, and spat over the side of his horse. "Found another one . . . over there a ways like he was carried away from the campsite. Old feller, a tinpan by the look of his duds, and the whitest white man I ever did see."

"What do you mean, Mr. Gamble?" Usher said.

"I mean he looks like the Mex we found, only whiter. Looks like every last drop of blood drained out of him. I can't find a gunshot or knife wound on him, just like t' other one."

"Take me to him." Captain Usher swung into the saddle and said, "Sergeant Martin, we'll noon here. Use the water from the canteens for coffee."

"There's a creek," Martin said.

"I know that, Sergeant, but I don't trust it. I wouldn't put it past King Fisher and his gang of desperadoes to poison the water."

"It's running water, Cap'n," Martin said. "It ain't easy to poison running water."

"Carry out my order, Sergeant." Usher looked hard into the noncom's hard eyes. "And take that smirk off your face. I will not tolerate dumb insolence."

Martin saluted. "Yes, sir. Anything you say, sir."

As he and Usher rode away, Gamble said, "One day you'll have to kill that man, Captain."

His jaw muscles bunched, Usher stared straight ahead and said nothing.

* * *

"Proud, what the hell are you doing?" Sergeant Rollo Martin said.

"Doing like the captain said, using the water from the canteens for the coffee."

"Use the water from the creek," Martin said.

"But—"

"But nothing. High and mighty Captain Usher is a drunken idiot. Use the creek water. We may need full canteens before this detail is over."

Corporal Ethan Stagg was a man with a full beard and shaggy gray eyebrows. Twenty hard years in the frontier army had taken their toll and had stooped his shoulders and made his face look like the cracked mud at the bottom of a dried-up pond. He said, "Before what's over? You got something in mind, Rollo? Something maybe we should all hear about?"

"I got nothing in mind, Ethan," Martin said. His eyes flicked to the troopers who stood to the corporal's right and watched their sergeant intently.

Stagg knew what that glance implied. "Don't you worry none about Booker and Vesey. They'll do as I tell them. Ain't that right, boys?"

The two privates nodded in unison.

Harvey Booker was a thickset man with iron gray hair, Clint Vesey a long, tall drink of water with muddy, unintelligent brown eyes. Both had served six years and were regarded by their superiors as below-average soldiers.

"Ethan, you've had a burr under your saddle since we left Fort Concho," Martin said. "If you got a gripe, let's hear it."

"No gripe, but I do got something sticking in my

craw," Stagg said. "A stolen thirty-thousand-dollar army payroll that by rights should be ours."

Martin smiled, then found his pipe and studiously considered the bowl before he said, "Last I heard, the payroll belongs to the army."

"And we're the army," Stagg said. "We got as much claim to the money as them bigwigs in Washington. We'll be the ones as finds it."

"Aye, and maybe some of us will die taking it back," Booker said.

Martin fingered tobacco into the pipe bowl. "Let me get this right. No, wait. Proud, are you in on this?"

"Damn right," Seth Proud said. "The army owes me that much and more, payback for all the rotten beef, wormy biscuits, and green salt pork it's fed me for the past ten years. And what about the alkali water I drank that gave me bad blood and running sores? I figure it's fair recompense for the long days, weeks, and months a-setting a McClellan saddle that galled my hide in the heat of the Staked Plains sun. And what about the Apaches? How many of us have seen the carcasses of men we bunked with and knew like brothers lying in the cold ashes of an Apache fire and the officer saying, 'Boys, it took this soldier three, maybe four days to die. Let this be a lesson to you. Save the last cartridge in the gun for yourself.' As if we didn't know that already."

Inspired by Private Proud's oratory, Vesey pulled up his shirt and showed the raw scar that ran from his navel to the bottom of his ribs on his right side. "A Mescalero woman done that to me with a Green River knife. Near gutted me, she did."

"Hell, Clint, you got that there cut in a brothel in Abilene," Stagg said.

"Bitch was still an Apache," Vesey said.

Martin joined in the laughter that followed and then lit his pipe, got it going with his second match, and said through a cloud of smoke, "You boys say we take back the payroll and then split it among ourselves?"

"Like Booker says, shared among them of us who're still alive, you mean," Stagg said.

Martin nodded and smiled as though the troopers had fairly stated their case. "I got two ways of thinking on this. The first is that I arrest all of you and see you hung by the thumbs and flogged to death at Fort Concho. The second is that I consider what you said about us having a rightful claim to the payroll money—a very profound statement, a soldier's way of thinking. I'll study on it tonight and give you my answer tomorrow."

"Captain Usher won't throw in with us, Rollo," Stagg said. "You come up with the right verdict and we'll have to do for him."

Martin smiled. "You mean I'll have to do for him."

"Whatever you say, Rollo. Whatever you say," Stagg said.

CHAPTER TWENTY-FIVE

"Somebody done for him, Captain, but I sure as hell don't know how." Luke Gamble said. With an irritable hand, he brushed away the fat fly that crawled across his face. "You seen any dead man look that white?"

"Bloodless." Captain Gregory Usher took a knee next to the naked body and stared into the man's dead face. "All right, old-timer, what killed you?"

"Not a mark on him," Gamble said, stating what Usher had already determined. "Maybe somebody smothered him with one of them feather pillows they got in the Denver brothels."

"Maybe," Usher said, "but judging by his appearance, he was wiry—one tough old buzzard. I'd expect to see some sign of a struggle."

"Then he just dropped down dead," Gamble said. "But that don't explain the Mex we found earlier."

"No it doesn't. Hello, what have we here?" Usher lifted the dead man's arm and closely studied the inside of the man's elbow. "There's a tiny red mark here that I can barely see. What do you make of that, Mr. Gamble?"

The scout kneeled and grabbed the arm. After a while he said, "Insect bite. Plenty of mosquitos around."

"Looks like a small incision to me," Usher said.

"What's that?"

"A cut. A very small cut."

Gamble said, "Well, that sure as hell didn't kill him."

"No, it didn't." Usher rose to his feet and, as eagerly as a baby seeks a feeding bottle, took a long swig from his flask and then wiped his mouth with the back of his hand. "I guess we'll never know what killed this man."

"Seems like," Gamble said, the smell of bourbon in the air around him.

Usher stared at his scout for long moments. "Mr. Gamble, are you a man to be trusted?"

"With little children and most animals. Beyond that, you never know where my loop will land."

"I have to trust someone," Usher said.

It was Gamble's turn to use his stare to peel the skin off the officer's face and leave the bare skull exposed. "Miss it, don't you, Gregory? You miss it real bad."

Normally Usher would have taken the use of his first name as gross insubordination, but he swallowed the slight because he needed this violent, conscience-less man for his gun skills and the strength of his muscular, brutal body.

"Miss what?"

"You know what you miss, Captain Usher. Don't play coy with me."

Usher did know. He remembered another time

and place, remembered men, women, and manners unknown to savages like Gamble but once so familiar to himself. He recalled the regimental balls in Washington. Beautiful officers in blue and gold. With sad, lovely faces, tall elegant women wore ball gowns so vivid, so colorful they looked as though they waltzed through rainbows. Drifting like ghosts among the guests, flunkies, black enlisted men in white jackets, carried silver trays of champagne. The drone of male voices and the crystal notes of female laughter entwined with the strings and brass of the infantry band. In moonlit terraces, deep in the shadows, the musky sweetness of a woman's naked shoulders, her skin like velvet on his lips, the tiny beads of sweat between her breasts, each as precious as a rare diamond.

Usher was lost in the memories.

"Ladies and gentlemen, take your partners for the Virginia Reel."

His partner smiled at him. It was a brilliant smile, white pearls in her pink mouth. She gave a tug on his arm, a not-so-gentle urging toward the dance floor.

"But Miss Lavinia" (or Miss Polly or Miss Charlotte) "I'm, all out of practice. . . ."

The sudden pop! of a champagne bottle . . .

Startled, Usher blinked his way back the present.

Gamble had just clapped his hands and he looked amused. "Where were you, Captain?"

Usher managed a smile. "Somewhere else . . . picking up the shattered fragments of lost dreams."

"You can't ever go back there," Gamble said. "Not after Dead Tree Pass."

"I know that. Don't you think I know that?" Usher again took solace in his whiskey flask.

Gamble grinned. "The Fall of the House of Usher. Ever read that story, Captain?"

The captain nodded. "I'm familiar with Mr. Poe's work. And yes, my house has fallen and with it what's left of my fragile sanity."

Gamble, a man he'd long considered an ignorant, illiterate lout, a brutish degenerate, surprised him. "'. . . an utter depression of soul which I can compare to no earthly sensation more properly to the after-dream of the reveler upon opium—the bitter lapse into everyday life—the hideous dropping off of the veil.'" The big scout smiled. "But no opium for you, Captain Usher, at least not just yet, though its time will come. For now, you are a reveler upon whiskey and you fill every sorrowing glass to the brim."

"What the hell are you, Mr. Gamble?" Usher said. "Some kind of poet?"

"My father was some kind of poet," Gamble said. "Poets make lousy farmers. That's why Ma died of neglect, and the day after we buried her, I blew his brains out. My father, Reynolds Gamble, smoked opium with Edgar Allan Poe in Baltimore the night before the great man died. Pa said Poe passed away whispering his name. I don't know if that's true or not."

Usher watched a hawk drop out of the immense sky and with incredible violence hit some crawling creature in the long grass. A squeal, a small death, and the day fell quiet again.

Smarting from the tongue-lashing he'd gotten from Gamble, Usher stared hard into the scout's face and said, "How the hell could someone like you be the son of a poet?"

"Because, *mon capitaine*, I hated Reynolds Gamble

like I never hated a human being before or since. All he was, I set out to be the opposite. Where he was weak, I am strong. Where he scribbled his doggerel while my mother died, I held her head in my arms and planned his execution. He presented himself up as a good man who was misunderstood, but I present myself a bad, violent man who everybody understands, including you. That's why you want me to help you steal the army payroll when we catch up with King Fisher and them."

"As I asked you before, Mr. Gamble, can I trust you?" Usher took a swig from his flask. "Give me a straight answer."

"No you can't trust me. Is that straight enough?" Then, before the officer could answer, Gamble said, "I'll help you gun them as need gunned and after that we'll talk about how we divvy the money."

"I'll settle for fifty-fifty," Usher said.

"Maybe so, but we'll discuss it when the time comes."

"Leave Sergeant Martin to me."

Gamble shrugged. "I don't care who I kill or who I don't kill. I never have." He smiled. "Now, shall we rejoin Sergeant Martin and the rest of the ladies?"

CHAPTER TWENTY-SIX

A strange procession headed northwest in the direction of Happyville. O'Hara, bellied down in the long grass, watched it go, his brow furrowed with concern. Where was Flintlock?

A couple riders led Sam's limping bay and behind them rolled a covered wagon drawn by a mule team. The woman up on the driver's seat held the reins with silver hands and beside her sat another female with a painted mask covering her face, bad omens that made O'Hara's stomach lurch. Even more disturbing, a badly misshapen dwarf wearing a top hat and goggles trotted alongside a massive wolf as though leading the way for the others.

But it was the great, growling wheeled machine with windows that struck fear into O'Hara's heart. Belching steam, it was as large as a locomotive without a tender, but it needed no rails. The machine's wheels, each as tall as a man and wide across as his out-stretched arms, crushed everything in its path—grass, small trees, and scurrying animals. The steam wagon left behind tracks that scarred the land to the depth of a foot, something that the constant traffic of a hundred horse wagons would have taken years to accomplish. On top of the wagon, just behind its glassed cabin and partially covered with canvas, angled the stubby barrel of a Gatling gun and a figure with one hand on its breech. It looked like a man, but it had the head of a bird with a great beak and round, staring eyes.

Impulsively, O'Hara clutched the Navajo shaman's medicine bag that hung around his neck, but it was his dormant Christianity, sometimes taught, sometimes beaten into him by Dominican brothers, that made him cry out in an agony of dread. "In the name of God, what wickedness is this?"

Sure he was watching a cavalcade of the damned, O'Hara's eyes reached out and scanned the wagon and the steam monster. Where was Flintlock? He saw no sign of him.

The warrior in O'Hara took over.

After the grotesque procession passed, he got to his feet, retrieved his horse from a thicket of brush and wild oak, and swung into the saddle. He slid the Winchester from under his knee and propped the butt on his thigh.

Sam Flintlock almost enjoyed the luxurious brass and red velvet interior of the Helrun's luxurious interior. He reclined in an overstuffed easy chair and next to him on a side table stood a crystal decanter and a couple long-stemmed glasses. He removed the stopper and sniffed. "Ah, sherry." He poured himself a glass and sat back to enjoy the ride, deciding he'd deal with his problems later.

Then trouble came looking for him.

"Rider ahead," Dr. Sarah Ann Castle said, looking at Flintlock over her shoulder. "Looks like a savage of some kind."

Flintlock sat up in his chair. *O'Hara.*

It had to be. He was the only savage around those parts.

"He's ordering us to stop," the doctor said. "Wait, Jasper Aston is going to talk to him. Obadiah, stand ready with the big gun."

"It's ready," le Strange said, his voice muffled behind his plague mask.

Wearing a black leather helmet and goggles pushed up on her forehead, Dr. Castle consulted the array of dials and valves on the panel in front of her. She pulled a lever, pushed another, and Helrun hissed to a shuddering halt. "King and Clem Jardine just left the wagon. Both are wearing their guns."

"Wearing guns? That will scare O'Hara all right." Flintlock said.

"Huh?" Dr. Castle said.

Flintlock let his feeble attempt at humor pass, then stared over the woman's shoulder through the glass. "The rider is a breed named O'Hara." To his surprise, he added, "He's a good friend of mine."

"Then I hope King doesn't kill him," she said. "He can be testy around strangers."

"Let me out of this thing," Flintlock said.

Steam hissed and a panel at the side of the passenger cabin swung upward.

"Be careful," she said. "Your friend looks like a desperate character."

Flintlock drained his sherry glass and stooped to leave. "He is," he threw back at the doctor as he stepped outside. "Believe me, he is." Flintlock had never doubted O'Hara's courage.

In times of trouble, the man was a rock. He was steady in a gunfight and could be depended on to stand his ground and get his work in no matter the amount of lead flying in his direction. O'Hara could understand a hired gun like Jasper Aston because he'd met his kind before, but nothing in his experience had prepared him for the likes of King Fisher and Clem Jardine. O'Hara's face was stiff with uncertainty, his knuckles white on his rifle.

It seemed to Flintlock that King Fisher might be talking, but the man's back was turned to him and he couldn't be sure. Seeking to head off any possible gunplay, Flintlock yelled, "O'Hara, over here!"

O'Hara's head turned in Flintlock's direction and Clem Jardine offered a fleeting smile.

Disaster struck.

Grofrec Horntoe had been holding back his wolf, but with his mouth twisted in a malicious grin, he let the animal go. Quicksilver went right for O'Hara's horse. The terrified paint reared just as the wolf hit and, surprised, O'Hara went flying off the back of his saddle. He triggered a fast shot when he struck the ground hard.

King Fisher suddenly had a Colt in his hand.

Stirrups flying, O'Hara's horse galloped across the flat, the wolf snapping at its heels.

"No! Don't shoot!" Flintlock yelled. He kneeled beside the dazed breed. "Are you all right?"

O'Hara shook his head, his eyes unfocused. "I thought Jasper might draw down on me, but I sure as hell didn't expect a wolf."

"You know him?" Flintlock said.

"Who, the wolf?"

"No, dammit, Jasper."

"Ran into him a few times along my back trail. He's fast with the iron."

"Set right there for a spell," Flintlock said. "I'll be right back."

Horntoe was giggling behind his hand when Flintlock grabbed him. A strong man and mad as hell, he lifted the dwarf bodily in one hand and carried him, kicking and cursing, to Fisher. "Rein in your dwarf, King," he said, dropping the little man at Fisher's feet.

"Grofrec, call back your wolf," Fisher said. "Now."

The dwarf, looking sullen, put two fingers into his mouth and let out a high, piercing whistle. Flintlock watched the wolf skid to a halt, turn, and trot back.

Still angry, Flintlock said, "King, if O'Hara had come up with a broken neck, you'd be looking for a gopher hole to bury your pygmy in."

"He amuses me, Sam. Court jester, you might say. That's why I gave him the name Grofrec Horntoe. Dr. le Strange says it's very droll. Can you vouch for the savage?"

"He's a friend of mine and he's only half savage. Isn't that enough?"

"Bring him over here. I'll question him," Fisher said.

Flintlock helped O'Hara to his feet and said, "King Fisher wants to talk to you."

O'Hara's eyes opened wide. "That's King Fisher?"

"What's left of him. Pretend you don't notice."

"Only a damned white man would say that."

CHAPTER TWENTY-SEVEN

The huge lens of King Fisher's right eye glowed green as he studied O'Hara. "Do I know you?"

The breed shook his head. "No. But I've heard of you. They say you're a cowboy killer."

"People talk," Fisher said. "Does my appearance disturb you? My eye? My hand?"

O'Hara nodded. "You're part man, part machine, like him." He used the muzzle of his Winchester to point to Clem Jardine. "God did not make you two like that."

"The Bible says he made man in His image. Maybe God is a machine," Fisher said.

"A machine does not have a soul," O'Hara said.

"And you think I have none?"

"Perhaps. It could be that your soul fled when you became more automaton than human."

"Automaton? You use a big word for a part savage," Fisher said.

"When I was a boy at the mission school, a monk called Brother Benedict was a watchmaker, but he also made little animals out of brass. They moved. Singing birds mostly, but once he made a bear that walked and danced. He called his creatures automatons."

King Fisher's immobile face could not register anger, but his voice rose to a shout. "You fool! You dare compare me to clockwork toys? I am the pinnacle of creation and as the sum of man's knowledge increases, I will be made even better. Little man, I'll still be alive when your grandchildren are dead and modern engineering may yet bring me immortality. What need for a soul then?"

Fisher's left hand, not mechanical and somewhat shrunken, reached over, opened a small valve on his wrist, and instantly released a hissing jet of steam. He closed the valve quickly and said, "There, now you've seen and heard my immortal soul."

O'Hara, openmouthed like an Inquisitor listening to heresy, could not bring himself to say anything.

Fisher did the talking for him. "Now, my Indian friend, the question is do I kill you or not?"

Flintlock said quickly, "King, I'd take a killing mighty hard."

"I'm sure you would, Sam. But if you did, I'd also have to kill you, and I don't want to do that right now. Take your friend's rifle and pistol."

O'Hara stepped back, his Winchester coming up fast. "You're not taking my guns."

King Fisher made two motions with his mechanical arm. The first was to shove his Colt into the holster on his hip. This was done at normal speed, but the second movement was so fast the human eye could not follow it. When the movement was complete, Fisher's articulated hand had grabbed O'Hara's Winchester by the barrel and tossed it aside.

Stunned, the breed shook the burning sting out of his hands and Flintlock, fearing another fancy move on King's part, removed O'Hara's Colt from his holster.

He handed the revolver to Fisher and said, "Mighty fast."

"And me only half-trying." Fisher looked at the people around him. "All right, we're moving out. Take your friend into Helrun, Sam. He looks like he needs a drink."

Flintlock nodded. "And I reckon so do I. I think we both just saw a ghost."

"They've caught up with your horse, O'Hara," Flintlock said, looking out the cabin window. "How is the sherry?"

"Is that what it is? Sherry wine?"

"Like it?"

"It's swill."

"And that's why old Barnabas told me to never to give firewater to an Injun. They don't appreciate good liquor. How were the ladies when you left?"

"I came to find you, Sam."

"I know that and I appreciate it. How are the ladies?"

"Still in the saloon. The town stinks worse now the bodies are rotting."

"I think King wants to settle there for a spell," Flintlock said.

"Then he'll die of smallpox."

Flintlock frowned. "Maybe he can't die. I don't know how much of his insides are made of brass."

"His human part can die, like any other mortal man," O'Hara said.

Sarah Castle turned from the controls. "Please don't discuss Mr. Fisher in my presence. If you have anything to say, then say it to him."

"There's smallpox in Happyville, for God's sake," Flintlock said. "A doctor should know she's headed for trouble."

"We can contain and then eradicate the epidemic," Dr. Castle said. "It is essential that the good townspeople return and the farming begin."

"What kind of farming? You can't plow around there," Flintlock said. "All you'll grow is rock and cactus."

"Then we'll just have to wait and see, Mr. Flintlock, won't we?" Sarah Castle paused, then said, "Hello, what is this?" and spoke into a speaking tube above the control panel. "Obadiah, do you see them? There's a large body of armed, mounted men approaching us."

Le Strange's tinny answer came back. "I see them. They look like Comancheros to me. I doubt that their intentions are friendly."

"Do you think King sees them?"

"I'm sure he does. Just keep driving, Sarah."

Flintlock leaned forward and peered through the front window. "They're not Comancheros. They disbanded and headed for the hills after ol' Quanah Parker surrendered in the winter of seventy-five and his starving Comanches went into a reservation. It looks to me like a bunch of other fellers in the same line of business."

"Those boys want something," O'Hara said.

"I figured that." Flintlock's hand strayed to his

waistband, but his gun was gone, taken by Fisher. "Sure is a passel of them, twenty-five, maybe thirty riders, half of them Americanos judging by their duds."

Le Strange's voice came on the speaking tube. "Sarah, King is signaling you to stop. He's bringing the wagon closer and I might be needed elsewhere so he's sending Max Eades to man the Gatling. Just keep Helrun locked up tight and stay right where you are."

Sarah Castle said, "Obadiah, wait."

But the man had already scrambled out of the gun turret and slid down the vehicle's side. He hit the ground running and headed for the wagon.

There was as yet no sign of King Fisher.

Flintlock glanced at the bandits. They had deployed in line and cut loose with a ragged volley. Bullets *pinged!* off the sloped side of the steam carriage, and Sarah Castle cried out as a round shattered the window to her right and burned across her forehead just under the brim of her leather helmet.

"Get your head down!" Flintlock yelled. He pushed the woman into her seat. He looked at the hatch that led to the gun turret. "Where the hell is Eades?"

The shooting became general as the horsemen advanced on the carriage and wagon.

Confined like a yolk in a boilerplate egg as he was in the close confines of the Helrun's passenger cabin, Flintlock could see little of what was happening outside. "O'Hara, get up there behind the big gun. I'll follow you."

As O'Hara scrambled into the hatch, Flintlock said, "Doc, are you all right?"

"It's just a bad bruise." With panic in her voice, Dr. Castle said, "I can't see King out there."

"I reckon Fisher can take care of himself." Flintlock climbed into the hatch.

O'Hara moved aside to allow him to sit in the leather seat. "Can you work this thing?" He jumped as a bullet *spaaanged!* close to his elbow, leaving a shallow gray scratch on the metal.

Flintlock's quick glance around him revealed that the bandits—in later years, winter yarning around a potbellied stove, he'd refer to them as the Sons of the Comancheros—had circled Helrun and the wagon. Several of their number had fallen and lay lifeless on the ground and it looked like Max Eades was down. The gunman's boot heels gouged holes in the dirt, a sure sign that he was gut shot and hurting. King Fisher, Clem Jardine, and Jasper Aston had backed against the wagon and were getting in some steady work. But the bandit numbers were starting to tell and their noose was tightening.

Back a ways and out of the line of fire, Flintlock thought he caught a glimpse of Barnabas. The old sinner grinned as he sat on the grass and peeled a ruby-red apple, a tight coil of skin dangling to the ground.

"Sam, damn it!" O'Hara yelled. "Shoot that fancy gun."

As bullets split the air around his head, Flintlock grabbed the Gatling gun and readied himself, gritting his teeth. The big gun was fed from a circular maga-zine named a Broadwell Drum after its inventor. Flintlock had seen a Gatling exactly like this one at Fort Bayard, up in the New Mexico Territory's Santa

Rita Mountains country. Usually seen on gunboats, the Gatling's two-hundred-and-forty-round magazine made it a fearsome weapon at sea or on land.

Luck was with Sam Flintlock that day.

About a dozen riders broke off from the fight and huddled around a man wearing a wide sombrero and an embroidered red shirt. They seemed to be getting orders, and now and then, they'd glance toward the wagon.

Flintlock sighted, turned the crank handle, and cut loose, the unique rattle of the big gun sounding like an iron bedstead being dragged across a knotted wood floor. The Gatling gun was an indiscriminate and inhumane killer, a destroyer of animals as well as men. When the six-hundred-round-a-minute hail-storm of .45-70 lead hammered into the assembled riders, shrieking and screaming men and horses went down like wheat before a reaper.

Appalled, Flintlock looked beyond the gun barrels at a gory tangle of dying, shrieking men and their kicking mounts . . . raw, bloody meat from a ghastly grinder. Dust and thick gray gun smoke writhed among the fallen as though their tormented souls desperately sought escape from the slaughter.

The man in the sombrero and red shirt, redder now, staggered to his feet, tried to say something, then fell on his back. Flintlock held his fire. He'd killed men before, but the dreadful execution he'd done among the bandits unnerved him.

The shooting came to a ragged halt. The surviving bandits, half their number dead or dying, including their leader, pulled back. The ferocity of the Gatling gun had taken the fight out of them.

"Sam!" Fisher yelled. "Finish them."

The bandits who could understand English threw down their guns and raised their hands. The others, bewildered by the suddenness and ferocity of Flintlock's attack, followed suit.

"They're done, King," Flintlock said.

Fisher's impassive face was incapable of showing emotion. He said, "They're done when I say they're done."

Already dismayed by the mayhem he'd wrought, Flintlock was not prepared for what happened next. No human being with a shred of decency could have been.

Fisher's mechanical arm hung by his side and its polished brass and network of thin bronze pipes gleamed like gold in the sunlight. A split second later, he was shooting, his self-cocking revolver vise-steady in his engineered hand. Six shots. Six empty saddles. Six dead men. All in the space of a single heartbeat. Flintlock was stunned that a Colt's gun could be made to shoot at that speed—like a burst from the Gatling.

Then horror piled on horror as the surviving bandits broke and ran.

"Clem," Fisher said.

Jardine drew and fired. His arm and gun hand were not mechanically enhanced, but he was a skilled gunman and shot two of the fleeing bandits out of the saddle.

When the racketing echoes of the shots died away,

King Fisher stiffly looked up at Flintlock in the gun turret. "Now they're done."

Flintlock studied what was left of the fleeing bandits. Their horses kicked up plumes of dust as they galloped across the flat. He saw no sign of Barnabas.

Fisher called out to the dwarf. "Grofrec, finish off the wounded. I don't want live enemies on my back trail."

The little man pulled a huge bowie from his belt, tested the edge with his thumb, and grinned. "Sure thing, Mr. Fisher." The dwarf, his wolf trotting beside him, hurried away to complete his task.

But even when shrieks of fear and pain rang out as Grofrec Horntoe began his throat cutting, Flintlock's attention was on Clem Jardine's wife kneeling beside the dead Max Eades. Only later did Flintlock find out that the gunman was her brother. She rocked back and forth and made low, moaning sounds behind her painted porcelain mask. After a while, she reached into the pocket of her skirt and took out a small, blue glass vial decorated with tiny silver skulls. She removed the stopper, a skull attached to the bottle with a thin chain, tilted her head and held the vial under her left eye, allowing drops of water to fall onto her mask and run down her cheek. She did this with the other eye until it seemed that tears streamed down her porcelain cheeks, rolling among the dice and the red and black hearts, clubs, diamonds and spades of playing cards. Blanche Jardine's wails grew in volume and she reapplied the vial and shed her unnatural tears several more times until her husband raised her to her feet and led her, stumbling, back to the wagon.

Grofrec Horntoe, his bared arms gory to the elbows, returned. "They're all dead, Mr. Fisher."

"What is the butcher's bill?" King Fisher said.

"Nineteen dead men and eleven horses," the dwarf said.

Fisher nodded. "Dr. le Strange, can Max Eades be saved?"

The engineer shook his head. "Even modern science can't raise a dead man. At least, not yet."

Fisher listened to that without comment and then said, "Grofrec, bury Eades. As for the rest, let them rot." Bending backward from the waist, Fisher looked up at Flintlock. "Sam, get the hell down from there. I want you and the Indian back inside Helrun."

The scrape with the bandits, more massacre than battle, weighed heavily on Flintlock, as did the killing of the wounded. He was angry, and that made him dangerous. He was by nature a man who could tolerate only so much sass before he snapped.

He let loose with a burst of Gatling fire, erupting a row of dirt Vs inches in front of Fisher. Noisily and dramatically, it emphasized his feelings. "King, I'm pretty damned tired of being ordered around. It ends right here."

"Sam, I thought we were friends," Fisher said. "I'm very disappointed."

"We're not friends, King, and we never were. Now order somebody to give our guns back to O'Hara and saddle our horses. Meantime, you stay right where you're at, King. If I need to cut loose with this thing again, you'll end up looking like a pile of scrap metal."

"Hurtful, Sam, very hurtful," Fisher said.

"Do as I say."

Fisher turned to Jasper Aston. "Bring their guns, then saddle the horses." He looked up at Flintlock. "Your horse is still lame, Sam."

"Then saddle another one." Loudly, looking down into the interior of the steam carriage, Flintlock said, "And lady doctor, get away from the bottom of the hatch with the derringer belly gun. If you shoot me, I'll still have time to chop up your boss."

Fisher said, "Sarah, can you hear me?"

"I can hear you," the doctor said.

"Put your gun away. Flintlock has never been known for his sanity, and he means what he says."

"Damn right," Flintlock said. "Right now I'm a crazy man."

"King, a shot to the femoral artery and he'll bleed out quick," Sarah Castle said.

"Not quick enough, my dear. Put the gun away."

The woman stood at the bottom of the gun hatch and looked up at Flintlock. She smiled and waved the derringer. "You're lucky, Mr. Flintlock."

He stared at her. "And so is your boss, lady."

CHAPTER TWENTY-EIGHT

"Why did King Fisher let us go so easily?" O'Hara said. "I mean, he let us just ride out of there."

"We're not that important to him." Flintlock drew rein, grateful to rest his right shoulder. His bay hated to be led and tugged at the rope halter constantly. "King lost his best gun and he wasn't anxious to lose another in a gunfight." He built and then lit a cigarette.

Ahead of him, the grassland stretched away flat and featureless except for a stunted mesa in the far distance that brooded over its lack of height. It was a landscape that offered nothing, promised nothing.

To Flintlock, it was nevertheless welcoming. He inhaled smoke deeply into his lungs and said, "That thing we met wasn't King Fisher. It's a freak. It's a freak in a freak show, one of them Barnum and Bailey creatures the picture magazines write about."

O'Hara managed one of his rare smiles. "Like Tom Thumb."

"Yeah. King Fisher's show has got itself one of

those, only his name is Grofrec Horntoe and he's an evil little son of a bitch," Flintlock said.

O'Hara turned in the saddle. "Why did the Comancheros attack us, Sam?"

"The usual reasons, horses and women."

"There were only a few horses and apart from Sarah Castle, the women were in the wagon."

"Helrun? Did they want the land locomotive?"

"Hardly. Bandits travel fast, hit fast, and then light a shuck. A thing like the Helrun would only slow them down. That is, if they could even get it to run. Close to thirty bandits, Sam. That many men were after something worth taking."

"What?" Flintlock said.

O'Hara shrugged. "Hell if I know, but the Comancheros reckoned it was worth fighting for."

"Money. Money is a thing they'd fight for, if there was a lot of it." Flintlock shook his head. "Beats the hell out of me. Maybe King Fisher is a secret millionaire and he carries his treasure with him."

"Could be," O'Hara said.

"But don't count on it," Flintlock said. "When I knew him, King never had two pennies to rub together. I doubt that he's rich. Let's ride. I'm sure the ladies will welcome us back with open arms."

"I wouldn't count on that either."

Biddy Sales said, "Hell, Flintlock, did you expect us to welcome you back with open arms?"

"Or open legs, maybe," Margie Tott said.

"Men always expect that," Jane Feehan said, giggling.

Biddy and Margie laughed, but Lizzie Doulan had closed down. She said nothing.

Flintlock stepped behind the bar and placed a bottle of rye and two glasses in front of O'Hara.

The breed poured for both of them and then said, "The stink of this town is even worse than I remembered."

"The dead still lie unburied," Lizzie Doulan said, breaking her silence. "Disease remains in the air like a yellow fog."

Flintlock retrieved his Hawken from behind the bar where he'd left it. He carried the rifle to the door and looked outside. "Well, there's still an hour of daylight left. Biddy, we'll set your wagon on its wheels now and ride out at first light tomorrow."

"We got visitors, Flintlock," Lizzie said. "At the livery."

Flintlock felt a pang of alarm. "What kind of visitors?"

"Former residents of Happyville," Biddy said. "A man named Adam Flood and his pregnant wife."

"Why did they come back?" Flintlock said. "Why would any man bring his pregnant wife to this hellhole?"

"Pregnant women have strange notions sometimes. She wanted her child to be born under a roof. She said the other townsfolk are camped all over and living mighty rough." Biddy saw something in Flintlock's eyes and said, "The rest won't come back until they're sure the smallpox is gone."

"How many and how are they surviving?" Flintlock said.

"Probably a couple hundred are camped out. Flood

says they're eating roots and jackrabbits when they can find them."

"A man can starve to death eating roots and rabbits," Flintlock said.

Lizzie nodded. "That's what Flood said. He says a lot of people are mighty sick, but they won't come back until they know the danger is gone."

"I want to get the wagon ready to roll," Flintlock said. "Then I'll go talk to this Flood ranny."

"What about?" Lizzie said. "His wife wants to give birth in the barn and he's got nothing else to say."

Flintlock frowned. "Yeah, well I'll talk to him anyhow. I think he's a damn fool."

Dusk deepened the shadows and ribboned the sky with red by the time Flintlock and O'Hara got the wagon back on its wheels. The oil lamps were lit in the saloon when he stepped inside and told Biddy that she and the other women should get ready to pull out at first light.

"Did you speak to Flood?" Biddy said.

"Not yet."

"Be careful, Flintlock. He's not a trusting man." She stared in the direction of the livery as though she could look through walls. "Rose Flood is hurting real bad. Don't tell her I said this, but I think she may not live."

"She's had a difficult pregnancy," Margie Tott said, her pretty face troubled. "She's very weak."

"I'm not much of a hand at birthing babies," Flintlock said. "But I'll talk to her."

Biddy nodded at the Hawken. "Then you'd better leave the cannon here. There's no point in scaring the poor woman to death."

Flintlock carried a lantern and a pint of rye as he walked to the livery, the lamp to make himself visible and thus seem harmless to the distrusting Flood. A few yards from the door he stopped and called, "Hello inside."

A man's voice answered, "Who are you?"

"Name's Sam Flintlock. I'm not from around these parts."

"What do you want? State your intentions and be warned. I'm armed."

"Came to ask how your wife is doing. I mean, with the baby coming an' all. Oh, and I got a pint of good rye with me."

After a long silence Flood said, "I could use a drink. My given name's Adam. Please come on in, but keep your hands where I can see them."

"I'll keep them on the bottle, huh? That set all right with you?"

Inside, a lamp glowed into life and Flintlock stepped into the flickering orange light. A tall, slender young man stepped out of the shadows, the Winchester in his right hand hanging at his side. Seeing Flintlock for the first time often unsettled folks. He looked like a buckskinned, frontier ruffian and the thunderbird tattoo on his throat did nothing to reassure the timid.

For a moment, Flood seemed taken aback, but

then he smiled and said, "Are you really interested in my wife's welfare or are you here for some other reason?"

"Yeah, to share a pint of whiskey." Flintlock took a knee beside Mrs. Flood. She was lying on a blanket in a stall that her husband had swept clean. "How are you feeling, ma'am?"

The woman looked at him with pained brown eyes. "The baby isn't right. I think she should be turned by now."

He smiled. "You're mighty sure it's a girl, huh?"

"Yes. I want a little girl." Rose Flood managed a slight smile. "I can dress up a little girl, put bows in her hair."

"You can at that, ma'am." After a few moments to sort out his thoughts, he said, "There's a doctor headed this way. Her name is Sarah Castle. She's with . . . other people."

Adam said, "Is she capable?"

"I reckon so. Capable enough that old Queen Vic set store by her." To add to the doctor's bona fides, Flintlock thought about saying, *And she was Jack the Ripper's lady friend.* But he decided against it. He raised the bottle. "May I beg your indulgence, ma'am?"

"Please do, Mr. Flintlock. I don't imbibe, but I'm sure Adam will appreciate a drink." The woman winced as a spike of pain hit her. "He's been through a lot, poor man."

"And so have you, Mrs. Flood." Flintlock used his big, scarred thumb to wipe sweat from the woman's temples. "But your pain will soon pass and when you see your baby girl for the first time, you'll forget all this ever happened. Pain has no memory, ma'am."

"You are very gallant, Mr. Flintlock." Rose held a rosary of pink coral in her hand, and the beads silently slipped through her fingers.

CHAPTER TWENTY-NINE

"Well, we sure as hell won't let them slip through our fingers," Luke Gamble said. "On account of how they ain't running."

Captain Gregory Usher looked around him at the evidence of slaughter. Hunch-shouldered buzzards squatted on the ground beyond the piled arcs of the dead, patiently awaiting their feast. "How in God's name did this happen?"

"Fisher's got himself a big gun," Gamble said. "Seems like these rannies came looking for the stolen gold and ran into a Gatling instead."

"I thought the missing payroll was a secret," Usher said.

"There are no secrets on the frontier, and especially in Texas where folks keep a close eye on the doings of Yankee soldiers."

Sergeant Rollo Martin stepped beside his officer. "Burial detail?"

"Hell, no," Usher said. "We'd be here planting stiffs for a week. Let them lie. They're not our dead."

"The men want to know if they can search the corpses," Martin said.

"Yeah, sure," Usher said, "but only to take what they can comfortably carry—watches and money and the like. A pistol, if there's one that takes their fancy."

After Martin saluted and stepped away, Usher glanced at the sky, where the sun burned like a white-hot coin. More buzzards had gathered, gliding gracefully in circles like skaters on a frozen blue lake. As squabbles broke out over the plunder, Usher stepped to his horse and untied his bandana. He soaked it in water from his canteen and retied it around his neck. "Does the Gatling gun spell trouble for us, Mr. Gamble?"

"Only if we charge them robbers a whoopin' and a hollerin' on horseback," the scout said. "We stay away from the kill-heaps gun and plug 'em any way we can. And call me Luke for chrissake."

Usher shook his head. "Damn it. I don't like this, Luke. The robbers have a Gatling gun. What else do they have?"

"We'll find out pretty damned soon and then we deal with it. The thing to do is to keep our heads." Gamble winked. "Greg."

Usher had no time to comment on that last. Behind him, angry yells led to a curse and then a revolver shot. As he turned, he was already undoing the flap of his holster.

Private Harvey Booker lay on the ground, blood already pooling under his gray head. Standing over him, smoking Colt in hand, was Private Clint Vesey.

Sergeant Martin grabbed the gun out of Vesey's fist

and then backhanded the soldier across the face. "You had no cause to do that."

Blood trickling from a cut on his lip, Vesey got up off the ground and said, "He grabbed a wallet right out of my hand. Damned piece of white trash said it was his."

"Where is this wallet?" Usher said.

Martin picked up the wallet from the ground and silently handed it to the captain. Usher quickly checked the contents and brought out two crumpled dollar bills. He glared at Vesey and said, "You killed a man for two dollars."

Vesey's muddy brown eyes glinted with defiance. "The wallet was mine by rights. I found it."

Usher looked around him. "Did you all see this?"

Booker had not been particularly liked, but the troopers nodded.

"It was murder all right, Captain," Martin said. "Private Booker didn't even reach for his weapon."

"Private Vesey, I will hand you over to the nearest civilian authority," Usher said. "Later you'll be transferred to Fort Concho to stand court-martial for murder."

Vesey's face was ugly. "Yeah? Well maybe I got some stories to tell to them court-martial fellers. Maybe I got stories about the stolen payroll and them among us who want it for themselves. Maybe the real thieves are right here among us. Maybe—"

A neat bullet hole appeared where Clint Vesey's eyebrows met above the bridge of his nose, and he dropped like a rock. Every head turned to the man who'd fired the shot.

Luke Gamble sat his horse, a smile on his face and

a thread of smoke curling from his gun. "Since I was once deputized by Judge Parker's court, I'm the nearest civilian authority and I judged this man guilty of murder. I therefore executed him."

The eyes of the surviving troopers turned to Usher. The flap of Martin's holster was open, but his hand stayed clear of his gun. Gamble had a reputation as a shootist and he was a man to step around.

Caught flat-footed, Usher said, "Mr. Gamble, we'll discuss this later, sir."

The scout gave a brief nod. "Suits me, Captain."

"'We'll discuss this later.' Is that it? Nothing more?" Private Seth Proud kicked a rock that bounced across the ground before losing itself in the grass. "It don't hardly seem fair."

"Fair?" Sergeant Martin said, keeping his voice low, out of earshot of Usher. "Life ain't fair, boy. Them as have, get. Them like us who don't have, get the end of the stick with the crap on it."

"Tell us what to do, Rollo," Corporal Ethan Stagg said.

"We stand pat. The bandits have a Gatling gun so for now we need Usher and Gamble. When the money is ours, if them two are still alive, we get rid of them."

Proud spat. "That damned Gamble. Killing Clint was a rotten trick."

"Clint was a piece of garbage and so was Booker." Martin grinned. "But I'll lift a glass to them when I'm spending their share of the payroll money."

Usher stalked toward Martin and the others and said, "You men quit gabbing and bury our dead."

"What about Gamble, Captain? He should help with the digging," Stagg said, his bitter eyes on the scout.

Usher said, "Corporal, the duties of an army scout are to discover and follow the enemy's trail, locate the enemy, and discover his strength. When required, discover the tribal affiliation of unknown Indians and to faithfully perform all other duties connected to military intelligence. If you don't already know that, you should. I cannot ask a scout to join a burial detail unless he expresses a wish to do so."

"And I don't wish worth a damn to do so," Gamble said.

"You heard the captain's orders," Martin said. "We'll cover them up any way we can." He stared at Gamble and their eyes met without hostility.

At that moment, the soldier and the scout understood each other very well.

CHAPTER THIRTY

Old Barnabas, in life as wicked as they come, stood under a gas lamp in an alley and called out to Sam Flintlock as he passed. "No, not there, idiot, over here."

Flintlock shoved his Colt back in his waistband and stepped to the alley entrance. "I knew where you were, Barnabas, but I didn't know who you were."

"Well, I'm me. Thanks to You-know-who, this here gas lamp comes all the way from London town. He says Jack the Ripper's cur dog cocked his leg on this lamp, but you can't believe a word he says."

There was no gas supply in Happyville, but the lamp glowed with a dim, greenish light as it had when it stood in Whitechapel Road. The light fell on Barnabas's cloaked shoulders and on the crown of his top hat. The old mountain man held a long, slender cane in his right hand with an ornate golden handle in the shape of a snarling Chinese dragon. When he moved, he revealed that the cloak had a bloodred lining in contrast to the dazzling whiteness of his frilled shirt collar and tie.

"Why the fancy duds?" Flintlock said.

Barnabas's face was tinted green from the lamp-light, his shadowed eyes and cheeks inky black. "We're all dressed up because there was a rumor that Jack the Jester was joining the fold, but You-know-who had it wrong as usual. Jack isn't due for a few years yet."

Flintlock said, "Well, I guess that's why God is in his heaven and Old Scratch isn't. It must have been a sore disappointment to you, Barnabas. I mean Jack not showing."

"Of course is was, but that's what hell is all about, Sammy. Disappointments . . . one after another. No dreams ever come true in hell, boy. Remember that."

A large white moth fluttered around the gas lamp and Flintlock said, "Is that a Happyville moth?"

"Nah, it's an East End of London, England, moth. Now listen up, Sammy. Do you want You-know-who's advice on how to get rid of the pregnant lady and the rest of them? I should warn you, Sam, you being an idiot an' all, that it involves a knife and some plucky work with a club."

"I'll handle my problems in my own way," Flintlock said. "Thanks all the same."

"Thought you'd say that, boy." Barnabas shook his top-hatted head. "Son, you just ain't too bright." His cloak swirled around him, flashing red. "Well, I got to go. I'll leave you with this thought, Sam—go find your ma. That Kingfisher feller plans to write his name across this here town and he'll dip his pen in blood. That's what he's all about, boy. B-l-u-d, blood." Barnabas put a cupped hand to his ear. "Hear that? It's the coppers. I got to light a shuck."

Flintlock stood to the side as Barnabas, his cape

billowing, ran past him and became one with the night.
The gas lamp glowed for a few moments longer . . .
and then winked out and vanished.

"How is she?" Biddy said.

"She's holding up but feeling some pain," Flintlock
said. "Right now I can't say the same about her husband."

"You got him drunk?" Biddy said, her eyes accusing.

"Only half," Flintlock said.

"You and O'Hara are pulling out tomorrow?"

"That's the general idea."

"I got news for you, big man."

"What's that?"

"The Indian doesn't want to go."

Biddy saw the question on Flintlock's face and said,
"He had a bad dream."

"O'Hara gets all kind of crazy notions about
dreams. He's very high strung, you know. Is there
coffee in the pot? I could sure use some."

"On the stove where it always is," Biddy said.

"Where is O'Hara anyway?"

"I don't know. Making big medicine somewhere, I
guess."

Flintlock took his coffee with him. He also carried
his Hawken. Old Barnabas's warning about King Fisher
had troubled him and suddenly the night seemed full
of hidden dangers.

Walking clear of the stores and buildings where the
smallpox dead lay unburied, Flintlock checked the

alleys—anywhere O'Hara might go to commune with the Great Spirit or whoever the hell he'd decided to commune with. A sudden noise in the narrow alley between a boarded-up hardware store and the New York Hat Shop attracted his attention. His Hawken up and handy, Flintlock took a step into the darkness. Had Barnabas come back?

"Bang, you're dead."

Something cold and round pressed into Flintlock's right temple just under the brim of his hat.

"O'Hara, someday that's going to get you killed."

"And someday you'll learn how to walk into a dark alley," O'Hara said.

Irritated, Flintlock said, "How about I blow a fist-sized hole in your belly with this here cannon, Injun? Just out of spite, like."

"You came too late to the dance, Sam. I already shot you dead, remember?"

Now even more exasperated, Flintlock said, "How come you're scaring all the women with your crazy talk?"

"What crazy talk?"

"About dreams an' sich." Flintlock looked to the west. A shooting star, bright as a hot coal, branded the night sky and he fancied that it would soon thump onto someone's tile roof in Old Mexico as a smoking, burned-out cinder. "And omens. Bad omens."

"Walk with me, Sam." After a few steps, O'Hara said, "In my dream we were walking across the prairie and then a man with the head of a bird flew from a wild oak tree and attacked the thunderbird on your throat."

Flintlock smiled. "Hell, O'Hara, I would've plugged

him for sure. I mean, flying down from a tree like that."

O'Hara ignored that. "I threw a lance at the bird man but missed and when I told him he was an unclean spirit and to leave you be, he said he wanted your blood. He said he needed it for the kingfisher."

Flintlock stopped, a spasm of unease niggling at him. "And then what happened?"

"The bird man filled his beak with blood and flew away and drops from his beak fell on me like a red rain. Sam, it was a dreadful rain and I fell on my face and begged the Great Spirit to protect me."

"And what about me?" Flintlock said, nettled.

"You lay on the ground on your back, and your throat was torn out and your face was white as wood ash."

Flintlock stopped walking. "O'Hara, did you eat Biddy Sales's beef and beans before you had that dream?"

"It wasn't Biddy's cooking that spoke to me, Sam. It was the voice of a spirit," O'Hara said.

"So what do we do about it?" Flintlock said.

"I don't know. The spirit doesn't advise. It warns."

"Biddy says you don't want to leave Happyville. Is that true?"

"I believe we'll be attacked if we ride into the open country," O'Hara said. "And I think the spirit warned of your death if we do."

"And if we stay here in town, King Fisher will kill us for sure," Flintlock said. "I don't know what he has in mind for Happyville, but now he knows we're in his way. It sure doesn't seem that we have much of a choice . . . damned if we do, damned if we don't."

"I'd rather take my chances in town," O'Hara said. "Out in the open, we'll be like ducks in a shooting gallery."

Flintlock shook his head. "Fisher will be slowed by the steam carriage and the wagon. If we ride out at first light, we can outdistance him and his big gun."

"I hope you're right," O'Hara said.

"So do I."

CHAPTER THIRTY-ONE

"Is it Brewster? Is it Charlie Brewster?" King Fisher said.

Clem Jardine palmed shut the telescope in his hand and said, "It's Charlie all right. He's made good time."

Fisher squinted into the heat haze. "How many does he have with him? Can you see?"

"I count ten," Jardine said.

Fisher nodded. "It's enough. Charlie hires only the best."

"Will he bring them in, King?" Jardine said.

"He'll round them up all right. He may have to gun a few to get the rubes to sit up and pay attention, but he'll bring them in."

"He's signaling," Jardine says. "He's seen us."

"Clem, those boys will be thirsty. Get the women to break out the whiskey jugs."

"Sure thing." Jardine hesitated a moment and then said, "How good is he?"

"Among the best there is, apart from me. Charlie is fast enough."

Jardine smiled. "Then he's as fast as me."

Fisher shook his head. "I don't know, Clem, but I think in a drawdown with Charlie, you wouldn't even come close."

If that hurt, Jardine didn't let it show. He called to the woman with the silver hands to get the jugs, enough for ten thirsty men. "It's Charlie Brewster and his boys."

The woman with the silver hands smiled but said nothing.

"Hell, King, when I first saw you I was took by surprise," Charlie Brewster said. "I mean that strange bug eye you got, and now you say you have a mechanical arm. I don't believe what I'm seeing."

"Believe it." Fisher waited until the big outlaw took a swig from the jug before he rolled up his right sleeve and showed the inside of his forearm. "My hand and forearm were hit with three bullets, pretty much shot to pieces. An engineer repaired my arm with steel and brass and it's as good as new."

Brewster's eyes got big. "Hell, King, can you draw with that thing?"

"Better than before. Maybe ten times faster."

The big outlaw smiled. "Ah, then I think I'll get the feller to do mine. I'm quick on the draw, but every men wants to be faster."

"Stick with me, Charlie, and that could happen. You'll still be slower than me, but ten times faster than you are now."

Brewster took another look at Fisher's arm and

then shook his head. "Ah, hell, I reckon not. I hit what I aim at and I'm content with that."

"You've killed eight men, Charlie," Fisher said. "Seems to me you're doing all right."

"Nine. A month ago down Fort Stockton way, I shot Diamond Johnny Hopewell. I reckon he figured I couldn't count up to five."

"Johnny always loved slipping that extry ace into the deck," Fisher said. "He was mighty slick with it, too."

"My bullet blew his watch clean into his belly. Undertaker said he was still ticking when he planted him." Brewster gave Fisher a sidelong look. "Passed a heap of dead men and horses couple miles east of here. That anything to do with the big gun you got on top of that armored stagecoach of yours?"

"Mexican bandits. They attacked us and the Gatling took them by surprise," Fisher said.

"They were surprised all right. Never knew what hit them. After the coyotes get through there's going to be ten acres of scattered bones back there."

Fisher waved a dismissive hand. "Like I give a damn."

Brewster smiled. "That's the King Fisher I remember. You always were a hard-feeling man." He took another long pull from the jug and then tugged at his bandana. "Damn, it's hot in this tent. Don't you feel it?"

"No, I don't feel it," Fisher said. "My blood is not good. It's thin."

Brewster used an end of his bandana to wipe his sweaty face. "Your blood is thin because you've spent too long in the Texas heat."

"Maybe so," Fisher said, his flat tone indicating that the subject was closed. "A thousand for you, Charlie, and five hundred each for your boys. Payable when the job is done. My offer hasn't changed."

"Round up a bunch of rubes and return them to . . . what the hell is the name of that town of yours?"

"Happyville."

"Yeah, that's right. Bring them back and everybody lives happily ever after, is that it?" The outlaw grinned. "Be happy in Happyville, huh?"

"Charlie, I don't give a damn if they're happy or not. I just want them there. And I want you to ride for the town this afternoon."

"You're in a big hurry," Brewster said.

"Damn right I am. I'll feel a sight better when you and your boys are in Happyville looking after my interests."

"We'll be there. Now for God's sake open the tent flap," Brewster said. "I'm dying in here."

Fisher pushed the flap open and then said, "This is a private talk, Charlie, so keep your voice low. There's bound to be a few fighters among the rubes. If they give you trouble, you kill them. No questions asked."

"I don't mind a killing or two," Brewster said. "But I sure can't figure why a bunch of storekeepers and pumpkin rollers are so damned important to you."

"I told you, Charlie. I have bad blood. That's why I need those people."

Brewster shook his head. "I still don't understand."

"You don't have to understand, Charlie. Just do your job and leave and I'll take care of the rest." Fisher thought about that last a moment. "But do your job well and there's always a possibility that I may offer you a new contract. I can make you rich, Charlie, rich and powerful beyond anything you can imagine."

"Tell me about it. That sounds real interesting."

"No, not now," Fisher said. "We'll talk about it at length in Happyville."

"All right, King, but for now change places with me. Let me sit by the flap where there's a breeze," Brewster said.

"We'll leave in a minute after you tell me if you're in or out."

"Of course I'm in, in for a thousand dollars. But I need to know more about the big contract you're offering before I can make a decision on it."

"Round up the citizens of Happyville and you'll soon find out, Charlie. I need them . . . to survive and if I'm to accomplish great things."

Brewster grinned. "What kind of great things. King?"

"You really do want to know, don't you? All right then, I'm talking about an outlaw empire, Charlie. Think of it." Fisher flexed his hand and it looked like an iron claw. "Given enough time, I can take over the whole country. The West first and then move east to the big cities where crime already flourishes. Within a few years, I can make myself the most powerful man in the United States and quite possibly the whole world." Fisher laid his withered left hand on Brewster's shoulder.

The big outlaw could not disguise his cringe.

"And you can be a part of it."

"Part of it, how?" Brewster said.

"You'll be the leader of my outlaw army," Fisher

said. "You will recruit others of your kind and lead them to rob and plunder far and wide. Soon the hick town of Happyville will become the new capital of the South, a metropolis grown rich as you and your thousands of fighting men fill its coffers with gold and silver."

Brewster looked incredulous, but with a straight face he managed to say, "And you, King? What will you be?"

"Why Charlie, what I've always been . . . King Fisher. Before, I was nothing, just a frontier ruffian destined to die with my beard in the sawdust of some saloon. Now that I'm returned to life, I see the way and the way is power."

"This country don't take kindly to kings with power," Brewster said.

"That does not concern me. They had a king once. They can have a king again."

Brewster grinned. "I got to hand it to you. When you plan a thing, you plan big. Now all you have to do is rule over them folks in Happyville, defeat the Texas Rangers, and then take on the whole United States Army." He shook his head. "That's a tall order, King, and suddenly I need another drink."

"Listen to me, Charlie. The Rangers are few in number and can be swept aside. The army has already fought one civil war and has no belly for a second. Some well-placed money in Washington will ease my way to the presidency, and then I will have no further need for private armies and criminality."

Shocked, Brewster said, "King, none of that is going to happen. What you're saying is impossible."

"It's not impossible. Throughout history people of humble origins have risen to great power. An orphaned peasant girl named Catherine became empress of all the Russias and our own Abraham Lincoln was born dirt poor in a log cabin. It can be done and I will do it."

"Whatever you say," Brewster said. "I wish you luck."

"You will join me in this great venture, Charlie?"

"Nope," the outlaw said. "Lookee here, King, here's how it's going to be. I'll round up your townsfolk for you and gun them as need to be gunned. Then you'll pay me and my boys and we part ways with no hard feelings. Are you all right with that?"

"I'm fine with that arrangement, but there's another, greater reason I seek power, Charlie. Are you willing to hear it?"

"I've heard some pretty wild stuff already," Brewster said, smiling. "I guess I can listen to a little more."

"I will use the modern engineering knowledge of this great nation to extend my life as long as possible," Fisher said. "Obadiah le Strange, my engineer, says a hundred more years is a probability and maybe even longer as our technical knowledge grows."

"Hell, you don't even talk like the old King Fisher I knew," Brewster said. "You don't want to share the jug and you haven't mentioned high-breasted women, not once. What's happened to you?"

"Do you really want to know, Charlie?"

"Sure I do. Tell me and maybe I can set you straight."

"I heard the screams of the damned in hell," Fisher said, his voice hollow, haunted. "I don't ever want to go back there. I want to stay away from that terrible place for as long as I can."

"Hah! So you got religion."

"No, not religion. I've found faith in modern science, Charlie, and I want what it can give me . . . immortality."

"You mean live forever? Well, you can't do that, King. No one can."

"There's a first time for everything. In this modern age if you think of a thing, engineers can make it happen."

Brewster held out the jug. "Here, King, take a swig of whiskey. It will do you good. Later, I'll tell you about a little Chinese gal I met over to Nacogdoches way. Why, she could—"

"Charlie, you don't understand, do you?" Fisher said. "That's my fault. I had no reason to believe you could grasp a concept that is way beyond the scope of your intelligence. Get out of here and take the jug with you. I'll talk to you later in Happyville."

Charlie Brewster needed no second urging. He stepped out of the tent, and the flap fell closed behind him. He stood for a moment and gulped fresh air, his mind feeling its way back to normal thought like a rational man who'd just walked out of an asylum for the criminally insane.

CHAPTER THIRTY-TWO

Sam Flintlock woke to the sound of men's voices out in the street. He grabbed the Colt lying at his side and padded on sock feet across the saloon floor.

O'Hara already stood at the door, staring out into the gray dawn. Without turning he said, "Riders. They're looking at the hanged man."

"Rangers?" Flintlock said.

"Nope. See the feller on the gray? That there is Charlie Brewster, as big and bad as I remember."

Flintlock's eyes almost popped out of his head. "Charlie Brewster . . . do you know how much reward money is on his head?"

"At a guess, thousands," O'Hara said. "But don't even think about it."

"Hell, he's a walking gold mine." Flintlock peered through the gloom, blinking his blurry morning eyes. "Nah, it can't be Brewster. He never leaves the Brazos."

"He has now," O'Hara said. "What's he doing here?"

"Who are those boys with him? Recognize any of them?"

"The one on the steel dust is Tom Hendry and the

feller wearing the fancy sombrero is Mexican John Reynolds," O'Hara said. "I don't know any of the others. Charlie never runs with that many riders. He must have something big in mind."

"Well there's one way to find out. Let's go ask him."

"Sam, be polite. Charlie don't take sass."

"Hell, neither do I." Flintlock donned his hat, pulled on his boots, and stuck his Colt into his waistband. He followed O'Hara out the saloon door into a misty morning that still held an evening chill.

"O'Hara! Is this one of your damned Indian tricks? Did you hang this man?" Charlie Brewster leaned forward in the saddle. "Come now, speak up."

"Good to see you, too, Charlie," O'Hara said.

"He was hanging when we got here a few days ago," Flintlock said.

Brewster, a bearded man with fierce black eyes and a knife scar on his left cheek, shifted his gaze to Flintlock and let it linger for a moment on the well-used revolver stuck in his pants. "Who you?"

"Me, Flintlock."

O'Hara said Brewster didn't like sass. Well he was getting some.

Recognition dawned on Brewster's face and he clarified things when he said, "Are you Sam Flintlock, the bounty hunter?"

"Yeah, that would be me."

"I reckon it should be you hanging from the rope."

"And I reckon a whole passel of outlaws think that way."

"Who hung this feller?"

"The town sheriff."

"Why?"

"I don't know," Flintlock said. "But I do know the feller had smallpox."

Brewster swung his horse away and waved to his men. "Git the hell back from there." Then to Flintlock again, he said, "Why does this burg stink?"

"It's the food you see rotting in the street and the dead people rotting in the buildings. Counting the sheriff, there's ten more and they all died of the smallpox. Oh, and another old-timer who knew he had the disease and shot himself."

"O'Hara, is this all true?" Brewster said.

"Flintlock speaks the truth. Can't you smell the death in the air you breathe?"

Brewster ignored that. "Where are the rest of the townspeople?"

"To the east of here, maybe ten miles or so," Flintlock said. "They're camped out in the open and probably starving by this time. If you and your boys came here to rob the bank, it's already been cleaned out."

Charlie Brewster wasn't listening. He looked beyond Flintlock to the boardwalk. "You got women here?"

Flintlock glanced behind him, then turned to Brewster again. "That there is Biddy Sales and we have three more just like her. Count the pregnant lady at the livery and we have five."

"It's a start," Brewster said. "I'm here to bring the folks all back to town."

Flintlock shook his head. "You're up against a stacked deck. They won't come in while the smallpox is here."

"If I have to, I'll shoot a few and the rest will follow," Brewster said.

"They're Texans. They'll shoot back, Charlie, and they won't follow worth a damn." The question formed on Flintlock's face a while before he asked it. "Who's paying you and your boys gun wages?"

Brewster hesitated a moment then said, "It's no secret, I guess. It's King Fisher. You recollect him?"

Flintlock nodded. "Me and King had recent doings, not all of them friendly. He tell you about getting attacked by Comancheros?"

"He didn't. Clem Jardine did. Me and Clem go back a ways."

"Why would bandits from south of the border, half of them Anglos, attack King's camp?" Flintlock said. "Women? Horses? He has few of either. So what does that leave?"

"Money?" Brewster said.

"Damn right. Those boys figured King had gold stashed away somewhere and they wanted it."

"King made his living as a gambler," Brewster said. "Gamblers don't get rich and if they do, they don't stay that way for long."

"Then maybe he robbed a bank," Flintlock said.

Brewster shook his head. "I would've heard about it. That's my line of business."

"Maybe not, Charlie," Flintlock said. "You lead such a sheltered life on the Brazos, hiding out from the law an' sich."

"An' sich are bounty hunters, huh?" Brewster said, his eyes hard and accusing.

"Yeah, there's always that possibility," Flintlock said.

"Not here there isn't. There will be no bounty hunting here."

"You're right, Charlie. I've got better things to do."

"Then state your intentions, Flintlock."

"O'Hara and me are headed for the Arizona Territory." Flintlock glanced at the flaming red sky. "Seems like a fair day ahead. I reckon we'll grab us some coffee and then be on our way."

Brewster didn't hesitate. "Not gonna happen that way, Flintlock. I've been studying on it, and I've decided that you stay here until the gather is finished. As a breed, bounty hunters are mighty cozy with the Rangers. Catch my drift? You could let something slip about what's happening in Happyville."

"I'm not on speaking terms with the Rangers," Flintlock said. "And neither is O'Hara."

"Then we'll let King Fisher decide whether you go or stay," Brewster said.

Flintlock shook his head. "Damn it, Charlie. King is crazy. He's not right in the head since that Dr. le Strange feller worked on him."

"I know King is loco, but he's paying my wages. He wants the people who lived here rounded up and brought back and that's what I'll do. He aims to build an outlaw empire and he needs the folks as . . . as . . ."

"A foundation," Flintlock said.

"Yeah, that's it. A foundation," Brewster said.

"But that's not the real reason."

"It's the one he gave me."

"He was lying to you, Charlie."

"Then what's the real reason?"

"I don't know."

Brewster smiled. "All right, Flintlock. When you

come up with the real reason, let me know. In the meantime, you stay real close."

The outlaw was about to swing his horse away, but Flintlock's flat, whispered use of his name stopped him. "Charlie."

"No!" O'Hara yelled. "Sam, let it go."

Flintlock's hand was close to his gun.

Brewster's eyes grew big. "Don't try it, Flintlock."

The attention of the dozen hard-bitten riders focused on Flintlock. Any one of them was as fast and deadly with a gun as he was and they'd be almighty sudden.

O'Hara stepped in front of Flintlock and said, "Charlie, Sam'l is a bear until he's had his coffee."

Brewster was not a humorless man and he grinned as he said, "Seems like you got a choice, Flintlock. You can draw down on a dozen of us, and die, or drink a cup of coffee and live."

O'Hara saw tension in Flintlock, a sure sign of that streak of recklessness that had several times before almost got him killed. "Sam, the Cheyenne say that the brave man does not yield to fear and neither does he surrender to anger. He is at all times master of himself."

"The Indian is speaking the truth, Flintlock," Brewster said. "Shuck the iron and you're a dead man."

"Charlie, never again tell me what I can and can't do," Flintlock said.

"Flintlock, I've got a dozen men at my back."

"I know. But I'll shoot you first, Charlie."

"I have no quarrel with you. We don't go back a ways over rocky ground. Let's keep it like that."

Flintlock looked into the faces of the hardcases

surrounding him and saw no friends but plenty of enemies.

Brewster defused the situation. "All right. I'm asking, not telling, you to stay in town until King Fisher gets here. As soon as the crazy man rides into Happyville, you ride out." He looked around at his men. "Boys, can I say fairer than that?"

Above the chorus of male voices assuring Brewster that he had honestly stated his case, Biddy Sales spoke up loud and clear. "Sam Flintlock, you're not going anywhere until Rose Flood has her baby." She stepped in front of him, her hands on her hips.

Flintlock turned to her, "Hell, woman, she's got a husband."

"Yes, she has, but he's not a gunman and you are."

"Look around you, Biddy. She's surrounded by gunman," Flintlock said.

"Yes, but I don't trust them," Biddy said. "God help me, I trust you."

"No harm will come to the pregnant woman, I assure you, miss," Brewster said. "Ain't that so, boys?"

Again Biddy's words rose above the chorus of agreement. "Mr. Brewster, your assurances mean little to me. When all is said and done, you are a frontier ruffian. Empty words are easy to speak."

"Hell, lady, so is Flintlock. He's a ruffian from way back."

"I'm aware of that, but better a ruffian I know than one I don't."

Lizzie Doulan stepped beside Biddy. The woman looked pale and drawn, her blue eyes strangely life-less. "Mr. Flintlock, please do the honorable thing and stay long enough to ensure the safety of the unborn child. It would be a terrible thing to turn your back on her now and live without honor."

"You tell him, girlie," Brewster said, grinning. "You and the other ladies are going to stick around for a while, ain't you?"

"*Hic manebimus optime*," Lizzie said.

Brewster was taken aback. "Woman, did you just cuss at me in some fancy foreign lingo?"

"I spoke in Latin. *Hic manebimus optime* means 'Here we will stay most excellently.' But its real meaning is that we will remain in place no matter the danger."

Brewster said something about how Mexican gobbledygook always did baffle him, but Lizzie ignored that and said, "Flintlock, what is your decision?"

Flintlock stared into the woman's eyes. It was like gazing into a misty, endless tunnel. *My God, what had those eyes seen?* "I'll stay until the baby is born and is safe." He frowned. "Now why the hell did I say that?"

O'Hara gave him a sidelong look. "Because you were allowed a glimpse of the spirit realm, Sam."

Flintlock grumbled something then said, "Hell, I need coffee."

CHAPTER THIRTY-THREE

"Hey, everybody, the circus is in town," Biddy Sales said, speaking from the boardwalk into the saloon.

Charlie Brewster and Flintlock joined her.

"It's King," Brewster said. He held a glass of whiskey in one hand, one of the saloon's five-cent cigars in the other. "He sure don't look well."

"Peaked," Flintlock said. "I'd say that's why he's riding the bed wagon."

King Fisher sat up on the wagon's seat, the woman with silver hands at the reins. The man's face was gray and drawn and every now and then he let his chin fall onto his chest as though his head was suddenly too heavy for his shoulders. Wrapped in a gray army blanket, he wore a turban of heavy blue wool and looked like a frail sick old man, a far cry from his vision of himself as master of the world.

O'Hara fixed his gaze fixed on the sickly creature in the wagon, "It's a time for vultures."

Brewster stared at him but said nothing.

"What the hell is that monster?" Biddy said.

Startled, Brewster said, "What monster?"

"The steam locomotive thing. It looks like a big iron egg. And there's a bird on top of it."

"That's not a bird. It's a man," Flintlock said.

"Why is he dressed like that?" Biddy said.

"Because he's going to rid this town of smallpox," Flintlock said. "At least that's the intention."

Biddy's face framed a question, but Flintlock ignored it. "O'Hara, did you reload the Hawken like I told you to?"

"I sure did, Massa," the Indian said, tugging his forelock.

"Then bring it here. If King Fisher gives me any sass, I'll blow a hole right through him. I swear I will."

"Yes, Massa."

Flintlock shook his head. "O'Hara, tell me again why I haven't put a bullet in you before now."

O'Hara didn't answer, but his hoot of delighted laughter sounded strange coming from a long-haired man who looked like a particularly mean Cheyenne dog soldier.

Attracted by the din of O'Hara's mirth, King Fisher's good eye angled to the boardwalk and an eyebrow crawled up his forehead when he saw Flintlock. Despite his apparent frailty, Fisher's voice was strong as he called out, "Sam Flintlock, we did not part on good terms. That has worried me. Made me uneasy."

"Your doing, King, not mine," Flintlock said.

"We will talk again once I rid this town of its pestilence."

"Looking forward to it, King," Flintlock said.

He watched Obadiah le Strange approach the wagon. The engineer had removed his bird mask and held it under his robed arm. He and Fisher conferred for several minutes, and then le Strange nodded and walked away and stepped onto the boardwalk. "Good to see you again, Mr. Flintlock."

"Yeah, you too, le Strange," Flintlock said.

The greetings from both men lacked in sincerity as they went through the motions for politeness sake.

"King asks that you point out the dwellings where the dead lie," le Strange said. "He means to quickly bring the pestilence to an end."

Over the young engineer's shoulder, Flintlock saw Dr. Sarah Ann Castle step out of Helrun. She and two of Fisher's nameless gunmen donned voluminous black robes and each held a bird mask under his arm.

"Dr. Castle," Fisher called. He had not yet stepped from the wagon. "Remove that abomination from the gallows. Cut it down. Mr. Brewster, report to Mr. le Strange for instructions."

The big outlaw grinned and nodded.

Le Strange continued. ". . . so that the bodies can be removed and burned, Mr. Flintlock, you understand."

"Just so long as you understand that I'll point from a distance," Flintlock said. "I don't want to get too close to those dead folks."

"That will be fine," le Strange said. "Dr. Castle and myself, along with a couple helpers, will do what has to be done."

"You mean the dirty work," Biddy Sales said.

"Indeed, that is the case, dear lady," the engineer said. "I only wish it could be otherwise."

"Le Strange, you got something for me?" Charlie Brewster said.

"Yes, Mr. Brewster. You see the rod and gun shop at the end of the street?"

"I see it."

"You and your men will tear it down board by board. Remove the guns if any remain and then drag the lumber somewhere, say a mile or so from town."

"Not our usual line of work," Brewster said. "It ain't the kind of job you give white men."

Le Strange nodded. "I realize that, but King deems it necessary. We need to burn the bodies of the dead, you see. And besides, this town will have no further need for a gun shop."

"How do you reckon that, le Strange?" Flintlock said.

The engineer smiled. "No one in this town will be allowed to own a gun except for Mr. Fisher's own police." The man's smile grew. "We don't need warriors in Happyville, Mr. Flintlock. We need a flock of sheep."

"I guess I take their guns before I bring them in," Brewster said.

"Exactly," le Strange said. "Anyone caught with a gun will face the most severe penalties. Happyville must be a quiet, safe, and contented town, ruled by King's strong hand."

"Here's your rifle, Sam." O'Hara glared at le Strange. "Unless you want to try taking this one."

Le Strange shook his head. "That will not be necessary . . . yet."

Dressed in black robes and beaked hoods, Dr. Sarah Castle, Obadiah le Strange, and the two gunmen followed Flintlock around Happyville like a flock of crows. He pointed out the houses where the dead lay and one by one the rotting bodies were carried out in blankets and dragged a mile distant from town. By nightfall, the gun shop that had yielded a single box of .22 cartridges had been completely pulled apart and the splintered timber piled high around the dead.

Le Strange lit the dreadful bonfire . . . visible from Happyville as a pillar of fire and smoke.

CHAPTER THIRTY-FOUR

"They're burning dead people," Luke Gamble said.

"You mean a dead person?" Captain Gregory Holden Usher said.

"Cap'n, look at my mouth. I said they're burning *people*."

Usher was appalled. "How many?"

"Judging by the stink and the height of the flames, a lot. Maybe a dozen."

"But . . . but why?"

"Your guess is as good as mine," Gamble said. "Maybe ol' King Fisher done fer more bandits."

"He's in the town?"

"Damn right he is, and plenty more with him. And he's got him some kind of steam locomotive that doesn't need rails. I seen it with my own eyes. Looks like a big egg."

"Ain't nothing like that possible," Sergeant Rollo Martin said.

Gamble's eyes hardened and his voice dropped. "I saw what I saw, Rollo. You callin' me a liar?"

"Sergeant Martin meant no offense," Usher said. "How many with Fisher?"

"Too many, Cap'n. And they ain't rubes. Look like guns to me."

"You were at a distance, Mr. Gamble," Usher said. "How can you be sure?"

"I used your field glasses, Captain. And I can tell guns when I see them. All them boys are well set up and they ain't riding Texas scrubs. There ain't a hoss worth less than a thousand in the whole bunch."

"Damn, that's bad news, rotten news," Usher said. "They've got to be more of Fisher's gang."

Sergeant Martin took the pot from the fire and said, "Here, sir, have some more coffee. Steady your nerves, like."

Usher's dark eyes glittered in the light of the flames. "My nerves are steady enough, Sergeant." Usher looked at Gamble. "How do we handle this?"

"What we don't do is stack ourselves up against a dozen hired guns," the scout said.

"Please don't tell me something I already know, Mr. Gamble. I need ideas."

"Sometimes the best idea is the simplest," Martin said.

"Let's hear it," Usher said.

"We become as bold as brass."

"Huh?" the officer said.

"We're the army, ain't we? We have authority around these parts. We just ride into town—"

"Bold as brass," Private Seth Proud said.

"Right you are, boy, bold as brass," Martin said. "We demand to search the Fisher wagon, find the gold, and then tell them to get the hell out of the way because we're taking it back to Fort Concho."

"And then we all get shot," Corporal Ethan Stagg said.

"You got a better idea?" Martin said.

"Your basic idea is a good one, Sergeant, if I had a whole troop with me," Usher said. "I say we don't ride in and lay all our cards on the table right away. Mr. Gamble, you and I will ride into the town and masquerade as a down-on-his-luck gold prospector and an army deserter. We will study the lie of the land, and by that I mean the location of the payroll."

Usher saw Gamble's face frown a question and he said, "I believe all those men you saw are newly hired mercenaries, men who fight for money, the only thing they care a hoot about. It's unlikely they know about the payroll, but we will mention it casually, inquiring if King Fisher is keeping it all for himself or sharing it. We will stir up unrest, Mr. Gamble, cause trouble. If my hunch is correct, our revelation will lead to gunplay and dead men. When the smoke clears we can meet up with Sergeant Martin, Private Proud, and Corporal Stagg and then claim what's ours."

"You mean claim what's the army's," Martin said.

"Of course," Usher said. "That's exactly what I meant. What did you think? That I'd run off with the thirty thousand?"

"It's a possibility," Martin said, hate loud and clear in his eyes.

Before Usher could respond, Gamble said, "It's thin, Captain. There's no way of telling if a gun battle will knock off enough of them boys to make it easy for us."

A smile tugged at the corners of Usher's mouth. "Mr. Gamble, you and I will also be shooting, discreetly of course, but at both sides. Between us, I think we can do enough execution to ensure that the hireling numbers are whittled down to size."

Gamble shook his head. "It's still thin . . . and damned dangerous."

"We want the money, Luke," Usher said. "Any great endeavor entails a degree of risk. Sergeant Martin, the original idea was yours. What do you think?"

Martin said, "I think I don't trust you, Captain Usher. If them boys in town believe one deserter, they'll believe four. I say we all go."

"The idea has some merit, Greg." Gamble saw the surprise in Usher's firelit face and grinned. "Deserters would be on first-name terms, don't you think? Besides, we can't keep on calling you *Captain,* because officers don't desert."

Martin's face was bitter. "Usher deserted his command once."

"You're not going to let me forget that, Martin, are you?"

"Not for as long as I live . . . or you live."

Usher tossed away his tin cup and rose to his feet. He undid his holster flap and said, "Maybe we should have this out right here and now."

"Suits me just fine." Martin went for his Colt, his draw slow from a flapped, butt-forward gun rig. The instant his hand grabbed the handle of his revolver he knew with awful certainty that he wasn't going to make it.

Luke Gamble had plenty of time . . . all the time in the world.

His bullet hit Martin square in the center of his chest before either the sergeant or Usher had cleared leather. Gamble put another round into Martin before the man hit the ground, but by then he was already dead.

Stagg and Proud, scared witnesses to Martin's death, didn't move. They'd thought the sergeant invincible, the toughest, meanest man in the United States Army, but Gamble disproved that in the space of two heartbeats.

Stagg, perhaps because of the stripes on his arm, found his voice. "Death on soldier boys, ain't you, Gamble?"

"Of late it seems like soldier boys are the ones giving me all the trouble," the scout said. He still had his Colt in his hand and his eyes steady on Stagg. "Call it, Cap'n."

"Put your gun away, Luke," Usher said. "Corporal Stagg—"

"Stow that, Usher. The name is Ethan. There ain't any of us in the army any longer."

"Man speaks sense," Gamble said.

"Ethan, a fourth split of thirty thousand is seven thousand five hundred dollars," Usher said. "A man can make a good life for himself with that kind of money."

Stagg's smile was thin. "Sure, I'm in until the day you"—he nodded to Gamble—"or him puts a bullet in my back."

"That won't happen," Usher said. "There's been enough bloodshed already. From now on we're partners, share and share alike . . . the dangers and the money. Priv—Seth—how does that set with you?"

The youngster glanced at the grinning Gamble and said, "It sets just fine with me, Captain."

"Call me Greg. As Ethan said, we're no longer army."

"We're outlaws," Gamble said.

"No," Stagg said. "We're deserters and if we're caught, we'll hang."

"We won't get caught," Usher said. "I will see to that." The evening was cool but a rivulet of sweat trickled from under his kepi and ran down his cheek. "Money has a way of staving off disaster."

"Wait." Gamble took a faded gray shirt from his saddlebags and tossed it into Usher's chest. "Officers don't desert, remember? You can't wear that blouse and shoulder boards any longer."

The scout waited until Usher changed into the collarless gray shirt and then shook his head. "Greg, as an officer and gentleman in dirty-shirt blue and gold you were quite the sight. But as a civilian, you sure don't stack up to much."

"Don't underestimate me, Luke," Usher said.

The big scout smiled. "I'll never do that, Greg. I reckon you're capable of anything."

CHAPTER THIRTY-FIVE

Out of consideration for the pregnant Mrs. Rose Flood, Charlie Brewster had ordered his men not to use the livery but to string a horse line on a grassy area behind the saloon.

King Fisher was not happy with that arrangement but seemed too sick to argue and remained in his wagon.

"How is she?" Sam Flintlock said.

Dr. Sarah Castle peered shortsightedly into the darkness outside the stable. "Oh, it's you, Mr. Flintlock."

"How is she?" Flintlock said again.

"The baby has not yet turned and it may be a very difficult delivery." The doctor lifted the makings from Flintlock's shirt pocket and began to build a cigarette. "I shouldn't smoke, but I do now and again."

Flintlock thumbed a match into flame and lit the woman's cigarette. Charlie Brewster and his noisy gunmen were in the saloon and he heard Biddy shriek with laughter, followed by Margie's strident cackle.

"Sounds like they're having a good time," Sarah Castle said. "Why don't you join them?"

"I have no friends in there."

"Where is your Indian friend? What's his name?"

"O'Hara. He's not much of a one for white men's saloons either. Some fellers object to an Indian being under the same roof and when they're drinking, it can get real nasty real quick, even if O'Hara is only half an Indian."

"You could almost be an Indian yourself," Sarah said. "How did you get the name Flintlock?"

"I'm named for this Hawken rifle I carry."

"Then your real name is Hawken?"

"No. My grandpappy named me for his flintlock rifle, seeing as how I never knew my pa's name. My father was a gambling man and when my ma got pregnant, he didn't stick around."

"Why didn't he give you his own name, that grandpa of yours?"

"He said every man should have his father's name. He told me he'd call me Flintlock after the Hawken until I found my ma and she told me who my pa was and what he was called."

"You ever find her?"

"No. I never did, but I'm still on the hunt for her. Or at least I was until O'Hara and me rode into Happyville."

"You were raised by your grandfather?"

"Yeah. By old Barnabas and some other mountain men. As parents go, they weren't much, a hard-drinking, whoring, brawling bunch of old sinners."

Sarah Castle smiled, her teeth very white in the moonlight. "Still, I'm very impressed that your grandpa was a mountain man. When I was younger I read some accounts of their adventures among the wild savages."

"Barnabas was with Bridger an' Hugh Glass an' them, at least for a spell. Then he helped survey the Platte and the Sweetwater with Kit Carson and Fremont."

"Strange, restless breed they were, mountain men."

"You could say that," Flintlock allowed.

The doctor peered hard at Flintlock's rugged, unshaven face and then his throat. "When we first met I noticed the big bird on your throat. Is there a story behind that?"

"I was raised rough," Flintlock said.

"Ah, old Barnabas did that to you?" Sarah said.

"Yeah, he wanted it done. When I was twelve years old, he got an Assiniboine woman to do the tattooing. As I recollect, it hurt considerable."

"What is it? Some kind of eagle?"

Flintlock began to build a cigarette. Without looking up from the makings, he said, "It's a thunderbird." He thumbed the match into flame and lit his smoke. "Barnabas wanted a black and red thunderbird on account of how the Indians reckon it's a sacred bird."

"He wanted it that big?" Sarah said. "It pretty much covers your neck and down into your chest."

"Barnabas said folks would remember me because of the bird. He told me that a man folks don't remember is of no account. He was a hard old man, was Barnabas, him and them other mountain men he hung with. A tough, mean bunch as ever was. But they taught me," Flintlock said. "Each one of them, in his own way, taught me something."

"Like what for instance?"

"I don't want to offend you, ma'am," Flintlock said.

Sarah smiled. "I'm a big girl. I've heard it all before."

"Well, they taught me about whores and whiskey and how to tell the good ones from the bad. They taught me how to stalk a man and how to kill him. And they taught me to never answer a bunch of damned fool questions."

The woman laughed. "Sounds like old Barnabas and his mountain man pals all right."

"One more thing, Sarah. If you save Mrs. Flood's life, they taught me to never forget a thing like that either."

Restless, unwilling to seek his blankets, Flintlock walked away from her into the moon-splashed night, past the tall wild oaks that grew, despite all the odds, at the edge of the street.

He was forty-two that fall, not forty as he claimed, short, stocky and as rough as a cob. A shock of unruly black hair showed under his battered straw hat and his eyes, gray as a sea mist, were deep set under shaggy eyebrows. His mustache was full, in the dragoon style made fashionable in Texas by the Rangers, and he walked with the horseman's stiff-kneed gait. If he'd chosen to, he could've sold his clothes, including his boots, for ten cents.

Flintlock was tough, enduring, raised to be hard by hard men but there was no cruelty in him. He had much honesty of tongue and a quick wry sense of humor.

Up until he'd used the Gatling gun he'd killed thirteen men—three as a lawman and the remainder since he'd turned bounty hunter. None of those dead men disturbed his sleep of nights and the only ghost he ever saw was that of wicked old Barnabas.

He saw him again.

The old mountain man balanced on his head in a patch of open, bottle-strewn ground between a couple stores, one of them with a sign in the window: BOOTS AND SHOES AT COST.

Flintlock bent over the better to see Barnabas's face. "You taking a different view of the world, old man?"

"Nah. Three-Fingered Johnny Reach teached me this. He says when the blood rushes to the head it gets into the brain and makes a man smarter. You recollect ol' Johnny, Sam?"

"I should. I was the one that shot two fingers offen him that time."

"He says you were the meanest man that ever collected a bounty on him."

"I didn't like him much. I always figured Johnny Reach was a disgrace to the bank-robbing profession. He had dirty habits. Now quit that stupid pose and stand on your two feet like a man . . . or a ghost . . . or whatever the hell you are."

"Testy, ain't we?" Barnabas did something fast and was suddenly standing again. "Why ain't you looking fer your ma, boy?"

"A situation came up," Flintlock said.

"That pregnant woman?"

"Her and other things."

"You-know-who said he'd tell you how to handle the woman thing."

"Barnabas, I don't need advice from Beelzebub, especially when it involves knives."

"And saws. I declare, but you was always an ungrateful whelp, Sammy."

"Why are you here, Barnabas?"

The old man made a face. "You always think it's about you, don't you, boy? Well it ain't. I was just passing this way and decided to stand on my head."

"I don't believe you, Barnabas," Flintlock said. "Say what you came to say."

"All right, Sam, here it is. If you don't get the hell out of this town, you'll be dead before the night of the next full moon. That's less than a week from now."

"I'll keep that in mind, Barnabas."

"You'd better, because I ain't joshing you, boy. Now beat it. I want to stand on my head some more. Hell, I feel myself getting smarter already."

Then the old man was gone and all that remained was the lingering smell of brimstone that always marked his departure.

It was Flintlock's intention to call it a night and return to the saloon, but he stopped in his tracks, his eyes on the looming bulk of King Fisher's wagon. An oil lamp burned inside and the canvas glowed with pale orange light.

He stepped closer, the old Hawken up and ready, wary of . . . he knew not what. He heard a woman in the interior sob and then a man talked low, soft, reassuring words. It was the voice of Obadiah le Strange.

Who was the woman and why was she so distressed?

Grofrec Horntoe appeared from behind the wagon, his restraining hand on the chain around his wolf's neck. Quicksilver carried its head low and a soft growl grumbled in its throat.

"You looking for something, Flintlock?"

"I thought I heard a woman crying." His voice sounded hollow in the darkness.

"Women cry all the time," Horntoe said. "Be on your way."

"Is she all right?"

"I said be on your way."

The wolf peeled back its lips and snarled, lunging. The chain around its neck chimed.

"The woman is sick, that's all," Horntoe said. "Women get sick, same as men."

Quicksilver's slanted eyes glowed red and Flintlock felt something spike in his belly. The feeling puzzled him at first, but then he realized that it was fear.

The woman's sobs had stopped and Flintlock recognized le Strange's sound of humming that was meant to be soothing.

Then he heard King Fisher's voice, loud and commanding, not the voice of a sick man. "Will she live?"

"She's a bleeder," le Strange said. "I knew that from before, but I had to take the chance."

"Can you stop it?"

"I need Dr. Castle," le Strange said.

"Grofrec!" This came from Fisher.

The dwarf said, "I hear you, boss." He never took his eyes off Flintlock.

"Bring Dr. Castle. Hurry."

"Right away, boss."

In the gloom, wolf and man were as one. Only Quicksilver's fangs gleamed amid the shadow.

"Will you give me the road, Flintlock?" Horntoe said. "Better for you if you do."

The wagon was silent. Flintlock lowered his rifle and stepped aside. "Little man, I swear I'll kill you one day."

"Or I will kill you." The dwarf grinned. "Quicksilver will tear the big bird from your throat. Depend on it." The smirking Horntoe dragged his snarling wolf past Flintlock. Man and animal smelled feral, wild, like the inside of a dragon's den.

Flintlock had not been asleep for long when he jerked into a sitting position, his frightened eyes searching the darkened saloon. Was it the wolf come for him? The one called Quicksilver? The one with a ravenous appetite for human flesh?

His head sank slowly back to the floor. Suddenly he was very tired, used up by the events of the past few days. He badly wanted this waking nightmare to end. He closed his eyes again, forced himself to empty his mind of all thought and for the rest of the night he drifted in and out of consciousness.

Once, in restless slumber, he saw his mother again.

Her hair was bright red, but her features were blurred because he could no longer remember her face. She was lost in a swamp and cried out to him. Suddenly, her hair was no longer red but gray, and she beckoned to him, her voice pleading, begging him to save her, her arms moving like willow branches in a wind.

He moved toward her, but slowly, slowly, as though he walked through thick molasses. He called out to her. "Ma, what's my name? Ma, tell me my father's name."

A mist came down like a gray cloud and his mother vanished from sight.

The dream within a dream ended.

CHAPTER THIRTY-SIX

O'Hara shook Sam Flintlock awake and handed him a cup of coffee. "I saw something this morning."

Grumpy, his mouth dry as mummy dust, Flintlock said, "Tell me in another hour when I wake up, huh?" But like all men who lived hard lives on the frontier Flintlock had conditioned himself to wake instantly and he was fully alert. He tested the coffee, made a face, and began to build a cigarette. "All right, now tell me."

"I saw a woman with silver hands." O'Hara stared at Flintlock, expecting him to register shock, or at least surprise, but he was disappointed.

"She lost her hands somehow and the engineer feller, le Strange, made her new ones," Flintlock said. "At least that's the story."

"Two of Charlie Brewster's men carried her out of Fisher's wagon," O'Hara said.

"Carried her out?"

"Yeah. And she was white as a boiled sheet."

"She's a white woman."

O'Hara said, "Then I reckon she was whiter than any white woman I ever saw."

"Did you see King?"

"Sure did. He was stomping around yelling orders. He wants all the bedding and furniture removed from the smallpox houses and burned and he told Adam Flood to get his wife out of the livery."

That last disturbed Flintlock, but he let it go. "Does King still look poorly?"

O'Hara shook his head. "No, he looks just fine. Well, as fine as a man with a tin arm and leg can look. Wearing his gun. I saw that."

Flintlock returned to the livery. "Why does he want Mrs. Flood out of the stable?"

"As far as I can tell, he wants to make room for his wagon and locomotive. By the look of things he's got the Gatling all loaded and ready."

Flintlock stubbed out his cigarette butt on the saloon floor, put on his hat, and then pulled on his boots. He rose, deciding to have it out with King about Mrs. Flood, but the smell of frying bacon stopped him cold and sent him toward the stove.

Biddy said, "This is the last of it, Flintlock, and there will be no more biscuits after these."

"Weevils in the rest of the flour." Margie wrinkled her nose. "It's disgusting."

Like Biddy and Jane Feehan, Margie's face was painted and she'd made an effort to make her clothes presentable. She'd hiked her skirt up a few inches the better to show her legs in her calf boots. The arrival of close to a dozen young, virile men had not gone unnoticed among the women. All, that is, except Lizzie Doulan. Her blond hair was unbrushed and she had dark circles under her eyes. The girl looked exhausted. She had the exhaustion of a person who no longer wanted to live. She looked as though every waking day was not be embraced with joy, but a thing to be endured.

Biddy handed Flintlock a biscuit and bacon, looked into his eyes, and said, "Lizzie is tired. She's been spending a lot of time with Mrs. Flood, poor thing."

Her next statement shocked Flintlock. "I'm scared. I saw two men out there in the street this morning. They didn't look human."

"King Fisher and Clem Jardine," Flintlock said. "Obadiah le Strange the engineer fixed them up with artificial legs and arms."

"And eyes," Biddy said.

"Both of them were shot to pieces. Le Strange saved their lives."

"He's not God. He's not even a doctor," Biddy said. "He's an engineer."

Flintlock took time off chewing to smile. "Tell him that."

"What is the metal egg? Is it a locomotive of some kind?"

"Yeah, but it doesn't need rails. King Fisher calls it Helrun, the Black Howler, and it's a machine to be reckoned with." Flintlock flashed back to the massacre of the Comancheros. "It's got a Gatling gun."

Lizzie Doulan spoke for the first time that morning. "A terrible evil has come to this town and it has trapped us here."

"We're not trapped," Flintlock said. "I'll shoot our way out of here if—"

A gunshot shattered the fabric of the morning and his words died on his lips.

Flintlock shoved his Colt into his waistband and

hurried out of the saloon and into the street. A crowd—Charlie Brewster, his men, and a couple other guns that Fisher had brought with him—had gathered outside the livery.

As Flintlock crossed the street, he heard Sarah Castle say, "Stand back. Give me room."

Brewster heard hurried footsteps behind him and turned. He stepped in front of Flintlock. "No, Sam." He jerked the gun out of Flintlock's pants and then with his mouth close to his ear, whispered, "You can't draw down on him. He'll kill you." Brewster stepped back.

Flintlock was facing him and a couple other gunmen. "Give me my gun, Charlie."

"You'll get yourself killed," Brewster said.

"Then I'll take it from you." Flintlock, his fists ready, moved in on Brewster.

The incident ended when King Fisher pushed his way through the crowd and stepped between the two men. His strange artificial eye glowing green, he said to Flintlock, "I will not tolerate defiance in a man. I made him aware of my feelings, but he chose to ignore me."

"Damn you. Who did you kill?" Flintlock said.

That question was answered by a woman's hysterical cry from the livery and in that moment Flintlock knew with terrible certainty who was dead.

"Listen to me, Sam," Fisher said. "I want to—"

"I'm all through listening to you, King." Flintlock brushed past the man.

Fisher threw at him, "Damn you. You'll regret this slight."

Flintlock ignored that and pushed his way through the circle of Brewster gunmen. Their hard faces revealed little, but the solemn silence they maintained as they stared at the lanky body of Adam Flood was suggestive of men who figured an injustice had been done. Rose Flood had thrown herself on top of her husband's body and she sobbed uncontrollably. An ominous pool of blood surrounded the pair, but Flintlock couldn't tell from whom it came. Perhaps from both . . . wounded husband and grieving wife.

He turned and said to a man standing next to him, "Get Biddy Sales. Tell her to hurry."

The man hesitated for just a moment and then flung himself through the crowd.

Flintlock kneeled beside the dead man and placed his hand on Mrs. Flood's back and whispered to Sarah Castle, "How is Adam?"

Before the doctor could answer, Rose lifted her tearstained face and said, "My husband is dead. Adam was murdered by that . . . that abomination."

An older man with eyes quieter than the others squatted beside Flintlock. "He had a Smith & Wesson belly gun in his pocket. He tried to run a bluff with the piece and King Fisher shot him."

"He draw down on Fisher?" Flintlock said.

"No, just showed it as a warning, like." The gunman shook his head. "Sure way for a man to get hisself killed."

Flintlock reached down and took a Smith & Wesson .38 from the dead man's pocket. He broke it open and said, "It isn't loaded."

The gunman sighed and rose to his feet. "Rube ran

a bluff with an empty gun and left his pregnant wife a widow." He shook his head. "Hell, I'm getting too old for this business."

Rose Flood screamed and screamed and as one, the surrounding ring of men shrank away from her, unable to face a thing so harrowing and so far beyond their experience.

"Make way there. Give her room to breathe." Dr. Castle pushed some of the onlookers out of her way. "You men be about your business and that includes you, Flintlock." She took a knee beside the screaming woman and the legs of her coveralls were instantly stained with blood. "Is Biddy Sales here yet? I'm sure she's seen a woman miscarry before."

Flintlock stumbled away with the other men then sought out Charlie Brewster and grabbed him by the shirtfront. "Give me my Colt, Charlie."

"Don't be a fool," Brewster said. "King Fisher will kill you. Nobody alive can shade him and I just saw that for a fact."

"Charlie, I won't ask you again." Flintlock turned away from the outlaw for a moment to yell, "One of you men give me a gun."

Brewster drew—practiced, fast, and smooth. The gun slammed into the side of Flintlock's head and dropped him like a poleaxed ox.

Flintlock didn't know what hit him.

The outlaw stepped back and saw O'Hara eying him. "You taking a hand in this, Injun?"

"Not this time," O'Hara said. "A couple of you men help me carry Sam into the saloon."

Suddenly, Rose Flood stopped screaming . . . but the resulting silence shrieked even louder.

CHAPTER THIRTY-SEVEN

Sam Flintlock woke to a splitting headache and the concerned, worn face of Lizzie Doulan.

She removed a wet cloth from his forehead and said, "Are you all right, Mr. Flintlock?"

Flintlock groaned. "What the hell did Charlie Brewster hit me with?"

O'Hara's voice sounded mildly amused. "His hogleg."

"Damn near killed me," Flintlock said.

"I guess he buffaloed you pretty good at that, Sam. You were so plumb loco out there in the street you didn't give him much choice."

"Hell, O'Hara, why didn't you plug him?"

"That would have been impolite, Sam. Charlie was only trying to help, being a good Samaritan, an' all."

Flintlock struggled into a sitting position. "I'm sure there's some Injun logic there. When I find it, I'll let you know." He pressed the heels of his hands into his eyes. "Damn. The whole room is spinning."

"It's dark out," Lizzie said.

O'Hara glanced at the railroad clock on the wall

that Margie Tott had compulsively kept wound. "It's near midnight, Sam. You've been out for hours." After a few moments, his voice was strangely expressionless. "You missed all the excitement. Mighty big doings in Happyville."

Outside, the wind, flecked with rain, blew hard and lifted shrouds of dust from the street. Flintlock cocked his aching head, listening.

"Mrs. Flood is dead and her baby with her," O'Hara said. "Bled to death while trying to birth that baby, or so Dr. Castle says. Happened a couple hours ago. Biddy told me the doctor did all she could."

Flintlock was silent for a while, absorbing that. Then he said, "King Fisher took three lives with one bullet."

"You could say that," O'Hara said.

"I hate this town," Lizzie Doulan said.

The skin tightened against the hard bones of Flintlock's face. "King just made himself a moving target."

"Just don't brace Fisher, Sam," O'Hara said. "I swear, I hear you talk about a drawdown and I'll give you another headache."

"There's more than one way to skin a cat," Flintlock said.

"Or a louse," Lizzie said. "Hear that sound out there?"

Flintlock listened into the night. "What is it? A woman sobbing?"

"Yes, her name is Blanche Jardine. She's—"

"I know who she is," Flintlock said.

"She's grieving for Mrs. Rose and her child," Lizzie said. "Her face is made of porcelain and she drops water on it for tears. The night before she died, Mrs.

Rose told Biddy she planned to call the baby Louisa if it was a girl or Jonas if it was a boy. It was a girl and Biddy says she'll put the names of all three Floods on the grave marker."

O'Hara said, "I didn't even know this town had a graveyard."

"It's small, to the north of town among some wild oak," Lizzie said. "There's only a couple graves and they're hard to find because of the brush."

"Now there will be five." Flintlock was not a man to be handled or helped, but he made an exception. "Help me to my feet, Injun." O'Hara, a man who'd shared the hardships of some of his most dangerous trails, was a man he respected. "I need to see if I can still stand."

O'Hara grabbed Flintlock by the arm and effortlessly raised him to his feet.

Doing what had become second nature to him, Flintlock's gun hand strayed to his waistband. "Damn him."

"If you're talking about Charlie Brewster, he gave me your gun. Told me to give it to you when you'd cooled down and were less liable to go off half-cocked looking for Fisher." O'Hara stepped to the bar, retrieved the revolver, and handed it to Flintlock. "Careful. Don't drop it."

Flintlock made a face, shoved the Colt into his pants, and half walked, half staggered to the door, which he pushed open a few inches. He leaned his shoulder against the frame and looked outside into the night. Wind gusted and a few raindrops pattered along the boardwalk and, across the street, the screen door of Muldoon's Hardware Store rattled on its hinges.

O'Hara stood behind Flintlock and said, "Four army deserters rode into town just after dusk. Well, one of them was a civilian scout."

"Did they have a story to tell?" Flintlock said.

"Not much of one. They said they'd come all the way from Fort Concho and have decided to head for Old Mexico. The scout said they plan to join Porfirio Díaz's army and live high on the hog for a spell."

Flintlock smiled. "And they'll desert from the Mexican army as well."

"Depend on it. They look like a shiftless bunch to me."

"Where are they now?"

"Camped out with Charlie Brewster an' them. When they heard about the smallpox they decided to stay well clear of the buildings."

"Can't say as I blame them," Flintlock said.

"Maybe them soldier boys will join Charlie's bunch," O'Hara said.

Flintlock shook his head and instantly regretted it. After the pain subsided he said, "From what I've seen of his boys, Charlie only recruits a better class of riffraff. I don't think he'll go for deserters."

Biddy, wrapped in a blanket, walked across the shadowed saloon floor on bare feet. "How are you feeling, Flintlock?"

"I've got a headache."

"We have a burying in the morning. You and your Indian better get some sleep."

"Why us?" Flintlock said.

"Because there's no one else."

Flintlock hesitated and Biddy said, "It takes a man to dig a hole big enough for two people and a baby."

"I'm not saying the words. I don't know the words," Flintlock said.

"We'll say the words, me and Lizzie," Biddy said. "We've heard them more often than was our fair share."

"Right after sunup," Flintlock said.

"That's early," Biddy said.

"Not too early," O'Hara said. "There's a reckoning coming soon."

Biddy was taken aback. "That's what Lizzie Doulan says, a reckoning is near. She told me there will be many dead in Happyville." She shivered and pulled her blanket closer. "Maybe we'll all get lucky and the dawn will never come."

CHAPTER THIRTY-EIGHT

The coming of the dawn found the battered whore wagon pressed into service as a makeshift hearse. But when the wheels got tangled in thick brush the bodies had to be unloaded and carried into the graveyard.

It took three hours of labor before Flintlock and O'Hara had dug a grave deep enough to accommodate the three bodies. After the earth had been shoveled over the mortal remains of Adam, Rose, and Louisa Flood, Biddy Sales and Lizzie Doulan said prayers for the dead, and then the women sang "Railway to Heaven," a new hymn recently penned by two devout Southern matrons.

> *Life is like a mountain railway.*
> *With an engineer that's brave.*
> *We must make the run successful,*
> *From the cradle to the grave.*
> *Watch the turns, the fills, the tunnels,*
> *Never falter, never fail.*
> *Keep your hands upon the throttle,*
> *And your eyes upon the rail.*

Revealing a whore's sentimentality, tears ran down Biddy's cheeks as she sang the chorus alone. Lizzie was too overcome with grief to continue and was comforted by Margie Tott and Jane Feehan, themselves in a considerable state of anguish.

> *Blessed Savior, thou wilt guide us,*
> *Till we reach that blissful shore,*
> *Where the angels wait to join us*
> *In thy praise forevermore.*

At the conclusion of the hymn all present—except O'Hara, who'd chanted and danced at a distance from the gravesite—agreed that the little Flood family had received a crackerjack send-off.

The sound of approaching horsemen attracted Flintlock's attention and his hand dropped to his Colt as Charlie Brewster and his men rode close.

When he saw the burial party at the grave, Brewster raised his arm and halted his cavalcade. He swung out of the saddle and walked toward the grave. Unusual for him, he wore two guns in crossed belts, a war sign Flintlock noted.

But the outlaw surprised him.

As his men sat their saddles and watched, Brewster walked to the graveside and without a glance in anyone's direction he removed his hat, bowed his head, and stayed like that for at least a couple minutes. Finally he replaced his hat, stepped away from the grave, and stopped beside Flintlock. "How's your head?"

"It hurts, Charlie. I owe you one."

Brewster smiled. "I saved your life. You'd have gone after King Fisher and he'd have killed you for sure."

"Maybe, maybe not," Flintlock said. "Where are you headed?"

"We're off to bring in the good folks of Happyville. King says the smallpox is gone."

"How does he know?"

"I guess the nice lady doctor told him." Brewster waved a black-gloved hand toward the grave. "This was none of my doing."

"You work for the man who did it, Charlie."

"Flintlock, I'll kill any man who comes at me with a gun in his hand, but I don't make war on women, especially a woman with child."

"How many men and women are you prepared to kill today, Charlie? Those townsfolk won't return to a plague town without a fight and you know it."

"As many as I need to. That's what King Fisher is paying me for. If they're willing to disarm and stay disarmed, maybe I won't have to kill any."

Flintlock was appalled. "You're really going to try taking away their guns?"

Brewster smiled. "King wants to be a dictator, boss people around. He can't get his way unless he disarms his people first."

"That is the way of dictators," O'Hara said.

"Injun, I know nothing about that," Brewster said. "I've never met one of them before." He turned his attention back to Flintlock. "Sam, if you're so concerned about the Happyville folks, get your horse and follow us. Maybe you'll learn something."

"Charlie, you've got nothing to teach me," Flintlock

said. "But I reckon me and O'Hara will join you and keep you honest."

Brewster glanced at the sky where scudding white clouds broke on the horizon like breakers on a beach. "Big wind and it's blowing from the east. I've heard that an east wind can drive men mad." His eyes hardened. "Don't let that happen to you, Sam."

The long grass tossed in the wind as Flintlock and O'Hara followed at a canter the tracks that cut across the flat. Brewster and his men were visible in the distance, like black ants crawling across a billiard table.

"Sammy, has it entered your thinking that there's two of us and a dozen of Brewster's boys and maybe half of them are faster on the draw-and-shoot than either of us?" O'Hara said.

Flintlock nodded. "I'm aware of that. It has entered my thinking."

"Ah, then that sets my mind at rest."

"We're not getting into a gunfight, O'Hara. Us just being there may stop a bunch of killings."

"Charlie Brewster will listen to reason. Is that it?"

"No, it isn't. But he knows if he guns people, I'd have the evidence to hang him."

"Hell, Sam, just about every lawman on the frontier wants to hang him and he's still kicking. You won't scare him."

Flintlock shook his head. "O'Hara, I don't know if it's the Irish in you or the Indian, but you sure don't take a sunny outlook on life."

"Let's just say that right now, when it comes to

Charlie Brewster and his boys, all I see ahead of us is doom and gloom."

"Just let me do the talking if such needs to be done," Flintlock said.

"And the shooting, if such needs to be done?"

"Leave that to me as well."

O'Hara nodded. "Well, there you go. Now I feel a sight better."

Flintlock turned his head. "You just made a good joke, right?"

"Wrong," O'Hara said. "It was you that made the joke, Sammy."

CHAPTER THIRTY-NINE

Captain Gregory Holden Usher stared into his coffee cup, his mind on King Fisher. He was filled with an odd kind of dread, like a man who has pursued heaven but then found himself in hell.

Fisher was like nothing he'd ever seen, neither automaton nor human but somewhere in between, a creature of flesh and bone and intricately wrought metal. The man's entire right side—arm, chest, and leg—had been forged from steel, brass, and bronze. It was a tangled network of tubes, valves, wires, and here and there, tiny dials no bigger than a man's pinkie nail. Usher had seen him in the company of a man named Clem Jardine, another metal man. Unlike Jardine, there was no metal on Fisher's face, but his right eye was peculiar, made of brass and what looked like colored glass.

Luke Gamble told him he'd heard of a Texas gunman by the name of King Fisher, but he'd been killed in San Antonio a year ago. Could it be the same man? No, that was impossible. It had to be impossible.

Usher looked up as Gamble stepped up to the fire

and squatted on his heels. The scout picked up a cup, tossed away some grounds, and then filled it from the pot.

"What did you hear?" Usher said.

"It was King Fisher who shot the rube and made his pregnant wife die of shock," Gamble said. "They're burying them now."

"Who's doing the burying?" Usher said.

"Does it matter?"

"I guess not. The riders have gone to bring back the citizens of the town. Seems that they ran away because of the smallpox."

"Yeah, that's Charlie Brewster's bunch that left to round them up. Brewster worries me."

"Why?" Usher said.

Gamble lit a cigar. "For an officer and a gentleman you're not too smart, Greg. Doesn't it occur to you that an outlaw like Brewster could be after the payroll?"

"I didn't know they were outlaws."

"What other kind of gunmen would Fisher hire?"

"Damn. There's a dozen of them."

"Eleven, counting Charlie."

"Do you suppose the money is in the wagon?" Usher said.

"It's there all right. That's why Fisher has two shotgun men guarding the livery."

Usher poured more coffee into his cup. "What do you think of him? Fisher I mean."

"I don't want to think about him."

"What the hell happened to him?"

"I don't know."

"He doesn't look like a man anymore."

Gamble looked Usher in the eye. "Listen up, Greg.

I've fit Apaches, Comanches, Cheyenne, and Sioux and I've killed as many white men in gunfights as you have fingers. I've been shot three times, knifed once, caught the cholera as a younker and lived to tell the tale. Them's my bona fides to prove that I'm not a coward. Well, King Fisher has made me a coward, because I'm scared of him."

"Stagg and Proud feel the same way?" Usher said.

"You see them setting here with us? They're hiding out in the saloon."

Usher nodded. "Then that settles it. We grab the payroll today and then light a shuck for Old Mexico." Usher smiled. "And we'll live like the gentlemen we are, Luke."

"I never laid any claim to be a gentleman and I reckon it's too late to start," Gamble said. "My share of the money will buy me whiskey and whores and that's all I ask." As cutting as a honed blade, he added, "You'll never recapture your glory days in Washington, Captain. We'll end up in the same stinking cantinas, drinking the same rotgut, and buying the same poxed women."

"If I thought that, I'd shoot myself," Usher said.

Gamble laughed but said nothing more.

"Here's how we get it done," Gregory Usher said. "We stroll up to the livery showing no guns, talk with the guards, and leave it to Luke to kill them."

"Kill them how?" Ethan Stagg said. "Shots will bring them tin men running."

"I've killed men with a knife before," Luke Gamble said. "I'll make it quick and I'll make it clean."

"Then what, Captain?" Seth Proud said.

"Call me Greg," Usher said. "I stopped being an officer when I tore off my shoulder straps."

"Then what . . . Greg?" Proud said, his young face flushing.

"We harness up Fisher's wagon while you and Ethan stand ready with your rifles. Then we light out of this town rich men and don't look back." Usher smiled at the doubt he saw in the faces of Stagg and Proud. "A simple plan is often the best plan."

By his own admission, Usher was no longer an officer and Gamble seemed determined to take charge. "Ethan, you and Seth saddle the horses. We'll want to dump the wagon and make the split as soon as possible. After that, we go our own ways. You follow me?"

"Got it," Stagg said.

"All right. Take the horses to the livery. Greg, there's a bottle of Old Crow in my saddlebags. Get it and then let's you and me go make friends with a couple o' guards."

CHAPTER FORTY

"They've stopped," O'Hara said.

"Looks like they found something," Sam Flintlock said. "Look, somebody's dismounting for a closer look. Well, let's go join the party."

Charlie Brewster and his men saw Flintlock and O'Hara from a ways off. The rider swung back into the saddle, but the outlaws sat their horses and waited.

The wind picked up stronger, making the prairie grass dance, and black clouds roiled the sky. The air smelled of ozone, but every now and again Flintlock caught a whiff of rot, of something long dead. O'Hara caught it, too, and he put the back of his hand to his nose and mouth.

They rode into a sand and gravel wash where there were few stands of prickly pear and the skeletal remains of an ancient cottonwood. After they regained the flat, they settled down to a trot and soon rode up on Brewster and his men.

A body lay on the ground, a heavy canvas satchel over its left shoulder. The man wore a Colt, and a Winchester lay close by.

"Dead 'un," Brewster said as Flintlock and O'Hara drew rein.

Flintlock controlled his prancing horse, upset at the nearness of death, and then studied the bloated corpse. Despite the black flies that crawled over the face, he recognized the man.

"Looks like you know him," Brewster said.

Flintlock nodded. "His name is Morgan Davis."

"Friend of yours?" Brewster said.

"No. He was a pimp and a lowdown back-shooter, and I badly wanted to kill him."

"Too late now," Brewster said.

"Seems like. What killed him?"

A man spoke up, the one who'd dismounted for a closer look. "Judging by his face, it was smallpox. Looks like he crawled a ways before he died."

"What's in his poke?"

"I don't know," the man said. "I didn't want to touch him."

"He would have to breathe on you to give you the disease," Flintlock said. "And he long ago used up his last breath." He swung out of the saddle, hooked the strap of the satchel with his toe, and dragged it off Davis's lifeless body. Flintlock kicked the bag and it made a soft, clinking sound. Taking a knee, he up-ended the satchel and tipped out its contents . . . a pile of gold watches, rings, brooches and about fifty dollars in coin and bills. "I should also have said Davis was a two-bit thief."

"Seems like he robbed the folks before he lit out," Brewster said. "He hasn't been dead long, a couple days at most."

Flintlock raised his nose and sniffed. "Then if it isn't him, what the hell is that smell on the wind?"

"Maybe the people Davis robbed weren't alive anymore," O'Hara said.

Flintlock said, "If he robbed the dead, wouldn't the living have stopped . . . him . . . oh, my God." He looked at Brewster. "They're all dead."

"No, it can't be." The big outlaw turned in the saddle and stared east across the flat as though he hoped to see hale and hearty people walking toward him. There were none. The only movement was the ripple of grass and the scurry of clouds . . . and the flash of lightning and bang of approaching thunder.

"They were crowded together and the sick spread the disease to the well," Flintlock said. "Chances are they had little food and water and didn't have the strength to fight the plague that had descended on them. Maybe they're all dead, Charlie. They aren't going back to Happyville or anyplace else."

Brewster managed a smile. "Or they're all sitting around fires, drinking whiskey and wishing they had shelter from this rain that's just started."

"There's one way to find out, I guess," Flintlock said.

"You heard the man, boys," Brewster said. "Let's go find the nice folks of Happyville. And remember, ride into the camp like we was visiting cousins. We don't want to alarm them. At least, right off we don't."

A man who rides a horse across the flat in a thunderstorm is always acutely aware that he is the tallest thing for miles around and it causes him no end of worry. Brewster, as uneasy as any, had his men dismount and lead their horses and Flintlock and O'Hara followed suit.

In a relentless raking rain, they began to find bodies, sometimes singly, others huddled together where families had perished. Smallpox was deadly. The people of Happyville had little defense against it. Crammed together, clinging to one another for comfort and support, they made themselves easy prey for a virulent, pitiless killer. Their camp was a field of bones where only the glutted vultures moved.

Moving through the rain with lightning flashes glistening on their wet clothing, Flintlock and O'Hara drew off at a distance, upwind of the dead.

Flintlock, badly shaken, tried to build a cigarette, but the downpour battered tobacco and papers from his fingers, and he gave up the unequal struggle. After a few minutes, a hollow-eyed Charlie Brewster joined them. His lips moved but no sound came. He made an effort and said finally, "Flintlock, I never seen the like. How many?"

"Hundreds. Two hundred at least. I think some of them already walked away from it and died somewhere else."

"Children," Brewster said, the dim, ashy light hardening in his eyes. "There are dead children."

Flintlock nodded. "Seems like."

Brewster said, "You seen that many dead white folk before, O'Hara?"

O'Hara shook his head. "When I was a boy, and old age was respected, I saw old white people sitting on sunny doorsteps, playing in the sun with the children until they all fell asleep. Then, at last, an old person would not wake up. But it was only one death, one white person. No, I have not seen that many dead white people before."

"You've never been in a war," Brewster said. "Many white people die in wars."

"This was not a war," O'Hara said.

"No it wasn't," Brewster said. "And I'm talking like a damned fool because I don't know what else to say."

Flintlock said, "I'm sure King Fisher will have plenty to say. Those people out there were to be the start of his empire. He'll be a mighty disappointed man."

Brewster said, "Do you think he's really King Fisher?"

"I think back in the day he was." Flintlock shook his head. "He isn't any longer."

"What is he?" Brewster said.

"Monster? Creature? Demon? Insane tin man? Take your choice," Flintlock said.

"Employer?" Brewster said, grinning.

As though the gods were angry over that statement, thunder crashed and the rain grew in intensity. O'Hara glanced at the sky and looked worried. The downpour was so heavy the horizon was invisible, lost in gray mist.

"I'm heading back," Flintlock said. "I plan to tell King the good news."

"I'm through here," Brewster said. "King wanted me to help found his outlaw empire and take over the entire nation with him as president. That doesn't set well with me. I like our country just the way it is."

O'Hara tore his gaze from the racked sky. "King

Fisher's dream is the vision of a madman. He fears hell and now plans to live forever."

"He told you that?" Brewster said.

"Me, he told me." Flintlock pointed to himself. "He said that after he got shot in San Antone, he died and got a glimpse of the condemned in hell."

Some of Brewster's men were listening and they eyed him with a *what-the-hell-did-you-get-us-into?* expression. Their concern did not go unnoticed.

"We're heading south, boys," he said. "Away from this damned rain and away from King Fisher."

Despite the miserable day, this drew a few cheers.

"All right, mount up," Brewster said. "And let's ride." He extended his hand to Flintlock. "Real pleasure to meet you, Sam. You ever want to get back into the bank-robbing profession, look me up."

"If hard times come down, I'll keep that in mind," Flintlock said.

"You too, O'Hara," Brewster said, touching his dripping hat brim.

He climbed into the saddle and he and his men rode into distance making their slow way through the raging day.

Flintlock watched them go and then said, "Right nice feller, Charlie, when he ain't shooting folks."

"I reckon so." O'Hara looked out over the lightning-glimmering grass. "What about the dead, Sam? Those people should have a Christian burial."

Flintlock nodded. "More burying than we can handle. First chance I get, I'll tell the Rangers."

"They can scrape the bones together," O'Hara said. "That's what will be left."

"You know the real tragedy here, O'Hara? It's the fact that all those people are dead and there's not a damned thing we can do about it."

O'Hara said nothing.

"All right then, there is one thing we can do," Flintlock said. "We can ride away from it and not look back."

CHAPTER FORTY-ONE

The thunderstorm that broke over Sam Flintlock and O'Hara had moments earlier erupted in the skies above Happyville as Ethan Stagg and Seth Proud saddled their horses. Cursing, the two men hurried the work, the four mounts made restive because of the thunder.

Trouble showed up in the small form of Grofrec Horntoe and his wolf. The dwarf was on the prod for no good reason other than he disliked the rain and bore a grudge against men of normal height. Rain drumming on his top hat, he watched Stagg and Proud for a few moments and then said, "What the hell are you two idiots doing? You can't ride in a lightning storm."

Stagg, a short-tempered man, was wet and uncomfortable and felt even less sociable than he usually did. "Beat it, Tiny. And take your damned mutt with you. It's scaring the horses."

Later, when men discussed the events in Happyville that day, some said Ethan Stagg didn't know the animal was a gray wolf and took the lobo to be a large dog. If he did, it was a mistake that killed him.

The long-barreled Colt in Horntoe's waistband looked like a cannon and the dwarf's face bore a mean, nasty expression. The muscles of his right forearm stood out huge, with thick veins, as he held Quicksilver's chain.

"You must be an Irishman," he said to Stagg. "Only an Irishman would be stupid enough to ride in a storm."

Thunder crashed and the rain lashed, hissing like a steam kettle.

Stagg dropped the saddle he'd just picked up and his face contorted with anger. "I won't tell you again, runt. Beat it."

"I'm going nowhere," Horntoe said. "Not so long as I can watch you."

"I'll bend you over my knee and take a switch to your butt, little man," Stagg said.

This made Seth Proud giggle and angered the dwarf.

"I'd like to see you try," Horntoe said.

And he released the wolf.

Quicksilver, instantly sensing which of the two humans was the most dangerous, went directly for Stagg's throat. The man collapsed and landed on his back, the snarling animal on top of him. At that terrifying moment, the wolf's slavering jaws just inches from his neck, Ethan Stagg knew he was in a fight for his life.

As Stagg battled Quicksilver, his already torn and bloody hands trying to keep at bay the wolf's relentless savagery, Horntoe grinned and jumped up and down and clapped his hands. "Git him, Quicksilver! Kill him!" he yelled.

Proud, his youthful face ashen, recovered from his shock and drew his gun.

"Shoot it off of me!" Stagg shrieked. The animal's fangs were tearing up the man's throat and its muzzle was stained scarlet. By a herculean effort, Stagg managed to throw the wolf off and it landed on its side. But instantly, faster than the eye could follow, he leaped on Stagg again and once more went for his throat.

Proud, his Colt in his fist, could not get a clear shot without hitting Stagg, and he ran around in the rain fussing, as useless a mother hen when the fox raids the chicken coop. Finally he fired and dirt kicked up inches from the battling Stagg's head.

"Damn you. Don't hurt my wolf!" Horntoe yelled.

The dwarf pulled his Colt, thumbed back the hammer, and two-handed it to eye level. His hurried shot missed but Proud did better. The youngster fired as Horntoe ran toward him, shooting as he came. Proud's bullet hit the little man square in the chest, a massive impact for such a small body. Horntoe screamed and fell on his back. He sat up, blood crimson in his mouth, and tried to work his Colt. He died in that position, sitting upright, staring through the rain with sightless eyes.

Quicksilver had finished killing Stagg, torn his throat out, and turned its attention to Proud. Terrified, the young man was not thinking straight, but he knew instinctively that if he fled, the animal would run him down and kill him. The animal was fast and charged Proud, a fanged, gray blur. Proud fired, missed, and the snarling wolf made its attack. Smaller and lighter than Stagg, the youngster collapsed under Quicksilver's weight but had time to fire one shot. In the wild, the wolf's prey usually died of massive blood loss, shock, or both. But with weaker prey, humans included, a massive lobo like Quicksilver was capable of biting a backbone in half. After firing, Proud turned his body away from the wolf's onslaught and thus the back of his neck was exposed. The animal bit down hard and crushed Proud's cervical vertebrae to splinters, killing him instantly.

The kill accomplished, Quicksilver did not savage Proud's body further. The wolf turned, saw Horntoe sitting upright and staggered toward him. But Proud's bullet had entered the animal's chest, destroyed its lungs, and delivered a mortal wound. Quicksilver collapsed and died just inches from the only friend and companion it had ever known.

Seth Proud's first shot had alerted the guards at the livery stable. They instantly lost interest in Luke Gamble's bottle of Old Crow, ran outside, and stared toward the campground, their Winchesters at the slant.

Gregory Usher, taken aback, stood undecided and looked toward Gamble for guidance.

The scout had already made up his mind. He drew and fired. Two fast shots. One dead guard, the other wounded, rolling around, clutching at his bloody side. Gamble didn't finish the man off. "Harness the horse to the wagon. We're getting out of here."

"You'll never make it out of Happyville, you damned

trash," the wounded man said through teeth gritted against pain.

"Neither will you." Gamble drew and shot the man with a killing bullet to the head. The scout looked at Usher. "I don't take sass from any man. Now, hurry."

Despite the rain and the roll of distant thunder, the old draft horse stood placidly in the traces until he was harnessed. Gamble climbed into the driver's seat and Usher followed him. The scout slapped the reins and the horse walked forward, and then launched into a shambling run as Gamble cracked the whip over his back. The wagon lurched down the street, its wheels throwing up great gobs of mud.

Usher saw the four women at the door of the saloon and they stared at him silently as the wagon rumbled past.

Gamble cracked the whip again and turned to Usher, grinning. "Well, Captain, how does it feel to be rich?"

"We won't be rich until we cross the Rio Grande," Usher said.

Thunder crashed and lightning lit up the sky. Gamble leaned out beyond the canvas cover and looked behind him. The women still stood at the saloon door but there was no sign of pursuit.

"We got it made, Greg," he said. "There's nothing between us and Old Mexico but grass."

Anxious as he was, Usher managed a smile . . . and wondered if he should shoot Gamble in the back before or after crossing the river.

CHAPTER FORTY-TWO

"Le Strange, you and Dr. Castle fire up the Helrun," King Fisher said.

"King, it will take an hour to heat up the boiler," Sara Castle said. "They'll have a head start."

"They've got a heavily loaded wagon pulled by an old nag," Fisher said. "On level ground the Helrun will catch up to them. Now fire her up, like I told you."

After le Strange and the doctor left, Fisher settled back in the barber's chair to let Blanche Jardine finish cutting his hair, which was thin and sparse and lifeless gray. "It will grow thicker soon."

The woman nodded, but behind her porcelain mask her acid-ravaged face might have borne any expression.

The door of the barbershop rang open, and Clem Jardine stomped inside, water running from his yellow slicker and the brim of his plug hat. The beautifully wrought brass plate that covered his chest and most of his face was beaded with rainwater, and his artificial metal leg was splashed with mud.

"Well?" Fisher said.

"Looks like Horntoe got into it with a couple of them deserters," Jardine said. "He's dead and so is his wolf."

"The deserters?"

"Both dead. Looks like the wolf done for both of them."

"Pity about Horntoe. He was a poisonous little gnome, but I was quite fond of him. His real name was Hugo Gerald. I liked the one I gave him better and so did he." Fisher brushed away an errant hair from his forehead with his badly shrunken left hand. "Clem, you'll join me in Helrun when I go after the robbers. We'll have some fun. Keep us amused until Brewster gets back with the flock."

Jardine smiled, the unarmored side of his face wrinkling. "*Flock.* I like that."

"We're dealing with sheep," Fisher said. "I'll bend them to my will or by the Lord Harry a bunch of them will swing from the same gallows. Now, go help Helrun get readied."

Jardine nodded and stepped to the door, his mechanical leg thudding on the floor.

"Wait," Fisher said. "Have you seen le Strange's plans for land crawlers."

"No. What are those?"

"Fast, steam-powered steel carriages that will carry a heavy cannon and go anywhere on flat or hilly country, destroying any army in their paths."

"Steel? We'll need a foundry, King," Jardine said.

"A town with an iron foundry and a railroad spur will be among my first conquests," Fisher said. "But that's for the future. As for now, be about your duties."

* * *

The rain had stopped, but the wind still gusted. Gregory Usher and Luke Gamble were an hour and a half out of Happyville and there was no sign of pursuit.

Gamble was in high spirits. "We'll cross the river and head into Chihuahua where we can shed the wagon and buy horses. A three-, four-day ride to the south is a silver boom town they call Hidalgo del Parral. I have friends there, including the commander of the local *rurales*." He winked. "And a few señoritas who are only as good as they have to be."

"Town sounds good to me," Usher said, smiling slightly. He had no intention of ever going there. After disposing of Gamble he intended to head for the nearest seaport and take a ship to Europe, perhaps Paris, where he could live once again like a gentleman.

The high wind rocked the wagon, and Usher fancied it felt like being shipboard on a steamer bound for the future . . . and the weight of the Colt on his waist reassured him that, "Gregory, all will be well."

Twenty-five minutes later, Gamble was the first to hear the roar of the pursuing Helrun. Ten minutes and twenty-seven seconds after that the Black Howler opened fire.

Chak-chak-chak-chak-chak!
A hailstorm of huge .45-70 bullets hammered into the wagon, splintered wood, shredded canvas, and tore into human flesh. Gamble's back was riddled.

The rounds went through him and punched a dozen great exit wounds in his chest, spraying fountains of blood and bone. Gamble threw up his hands, stood for a moment staring at Usher in horror, and then toppled over the side.

The horse went down, screaming. Usher jumped free of the wagon, rolled and jumped to his feet. He was unhurt, but the great, roaring steam locomotive just a dozen yards away, looked like a thing out of his worst nightmare.

"No!" Usher yelled, talking only to metal and glass. "I surrender!"

King Fisher, up in Helrun's gun turret, watched the slim, dark-haired man raise his arms and heard him frantically yell his surrender.

Fisher giggled, aimed, and cranked the Gatling's firing handle.

Bullet after bullet slammed into the man and made him dance like a rag doll, his arms and legs moving every which way to the rhythm of the gunfire. Finally Usher's tattered body fell and all his splendid dreams died with him.

King Fisher had le Strange and Jardine transfer the money chest from the wagon to the Helrun and then he profusely thanked Dr. Castle for her superb handling of the machine. Still buoyed by the success of his attack, he asked le Strange if adding a second or even a third gun turret to the Helrun was possible.

The engineer assured him that it would be a relatively simple matter.

Fisher said, "Excellent. I want a terror weapon, a

killing machine that will ensure my victory over any enemy."

Le Strange nodded. "Yes, a triple-turret Helrun could fulfill the role, but we'd need a lot more of them."

"Yes, and that means foundries and metalworkers." Fisher saw skepticism in le Strange's face and said, "Dream big, plan big, Obadiah. That steam turbine expert . . . the Ripper . . ."

"Professor Tynan?"

"Yeah, him. Can we bring him here from England? Plenty of whores in the West to keep him amused. Hell, we have four in Happyville."

Le Strange shook his head. "I don't know. Dr. Castle corresponds with him. She would know better." For a moment the engineer seemed wistful. "Professor Tynan has a brilliant mind. It's a pity that such a technologist is locked up in a dungeon somewhere."

"Then we must free him instanter, Obadiah. I will put him in charge of Project Helrun and supply him with all the men and money he needs." Fisher waved a negligent hand. "And women for his biological experimentation, of course."

"Dr. Castle and I made contacts in London, some at the highest levels of government," le Strange said. "Once things settle down in Happyville, I will instigate an inquiry into Professor Tynan's whereabouts and how we can best obtain his release."

Fisher said, "My dear le Strange, things have already settled down. Once Brewster returns with the people we can start to put my plans into operation. Of course, food supplies will be our first concern, but once that is out of the way, we begin to lay a

foundation for . . . a foundation for . . . foundation
for . . . empire."

King Fisher reeled and laid a hand on the side of
Helrun to steady himself. Le Strange caught him
before he fell and gently lowered him into a sitting
position.

"Bad blood," Fisher said, his voice weak. "She had
bad blood."

"You're fevered." Le Strange turned his head and
yelled, "Dr. Castle!"

Sarah Castle, obviously alarmed by the panic in
le Strange's voice, hurried from Helrun's cabin and
kneeled beside Fisher, who was semiconscious, short
of breath, and complaining of abdominal pain. After
sounding the man's heart, the doctor looked at le
Strange and said, "The woman's blood was bad. I'm
going to bleed him and then replace his blood with
some of mine." Her eyes accusing, she said, "Obadiah,
there are major flaws somewhere in your engineering.
King is sick from bad blood, and for the past couple
days I feel my heart faltering."

"Don't concern yourself, Sarah. Engineering created your heart, engineering can repair it," le Strange
said. "Now, can you save King?"

"I believe so, but this reaction to a transfer is the
worst he's ever had. Help me get him into Helrun and
pray it isn't too late."

Le Strange frowned. "Doctor, we're scientists. We
have no need for prayer."

CHAPTER FORTY-THREE

"I guess we should say a prayer for this woman, O'Hara," Sam Flintlock said. "Do you know any?"

"God grant this woman eternal peace," O'Hara said as Flintlock removed his hat. "May she follow the buffalo herds."

"That's it?" Flintlock said.

"It's enough," O'Hara said.

"A half-breed prayer if ever I heard one," Flintlock said. "But you're right, it will do, get our message across."

The grave of the woman with the silver hands had been hastily dug a mile or so north of Happyville. Her beautifully crafted hands lay on top of the shallow mound.

Flintlock ran a hand through his hair and then replaced his hat. "King Fisher murdered this woman, but I don't know how. Her face was white, white as bone."

O'Hara picked up the silver hands and examined them. The fingers and thumb were articulated and a complex series of wires and rods had attached them to the muscles and tendons of the forearms.

"Pah! These are filthy things." He tossed the hands back on the grave. "Only the Great Spirit can make a woman's hands."

Flintlock nodded. "Yeah, that's always been my way of thinking." He gathered up the reins of his horse and glanced at a threatening sky the color of gunmetal. "I was always told it never storms in West Texas."

"Coming down from the New Mexico Territory, Sam, and that's mighty unusual at this time of the year. A big blow moving in from the western ocean, maybe so."

"Whatever it is, it looks like rain," Flintlock said. "We'd better head for town."

"What the hell?" Flintlock said. "Everybody's gone."

"Seems like," O'Hara said.

The livery stable was empty, Helrun and Fisher's wagon gone, but two dead men lay sprawled in the dirt outside. Flintlock dismounted and studied the bodies. "Both shot, O'Hara. One of them in the back."

Biddy Sales, the three other women in tow, crossed the street, hiking up her skirts free of the mud. "You and the Indian always manage to miss all the excitement, Flintlock." Her angry eyes told him that this was an accusation.

"We had some excitement of our own," Flintlock said as rain pattered around him. "We can exchange stories in the saloon. Right now I need a drink."

All six moved quickly to the saloon.

He and O'Hara sat at a table, sharing their company with a bottle of Old Crow. Biddy wrapped up her account of the gunfights and the escape of the army deserters with the wagon and Fisher's pursuit.

"After that, I don't know what happened," she said. "Fisher lit a shuck in the big locomotive thing, following their tracks."

Flintlock made the connection quickly. "I didn't know King had stolen an army payroll. Damn. That's why those Comancheros attacked us. They didn't want horses and women. They wanted the payroll."

"Correct and correct, Flintlock," Biddy said. "You're such a clever boy."

"And I'm willing to bet the army deserters knew about the money," Flintlock said.

"That would be my guess," Biddy said.

"Did you see the bodies? Is the wolf dead?" Flintlock said.

"Yeah. The wolf done for two of them soldier boys, but not before one of them got a bullet in Horntoe," Biddy said.

Margie Tott made a face. "I hated that little midget. He was always trying to grab my ass."

Biddy nodded. "He was a horny little cuss. His name suited him, I guess."

"He's better off dead," Lizzie Doulan said. "He had no life to speak of."

"Takes one to know one, Lizzie, huh?" Margie said.

"Margie, leave her be," Biddy said.

"It's all right," Lizzie said. "Margie is right. I want so badly to be dead."

Blanche Jardine sat at another table and shuffled a pack of cards. Behind her painted mask, her eyes moved to Lizzie and she said, "That makes two of us, honey. Seems that everyone who visits Happyville is either dead or wants to be."

"I don't," Biddy said. "Neither does Margie or Jane." Then, an edge to her voice she said, "Must you wear that damned mask?"

"I was a faro dealer at the Silver Horseshoe in Denver and a sore loser threw acid in my face," Blanche said. "Yes, lady, I have to wear this mask. You don't ever want to see what lies under it."

"Hell, I do," Margie Tott said, her pretty face eager.

"No you don't," Biddy said. "Adults are talking, Margie, so sit there quietly and drink your gin."

The girl pouted her annoyance but said nothing more.

Biddy directed her attention to Flintlock. "When is Charlie Brewster bringing in the townspeople?"

"Never." He had taken the time to reload his Hawken with powder and ball and it lay across his thighs, mostly hidden by the table.

"What does that mean?"

"It means they're all dead. Killed by the smallpox, unless a few of them made a run for it and died somewhere else."

All four of the women were shocked.

Biddy gasped and lightly touched her left breast, a thing she did when she was under duress. "Oh my God." As though she'd just remembered, she added, "Now what will King Fisher do?"

"I don't much care since he will answer to me," Flintlock said. "After that, he won't much care either."

Blanche Jardine spoke up again. "Flintlock, you're a fool. Didn't you see the skulls of men killed by King the first time you rode into our camp with Grofrec Horntoe? No one can beat King on the draw, and there's no one alive who can outshoot him. He was created by science and only science can destroy him." Then, as though she'd been taught to say the words, she added, "One day King Fisher will be the master of the world."

"Hell, lady, he ain't even master of Happyville, Texas," Flintlock said.

"I heard what you said about the people," Blanche said. "King will find more in another town. He has recruited the bandit chief Charlie Brewster and his gunmen to be his strong right hand."

Flintlock shook his head. "Charlie isn't coming in either. Last I saw of him, he was headed for Old Mexico."

Her mask was expressionless, but the way Blanche slammed her cards onto the table revealed her agitation. After a while she said, "King will hire more men and find a way. He always does."

"If he lives long enough," Flintlock said.

CHAPTER FORTY-FOUR

Dr. Sarah Castle removed the silver tube from her forearm and then the one from King Fisher. "The transfer is completed."

She felt weak and light-headed, but King Fisher's breathing was better, and he no longer seemed to be in pain.

The silver tubes were connected to a length of India rubber tubing with a stopcock at both ends and a bulb in the middle. When the doctor squeezed the bulb it acted as a pump to expedite the flow of blood from donor to recipient. The apparatus was state of the art and was hailed by surgeons in England and France as a great step forward in modern medicine. But clotting was always a problem, a complication le Strange intended to remedy after more research.

As he took apart the apparatus for cleaning, he could not understand why King Fisher's own body destroyed its own blood, necessitating what the European doctors were calling *transfusion*s every week or so. The man's metal parts were expertly engineered, some major organs replaced by exquisite replicas made of brass and in some cases bronze. His blood circulated but self-destructed and the problem had to be corrected soon if King was to take his rightful place in the world. And, as le Strange and Dr. Castle had learned, transfusions could be dangerous. Some people had bad blood and it made King very sick. That was another problem but nothing that modern science could not solve.

Dr. Castle poured herself a glass of red wine, drank it down in one gulp, and poured another. She looked at her patient, who lay on a fold-down metal cot, and said, "King, can you hear me?"

The man nodded.

"How do you feel?"

"Better. Stronger."

"Lie quietly for a while and then I'll give you some wine," the doctor said.

"We must return to Happyville," Fisher said. "My people may already be there."

"We'll be there before nightfall," le Strange said. "King, you'll be welcomed by an adoring crowd as their savior."

"And that is my right," Fisher said. "Using Charlie Brewster and his ruffians as my blunt instrument, soon Happyville will be a major city and manufacturing town. The railroads and industrialists will beat a path to my door, urging me to join the Gilded Age." He grabbed le Strange's hand. "Imagine it, Obadiah. We'll do business with the likes of Cornelius Vanderbilt and J. P. Morgan and be richer than either of them."

Sarah Castle smiled. "King, I can tell you're starting to feel better."

"Dreams of an empire always make me feel better," Fisher said.

"Here, drink this." She passed Fisher a glass of wine. "Later, I'll get some nutrient fluid into you."

"Vile swill," Fisher said.

The doctor nodded. "But necessary."

Stronger, at least temporarily, King Fisher gazed through the polished windshield of the Helrun. Alarmed, he turned to le Strange, who sat behind him with Clem Jardine. "Obadiah, give me the field glasses."

Sarah Castle knew what was troubling him. "Brewster is not back yet, King. He's probably slowed by the townspeople."

"Deserted," Fisher said. "Happyville is deserted. Wait. I see Sam Flintlock. Maybe he can tell us what the hell is happening."

"King, Flintlock is no friend of yours," Jardine said.

"I know that. He badly wants to kill me since I gunned the rube with the knocked-up wife. Well, I plan to kill Mr. Flintlock at the first opportunity, but not today."

Rain spattered Helrun's windshield and as the day faded, the sky looked like a gray wash on watercolor paper. Sarah Castle steered the vehicle into the livery. She'd pulled back her hair and tied it at the base of her neck with a scarlet cravat, a gift from an admirer, a British cavalry officer she'd met during her time in London. The woman was very pale, and her full lips had a bluish tinge. Helrun's steering was heavy and her left arm pained her.

"I'm going to talk with Flintlock," King said. "Clem, come with me and stay close. I don't trust him."

"Sure thing, boss. I'll keep a close eye on him. Bounty hunters like Sam Flintlock are full of fancy moves."

To everyone's surprise a sudden crash of thunder exploded in the dark sky and lightning shimmered.

A moment later, Dr. Sarah Castle fell against the side of Helrun and said, "Obadiah, I'm having a heart attack."

"Damn you. Not now!" King Fisher rounded on the woman. His voice was venomous. "I've no time for this."

Obadiah Le Strange helped the unconscious woman to the stable floor. "King, you can't choose your time to have a heart attack."

"Well, get it repaired or whatever the hell you do, Obadiah. I have much more important business that needs attention."

Le Strange cradled Sarah's beautiful head in his arm and for the first time he realized that in King Fisher he'd created a monster.

CHAPTER FORTY-FIVE

Sam Flintlock handed O'Hara the Hawken and took the Winchester in return. The Hawken's .50 ball could drop any man, but King Fisher was not just any man. He was a thing of metal and flesh and would be hard to kill.

The persistent thunderstorm hung around and lightning lit up the sky as Flintlock stepped onto the boardwalk. He held the rifle across his body at belt buckle level and watched Fisher. Beside him, the thick mud of the street was giving Clem Jardine's artificial leg problems and he walked hesitantly with a dragging gait.

"That's far enough, King," Flintlock said. "We got something between us that needs settled. Might as well get it over with."

"Sam, will you leave me out in the rain?" Fisher said.

"I sure will. You're lowlife trash, King, and you always were. Nothing has changed."

Fisher's face could not show any expression, but his body stiffened. "I've killed men for less than that."

"Much less. Yeah, I know."

"We've become enemies because of a damned rube," Fisher said. "Man, let bygones be bygones."

Thunder rolled, imperious and uncaring, and lightning gouged the sky like a roweled spur along the flank of a black horse. Somewhere, a stray dog barked, catching the scent of hungry coyotes prowling the flat.

King Fisher was rattled, and Flintlock decided to rattle him some more. "Got news for you, King."

Fisher was close to a draw and Flintlock knew it. His finger was inside the Winchester's trigger guard and he'd taken up an eighth of an inch of slack. There was no going back from this. King Fisher must not be allowed to live, so either he or Flintlock must die right there in the street, in the rain, and in the falling darkness. If he'd been a gambling man, he'd give odds of ten to one against himself. But probably his chances of killing Fisher were one in a hundred.

"What news do you have for me, Sam?" Fisher said.

"All the people who lived in this town are dead of the smallpox."

"You're a damned liar. Where is Charlie Brewster?"

"Headed for Old Mexico. He doesn't like you much, King."

Sweat broke out on Fisher's forehead. He swayed on his feet and his breathing came in short, sharp bursts. "I'm . . . I'm going to . . . going to kill you . . ."

He dropped heavily to the ground and sat in the mud.

Footsteps squelched behind him and he turned his head. "Le Strange, help me. Bad . . . bad blood . . ."

His face like stone, Le Strange said, "Sarah is dead. She died in pain."

"Help me," Fisher said. "Oh my God, she didn't . . . didn't . . ."

"Give you the transfusion, King. No, she didn't," le Strange said. "The wine was what helped you feel better."

"Bitch!" Fisher screamed. He glared at le Strange. "Get one of the whores. Use her blood. Save me, le Strange."

"Rose Flood died because of you, King," le Strange said. "Sarah wanted to save the woman and her baby, but you killed them both. She could not forgive that."

"Damn you!" Fisher said. "You knew! You knew the woman didn't transfer her blood to me."

"I didn't know for certain, but I suspected it," le Strange said.

"Why didn't you tell me?"

"Because I'd come to realize that I'd created a monster, and it was up to me to destroy it."

"No, that's not how it works, Obadiah. In King Fisher's world the creation destroys the creator."

Two things happened very quickly.

Fisher's mechanical arm blurred as he drew and fired. Flintlock saw the movement and he immediately triggered the Winchester.

Fisher's bullet hit le Strange high in the chest. A split second later, the .44-40 rifle round slammed into Fisher's right shoulder. The man screamed in pain and rage and tried to bring up his Colt. but he was done for. Flintlock's bullet had shattered the wires and copper tendons of Fisher's arm and he could not lift his gun. The revolver fell from his convulsing fingers and splashed into the mud.

"Damn you, Flintlock!" Fisher yelled. "Don't shoot

any more. My life is in danger and you must save me."
He tried to struggle to his feet, but Sam Flintlock,
never the most merciful of men in a gunfight, ignored
his plea and pumped two bullets into him.

The first round staggered Fisher, but he rode the
second into hell.

There has been much speculation as to what King
Fisher saw in the moment of his death. It is said his
shriek of fear was the loudest that ever came from a
man's throat. Did he scream when he caught his first
sight of the gates of hell? Like all of the West's great-
est mysteries, speculation is useless because we will
never know the answer.

What is certain is that Fisher's primitive howl of
terror saved Sam Flintlock's life.

Stunned by the death of le Strange, Clem Jardine
had been slow to react, but Fisher's scream galvanized
him into action. He drew and fired at Flintlock.

It would have been an accurate, perhaps killing
shot, had not Lizzie Doulan cried out, "No!" and
thrown her body in front of Flintlock. Jardine's bullet
crashed into her chest just under her right armpit.
She was a thin girl, and the .45 exited just above her
left breast, after destroying a massive amount of tissue
and bone.

Flintlock held her as she sank to the boardwalk. To
his right, he heard the bark of O'Hara's Colt—three
shots, cadenced but very fast. Jardine was hit twice,
both shots to the torso, and he fell facedown in the
mud. His metal leg jerked for a few moments and
then was still.

For a long while Happyville lay in hollow silence,

the only sound the soft hiss of the rain and Lizzie Doulan's even softer breathing.

Biddy kneeled beside her and said, "Why did you do such a stupid thing?"

Lizzie smiled. "Flintlock's life is more worthy than mine."

"Some people would argue on that point." He brushed a tumbled wisp of hair off her forehead.

She turned her head and looked at O'Hara loading fresh shells into his Colt. "Come talk to me, Indian."

O'Hara holstered his gun and kneeled beside her. "What do you want from me?"

Lizzie's frail hand reached out and bunched in O'Hara's shirt front. "Am I dying?"

"No. You're not dying," Biddy said. "I'm going to take good care of you."

"Woman, don't close your eyes," O'Hara said. "Hold my hand and keep holding even when you've gone away from me. Look around you. What do you see?"

"The sky. I see the sky."

"Tell me about it."

"It's beautiful. The sky is beautiful. More beautiful than I've ever seen it . . . shining like gold."

The sky was black, the clouds in constant movement as though they boiled in a cooking pot, but O'Hara seemed satisfied with Lizzie's answer.

"You sacrificed your life for another, and this is good," he said. "I think your time has come."

"After all these years—decades and centuries— God will let me die? Oh say it is so, O'Hara."

"It is so. Your eyes now see only beauty. The long darkness and all the ugly memories are gone."

"Tell me how to die, O'Hara," Lizzie said. "Show me the way."

O'Hara smiled. "Woman, be not like those whose hearts are filled with fear of death so that when their time comes they weep and pray for a little more time to live their lives in a different way. The Great Spirit has answered your prayers and rewarded your suffering." He gently squeezed Lizzie's hand. "You have sung your death song and now you must die like a hero going home."

A trickle of blood ran from the corner of her mouth, but her smile was sweet. "Yes, I'm going home."

Lizzie closed her eyes and died and O'Hara held her hand for a long time.

Blanche Jardine kneeled in the mud beside the body of her dead husband. She turned her face mask to the rain and had no need for the bottled tears she kept in the pocket of her dress. She refused to leave Happyville with Flintlock and the others and was still there when the town burned.

No one ever knew what became of her.

CHAPTER FORTY-SIX

Happyville was a town of the dead.

Flintlock and the others buried Lizzie Doulan in the cemetery, removed the army payroll from Helrun, and carried the remaining bodies, including King Fisher's withered corpse, into the livery stable that was then set on fire.

As they rode away from the town, one of the dead guards' mounts pressed into service as a packhorse, Flintlock looked back at the burning stable and said, "The fire is spreading."

"The best thing that could happen," Biddy said, drawing rein. "I hope the whole sorry place goes up."

Despite occasional rains, Western towns were tinder dry and fires quickly spread. Happyville was destined to burn down to its foundations, its ashes blown away by the prairie winds until no sign of the town or the people who lived and died there remained.

* * *

After three days of westward travel across the Great Plains, Flintlock and the others crossed the Pecos. It was only when they camped the following night that the subject of the army payroll was broached.

"What are we going to do with it, Flintlock?" Biddy said. "Thirty thousand dollars is a pile of money."

Smoothing her stocking over a shapely thigh, Margie said, "Split five ways that's . . . that's . . . well, it's a whole lot of money."

"Six thousand dollars, Margie," Jane Feehan said.

"Right. I told you it was a lot of money," Margie said.

"We give it back, I guess," Flintlock said.

Biddy said, "The army has plenty of money and we're poor people. We need six thousand dollars more than the soldier boys do." She touched her breast. "What does the Indian say, Flintlock?"

"I don't know. I haven't asked him."

"Where is he? Skulking around somewhere as usual?"

Flintlock nodded. "O'Hara is out there in the dark. He says money attracts outlaws like the smell of rotten meat attracts rats." He tossed a stick onto the fire. "I think maybe we should ride deeper into the timber country, maybe even cross the border into the New Mexico Territory. I mean, get the money and ourselves the hell out of Texas."

"We've got no pressing business anywhere," Margie said. "I guess New Mexico is as good a place as any . . . just so long as the payroll goes with us."

Jane Feehan said, "You're such a whore, Margie."

"Takes one to know one, Jane."

Flintlock said, "I'll study on this payroll thing for a spell." He rose to his feet and took up the Hawken. "It's time to take a look around anyway."

"In the dark?" Biddy said. "You're as bad as the Indian."

"O'Hara has a nose for danger. He can smell it."

"Like outlaws smell money," Biddy said.

"Something like that." Flintlock stepped out of the firelight, halted among a stand of wild oaks, and let his eyes become accustomed to the darkness. Behind him, he heard Margie Tott say something and it must have been funny because the other two women laughed.

He stepped deeper into the trees, angry that money could be such a temptation to a man. Like all bounty hunters, he had a fair amount of dealings with lawmen and for the most part he admired them, especially the forty-dollar-a-month cow town marshals who had to deal with young men wilder, a lot more dangerous, and harder to handle than the steers they drove. In his earlier years, Flintlock had stepped lightly onto the lawless side when times were hard, but for the most part he strived to stay on the straight and narrow.

But thirty thousand dollars in Yankee money was a temptation to be reckoned with, an enticement for any man.

Old Barnabas stood in a clearing gazing at the stars with a brass telescope as big around as a cannon barrel. Flintlock ignored him and was about to turn and walk back to the fire when the old mountain man's voice stopped him. "You ever seen the moon through a telescope, Sammy?"

"Can't say as I have."

"Well, you ain't seeing it now. Stargazing is for smart folks and not fer the likes of you. On your way to find your ma, are ye?"

"That's the general idea," Flintlock said.

"You-know-who says you done well in Happyville, added considerable to the slaughter, you did. He's so pleased he's got advice fer you about the army payroll."

"I don't want his advice," Flintlock said. Then, racked with doubt as he was, he said, "What is it anyway?"

"Mars, now that's an interesting planet," Barnabas said. "It's got canals, or so some Italian feller says, but I can't see them. And neither can you because I'm not letting you look because you're an idiot."

"Then I'll be on my way, Barnabas. As always it's been a pleasure to talk with you."

"Wait, don't you want the advice from Himself, Sammy?"

Flintlock hesitated, then said, "All right, Go ahead."

"Well, he said, 'Tell the idiot—'"

"That's it. I'm out of here," Flintlock said.

"All right, all right. I'll just give you the gist of it. Does that set nice with you, Sam?"

"Let me hear it," Flintlock said.

"He says you should gun the three women and the half-breed and keep the army money for yourself. Spend it all on whores and whiskey, mind you, and when the money is all gone and you're sick and broke, blow your brains out with the Hawken."

"Old Scratch never gives good, friendly advice, does he?" Flintlock said, smiling.

"That's because he ain't good and he ain't your friend."

"And what do you think, Barnabas?"

"Keep the money for yourself and go find your ma," the old man said. "Later you could maybe buy a ranch and settle down with a good woman, if any will have you. That's my advice, but you won't take it because you're an idiot. Now I got to go. I'm headed for Italy. I need to talk to that Italian feller about the canals on Mars." Barnabas lifted his telescope and walked into the darkness.

Flintlock called after him, "You'll scare the wits out of the Italian. I mean, you being dead an' all."

"Serve him right. I don't like Italians. Hell, I don't like anybody." Barnabas vanished in the gloom.

Flintlock looked up at the night sky, but he couldn't find Mars or its canals . . . and he saw no answer to his problem.

CHAPTER FORTY-SEVEN

O'Hara shook Sam Flintlock awake and immediately made a hushing motion, his forefinger to his lips. Leaning close, he whispered in Flintlock's ear, "Five. On foot."

The fire had burned down to a few cinders and spread little light. Flintlock nodded and rose to his feet. He took up his Winchester and they stepped on cat feet into the cover of the wild oaks.

The three women slumbered on . . . bait in a trap.

Tense time ticked past. . . .

One stirred under her blanket and talked softly in her sleep. An owl flew close to the firelight and then turned away, gliding through the oaks like a gray ghost.

Flintlock turned and his eyes sought O'Hara's in the gloom. He scowled his face into a question and the breed nodded.

"Five," he whispered.

Flintlock shook his head. In the dark of night, even an Indian could see things that were not there.

Then, like the parting of a black curtain, figures

appeared from the sullen blackness. Flintlock tensed, his knuckles white on the Winchester. He waited . . . letting them get closer and into the dim circle of the firelight. Beside him, O'Hara was on one knee. Like Flintlock, he was ready.

One of the intruders, a buckskinned man with long hair falling over his shoulders, stepped silently to the nearest woman, the long-barreled Colt in his hand ready. Flintlock saw the gleam of the man's teeth as he identified the sleeper as a woman. He bent over, reached out with his left hand, and jerked the blanket off Biddy Sales's body. The spiteful bark of the Remington derringer in Biddy's hand shattered the quiet of the night and her assailant died with a .41 caliber bullet between his eyes.

"That ripped it!" Flintlock said.

For a long moment the element of surprise froze the other four men in place—time enough for practiced gunmen like Flintlock and O'Hara to take full advantage of the confusion.

Flintlock jumped to his feet and shot at the man nearest to him, then fired at another. O'Hara engaged the other two. Flintlock's first target fell, but the second, a lanky towhead, stepped back and got his work in with a Colt. Bullets splitting the air around him, Flintlock quickly retreated to an oak and returned fire.

O'Hara's targets stood their ground and fired steadily, but one made the mistake of going too close to Biddy and she dropped him with a shot to his knee. Her derringer empty, she rolled away. The wounded man roared in anger and leveled his revolver at her.

O'Hara fired and hit the man, who threw up his arms and fell on his back.

His rifle giving him the advantage, Flintlock's fire finally took effect and he scored a solid hit on the towhead as the man desperately tried to reload his Colt. The remaining would-be robber turned and ran, but Flintlock and O'Hara fired at the same time and dropped him in his tracks.

Gun smoke drifted across the clearing as Flintlock looked around him and counted the cost of the night's work. All five of the attackers were down— dead or wounded—but he and O'Hara were unhurt. Biddy's anguished wail told him that they had suffered a terrible loss.

Margie Tott was dead.

The girl had caught a stray bullet as she rose from her blankets and her small body lay cradled in Biddy's arms. Biddy's face was buried in Margie's hair and her shoulders moved as she sobbed.

Flintlock shook his head. "Damn. Damn it to hell."

"Sam, this one is still alive," O'Hara said. He kneeled beside the first man Flintlock had shot.

Enraged over the death of Margie, Flintlock racked a round into the Winchester. "I'll finish the son of a bitch right now."

O'Hara jumped to his feet and grabbed him. "No, Sam. He's just a boy."

"Old enough to try to kill us." Flintlock brushed O'Hara aside and stepped to the wounded boy. Once glance told him that the youngster had a sucking chest wound and was close to death. The muzzle of the Winchester was inches from the boy's face. "You came after the payroll."

The kid managed to smile. "Everybody is after the payroll."

"The word got around, huh?" Flintlock said.

"There's a lot of poor people in Texas, mister, and no man should have thirty thousand dollars all to himself." The youngster coughed and sudden blood stained his lips. "It just ain't decent. My pa said . . ."

Flintlock was not destined to know what the kid's pa had said. The boy, about eighteen years old by the look of him, died without imparting that information.

O'Hara had stepped away and checked on the other men. Returning to Flintlock, he said, "Seems like it was a family affair, Sam. We got a grandpappy and this boy's pa, looks like. Maybe his older brother and one real old coot over there who could be the great-grandpappy of all of them."

"All dead?" Flintlock said.

"Yeah, all of them. Good shooting, Sam."

"You too, O'Hara. Good shooting."

"They look like poor folks," O'Hara said.

Flintlock nodded. "A lot of poor folks in Texas. They wanted the thirty thousand."

"Seems the payroll money always comes at a high price to them that wants it."

"King Fisher started it," Flintlock said. That statement didn't really mean anything, but it was something to say.

"And you finished it, Sam. Or is it finished yet?"

"I sure hope so."

"What will you do with it?"

Flintlock had been staring at Biddy Sales. "Huh?"

"What will you do with the money?" O'Hara said.

"Buy a ranch." He stared into O'Hara's eyes.

O'Hara nodded. "Blood money. It will fertilize the graze."

"Or I'll give it back to the army," Flintlock said.

"You got a decision to make, Sam."

"O'Hara, what do you think?"

"I never in my life wanted something bad enough to steal it. That's what I think."

"Does that include thirty thousand dollars?"

"Maybe it does, Sam." O'Hara stepped away from Flintlock and kneeled beside Biddy. He said soft words to her that Flintlock couldn't hear.

Blood money. Flintlock decided O'Hara had been right about that.

But blood would leave no stain on silver and gold.

CHAPTER FORTY-EIGHT

At first light O'Hara rode into the flat and brough in the dead men's horses, five rough-looking mustang only two of them with a saddle.

Margie Tott, wrapped in a blanket, was laid to re in a shallow grave, her only marker a bow of the re ribbons she'd often worn in her hair. Within a fe years, there would be no trace of her burial place, a was the way of the Great Plains.

It was not yet noon when Flintlock and the other saddled their horses. Biddy and Jane were quiet for while.

Biddy finally voiced the thought that was uppe most in her mind. "Flintlock, if you'd just ridden on none of this would have happened."

"And if Morgan Davis hadn't bushwhacked me, Flintlock said.

O'Hara said, "It was our destiny to meet in such way and nothing could change it, just as the man bor to be hanged will never drown."

Biddy finished tightening the cinch then turned t Flintlock again. "So where does destiny lead us now?

"Across the border into New Mexico Territory.)'Hara says he recollects that there's a settlement by he name of Nube Blanca on the east bank of the ecos. It's just a plaza and a few buildings, but it has cemetery. I'm all through leaving dead men without Christian burial."

"I never took you for a gospel wrangler, Flintlock," ane said.

"I'm not, but somewhere along my back trail I eckon learned the difference between right and vrong." O'Hara's raised eyebrow at that statement ir- itated Flintlock and he said, "All right, Injun, help ne get them dead men loaded."

"Be glad to help, Sammy, now you found religion, n' all."

"Not hardly," Flintlock said, mad clean through.

Nube Blanca was a small, dusty adobe village situ- ted about a mile east of the Pecos. The walls of the uildings immediately surrounding the central plaza eflected the red glow of the evening sun. In shadow, he outlying adobes were like a collection of old men n white nightshirts who'd wandered into the piñon .nd juniper and lost their way.

A crowd gathered as Flintlock and the others rode n, trailing five dead men facedown across their .orses. Most of the upturned faces were Mexican, but .ere and there a white face showed.

It was a big white man—huge in the face and .elly—who stepped out the crowd in front of Flint- ock's horse. He carried with him an air of authority that was explained by the tin badge pinned to th front of his hat. "What are you bringing us, mister?"

"Dead men for burying," Flintlock said.

"Anybody I know?"

Flintlock shrugged. "Take a look." He saw th badge more clearly and added, "Mayor."

The mayor grabbed each of the dead men by th hair and yanked up their heads then stepped back t Flintlock. "Nobody I know. What happened?"

"They tried to rob us," Flintlock said.

The big man cast his eyes over Flintlock and th others, a shabby, dusty bunch. He lingered on th women a few moments longer than was necessar then said, "Them boys sure set their sights low, didn they?"

"I figure they reckoned we had more than the had," Flintlock said.

"And that wasn't much. Name's Arch Hooper. I'r the mayor of this town."

Flintlock looked around him. "It ain't much."

"It'll do. We got a cantina and a place for tired me to sleep. If you plan on planting them boys here, will cost you a dollar a head." Suspicion dawned o Hooper's fat, sweaty face. "Here, you ain't on th scout, are you?"

"Can't say as we are," Flintlock said. "The cost c burying dead men comes high in this burg."

"Take it or leave it. Of course, for a dollar you ge the planting done. Hey Pedro, come over here." Afte a small, solemn man with sad black eyes joined hin Hooper said, "This here is Pedro Gonzalez. He take care of the graveyard and buries the stiffs. If you wan to hire him, do it quick before them rannies start to stink."

The gravedigger whispered something into Hooper's ear.

The mayor looked surprised. "Pedro says he'll bury your dead in green pine boxes in return for the mustangs and saddles. Hell, he can't be fairer than that. Say, what's your name, feller?"

"Sam Flintlock."

"Right pleased to make your acquaintance, Sam. You can introduce me to your friends later. Now, what about Pedro's proposition?"

"I don't have any choice. Tell Pedro he can have the horses and traps. And tell him he's a robber and that I've seen men hung for less."

Hooper smiled. "No need to tell him. Pedro speaks American as well as you do."

The little Mexican took the lead rope, grinned at Flintlock, obviously holding no grudge, and led the horses with their grim burdens toward the graveyard at the edge of town. A couple other Mexicans, apparently his helpers, ran to join him.

"The cantina is right over there." Hooper pointed the way. "The grub is good and Diego Santos will provide you all with a place to bed down." The mayor beamed. "Is there anything else I can do for you, Mr. Flintlock?"

"Yeah, you can tell me if Diego is another robber."

"Oh, no, he's as honest as the day is long. Of course, he'll have to charge you for your horses and baths for the ladies."

"The ladies don't need no bath," Flintlock said.

"Oh yes we do, Flintlock," Jane Feehan said. "And you could do with one yourself."

Flintlock gave O'Hara a long-suffering look. "Let's go arrange baths for the ladies."

Biddy said to Jane, "It's about time he acted like a gentleman, isn't it?"

CHAPTER FORTY-NINE

Sam Flintlock walked into the cantina, a malodorous room with an area curtained off and to one side, and saw trouble. Beside him O'Hara stiffened, seeing what Flintlock saw and not liking it.

"Howdy boys," said the man sitting at the corner table. "Flintlock, you look as disreputable as ever. I really must give you the name of my tailor. O'Hara, you still haven't been hung. Well, that's good news."

"I want no trouble with you, Nate," Flintlock said. "I got enough of them already."

"No trouble, Sam," Nate Rocheford said. "If you think I'm still sore about the little fracas we had in Denver that time, well forget it. I know I have."

"I put a bullet into you, Nate. I never pegged you as that much of a forgiving man."

Rocheford waved a hand up. "Water under the bridge. When two bounty hunters go after the same man there's bound to be a little friction. Of course, you shot me when I was drunk."

"We were both drunk that night."

"Then it evens out, and that's why I say let bygones be bygones." Rocheford called out, "Can we get another bottle over here?" He waved to the chairs opposite him. "Please be seated Sam. You too, O'Hara."

Flintlock adjusted the lie of the Colt in his waistband and sat. O'Hara remained standing. Nate Rocheford had been a rancher, peace officer, hired gun, and latterly a bounty hunter. He was fast with a gun and was said to have killed eight men. O'Hara didn't trust him.

Despite the heat and dust of the trail, Rocheford's black broadcloth frockcoat, white shirt, and red tie with a four in hand knot were immaculate, in sharp contrast to Flintlock's shabby buckskin shirt and canvas pants.

Diego Santos laid a bottle of tequila and glasses on the table and then said to Flintlock, "I've arranged for the ladies' baths, señor, and provided them with a bar of Pears soap, the favorite of the beautiful Miss Lily Langtry."

"Make sure Mr. Flintlock's ladies have their privacy, innkeeper," Rocheford said.

"They're not my ladies," Flintlock said, scowling.

"I will indeed," Santos said, bowing.

When the man left, Flintlock said, "Why are you here at the edge of the world, Nate?" He smiled slightly. "By the way, if I see your gun hand slip under your coat, I'll shoot you. Or O'Hara will."

Rocheford poured drinks with his right hand. "Sam, what were the chances of us meeting like this? Pretty damned slim, I'd say. If I held a grudge about the Denver shooting, I would have settled it with you a long time ago."

"Then why are you here?"

"I was told that a man answering the description of King Fisher was wanted in connection with the theft of an army payroll. I knew King was dead, so I figured it was some small-time imposter using his name. The army is offering a five-thousand-dollar reward for the capture of Fisher and the return of the payroll, so I went after him."

Flintlock downed his tequila and refilled his glass. "It still doesn't explain why you're here."

"You haven't told me why you're here either," Rocheford said. "But that's something you'll tell me in your own good time. In answer to your question, Sam, I tracked Fisher to a burned-out burg they used to call Happyville. The Texas Rangers were already investigating the fire. Evidently the smoke could be seen for miles and a few people died. The Ranger sergeant I spoke with said Fisher had probably slipped into the New Mexico Territory and taken the payroll with him. I started here, asking around, trying to pick up a lead, but so far I've had no success."

"King Fisher is dead," Flintlock said.

Rocheford nodded. "I knew that. He was killed with Ben Thompson in San Antone. I'm hunting an imposter."

"King didn't die in San Antone. I killed him myself in Happyville."

Rocheford's face registered shock and surprise and that pleased Flintlock. The man's cocky self-assurance irritated him and was one of the reasons why he'd shot him in Denver.

"Sam," Rocheford said after he'd recovered his

poise, "I'm not catching your drift. You want to explain to me how you came to kill a dead man."

"It's a story that's long in the telling," Flintlock said.

"You know how long women spend in a bathtub?" Rocheford said. "I'd say we got nothing but time."

Flintlock nodded. "All right. Here it is . . ."

And he told his story.

When Flintlock's talking was done, Nate Rocheford sat erect and gripped the arms of his chair, thinking through step-by-step what he'd been told. After a while, he shook his head and said, "Sam, I'm not going to call you a liar, but metal men and an infernal machine are hard to take."

"King was only part metal and he was a wonder to behold," Flintlock said. "But in the end his body betrayed him and his blood turned bad. If I hadn't shot him, he would have died anyway."

O'Hara said, "Sam speaks the truth. You've read about it in the newspapers, Rocheford, how far modern steam engineering has come. It is the people who can't keep up. You saw the Helrun?"

"What was left of it," Rocheford said. "The Rangers said it was a city streetcar that someone wanted to live in, sort of a house on wheels."

Flintlock shrugged. "Did they mention the Gatling gun?"

Rocheford shook his head. "Nobody saw a Gatling gun."

"Then it had been stolen."

"Maybe so. In the last few days, once the word got

around, plenty of people have scavenged that town."
Rocheford poured himself a drink. "Where's the
money, Sam?"

"Out there on the packhorse."

"What do you plan to do with it?" Rocheford said.

"I don't know yet," Flintlock said. "Don't get any
ideas, Nate."

Don't concern yourself with that," Rocheford said.
"Robbing army payrolls is not in my line of work. A
bounty hunter keeps on speaking terms with the law,
and that includes the army . . . navy, too, if I've got a
job on the coast."

"I know all that," Flintlock said. "I'm in the same
line of work."

"Here's the thing, Sam. Since you mentioned Charlie Brewster, I've got bad news for you," Rocheford
said. "Charlie bumped into an army patrol this side of
the border and for a spell things, looked bad for him,
all those wanted dodgers and the like. But Charlie is
smarter than a tree full of owls. He made a deal with
the man in charge that in exchange for free passage
to Old Mexico, he'd tell him all he knew concerning
the whereabouts of the missing payroll. Well, since the
army wasn't really interested in arresting Charlie and
his boys, they cut the deal. Now the army knows where
the payroll was headed and since it can never keep a
secret, so does everybody else. They offered five thousand for the return of the money and now everybody
and his brother is searching for it, outlaws who want
the whole shebang, frontier riffraff who'll cut a throat
for ten dollars, and a few honest men like myself who
are willing to settle for the five thousand. The bottom

line is that as long as you have the money, you've got a target on your back."

"I'll keep that in mind," Flintlock said.

"I guess you have to decide if thirty thousand dollars is more valuable than your life."

"What do I tell the army? Say I was keeping it safe for them?"

"As good an explanation as any. The army wants its money back and it won't ask too many questions about how you came to have it." Rocheford grinned. "Hell, Sam, I bet some general will give you the five-thousand-reward and maybe a gold medal."

"And what about you, Nate? You'll lose out on that deal."

"Well, I could arrest you, Sam, take the money back to Fort Concho myself, but then I'd be a target. I'd say the odds of me getting even halfway there without a bullet in my back are pretty slim."

"I'd say the odds of you arresting me are pretty slim, as well," Flintlock said.

O'Hara smiled. "Sam speaks the truth."

"I figured that. I'm willing to sit this one out," Rocheford said. "I guess I'll eat some beef and frijoles, have a good night's sleep, and ride out in the morning. How does that set with you, Sam?"

"O'Hara will keep you honest, Nate. He never sleeps."

"That's fine by me. You put me on my back for six weeks, Sam, but I don't mean you any harm." Rocheford rose to his feet. "Ah, the ladies are joining us, and very pretty they look, too."

"Nate," Flintlock said. "If you come across an army patrol, tell them where I am."

Rocheford seemed a little surprised. "You sure?"

"Yeah, I'm sure."

"Then I'll do it."

"I never intended to keep the damned money anyway," Flintlock said.

"Sam speaks the truth," O'Hara said, his face empty.

CHAPTER FIFTY

After joining Flintlock and O'Hara for a supper of beef, peppers, and beans, Biddy Sales and Jane Feehan called it a night. Both had damp hair and smelled of Pears soap and Flintlock was forced to admit that when they weren't covered in mud or dust, they were mighty fine-looking women.

An adjoining adobe behind the rear of the cantina was partitioned off into three small rooms, each with a cot, a dresser, and in one corner a kiva fireplace. Nate Rocheford had already moved into one and it had been agreed that Biddy and Jane would share another and Flintlock and O'Hara the third. Since O'Hara rarely slept in a bed, Flintlock was happy with the arrangement.

Packed into saddlebags and flour sacks, the payroll money was carried into Flintlock's room and stashed in a corner. There was no lock on the door, only a flimsy wooden bolt. A narrow porch ran the length of the building and large clay ollas beaded with water were suspended from crossbeams outside each room.

Taking his rifle and a blanket, O'Hara said he'd

stand guard on the roof. Flintlock told him to be careful and not to raise any false alarms since Nate Rocheford was a light sleeper and inclined to shoot first and count heads later.

O'Hara frowned. "Sam, if you hear me yelling for help, it won't be a false alarm."

"Just don't go cutting loose at shadows and the like," Flintlock said. "Injuns see all kinds of boogeymen in the dark, and that's a natural fact."

"I won't shoot until I see the whites of their eyes," O'Hara said, "unless I see a bandit carrying your scalp. Then I'll plug him right off."

"Well, that sets my mind at rest. You're a good friend, O'Hara."

"Hell, Sam, I'm your only friend." O'Hara opened the door and vanished into a night made bright with columns of moonlight.

Flintlock moved his pillow to the bottom of the bed so he'd face the door when he lay down. He removed his gun belt, spurred boots, and hat and then stretched out on the cot, his Colt by his side. A weariness in him, he closed his eyes and soon slept.

It had been an hour since his last customer left and Diego Santos decided it was time to close up shop and seek his bed. He blew out the oil lamps until only the one behind the bar was still lit. He stepped through shadow to extinguish it but stopped in his tracks when the door opened and two men stepped inside.

Apart from the age difference, they looked like identical twins, tall, rangy men wearing slickers. Both had cold blue eyes and sported large dragoon mustaches and scowls.

"I'm sorry gentlemen but I have no rooms and the kitchen is closed. I can bring you tequila."

"Later." The older man reached inside his slicker. "Man carries his gun here. Where is he?"

Seeing that, Santos made the dreadful mistake that could have spelled the end of Flintlock. He thought *carries his gun here* meant *shoved in the waistband.* "Ah, that would be room two. The gent carries a gun just like you said. Do you wish to speak with him?"

"Yeah, but we want to surprise him," the older man said. "We're kin of his. How do we get to his room?"

"I don't think he'll want to be disturbed at this late hour, señor," Santos said.

"He'll want to see us," the younger man said. "His mother passed away, and he'll want us there to comfort him in his time of need."

"Oh, I see, then that makes a difference. Just go out the back door and the rooms are facing you." Santos said, "Room two is in the middle, of course."

The younger man nodded. "Much obliged."

Like all men who have spent time on the scout, Sam Flintlock was a light sleeper, never quite crossing that misty line between wakefulness and deep slumber.

From outside, a dull thud followed by a whispered curse woke him. He grabbed his Colt, silently rolled out of bed, and crouched in shadow against the far wall. A moment later wood splintered as a booted foot kicked in the door and a man charged inside. The intruder hesitated for a second while he tried to locate his target.

It was all the time Sam Flintlock needed.

He fired once into the man's dark silhouette, heard a cry of pain, and fired again. It was a miss as the man sank slowly to the floor, thumbing off shots, shooting at shadows. A bullet burned across the meat of Flintlock's bicep as a second man barged into the room, stumbled over his fallen companion, and cursed as he held onto the doorjamb for balance. Flintlock fired two shots very close together, his target a shifting mass of blackness. This time there was no drama. Hit twice, the second man fell heavily to the wood floor of the room, made a small groaning noise, and then was silent.

Nate Rocheford's voice came from outside. "Sam. Are you all right?"

"I guess. I'm lighting the lamp."

The oil lamp flared into life and spread a sickly yellow light over the two men on the floor. Both were dead, big, fine-looking fellows who'd been in the prime of life.

Flintlock looked at Rocheford standing in the doorway. "I guess they heard about the money," he said, his voice flat.

Rocheford kneeled and studied the faces of both men. It didn't take him long to make up his mind and rise to his feet. "That's Oban Polk and his brother Yates. I killed their oldest brother Eldon in a street fight down Fort Stockton way. That was four months ago, and the Polk brothers have been dogging my back trail ever since."

"So it was nothing to do with the payroll?" Flintlock said.

"No," Rocheford said. "More like a case of mistaken identity. These boys went to the wrong room." The bounty hunter smiled. "Boy, did they ever."

Biddy Sales and Jane Feehan, wearing earrings and little else, crowded into the room. So did O'Hara and Diego Santos.

Flintlock, angry beyond measure, vented his spleen on the little Mexican. He grabbed the man by the front of his shirt and said, "Why did you send those damned assassins to my room?"

Santos, his eyes popping, spread his arms. "They told me they were kin of a man who carried his gun . . . here." The little man moved his hand across his belly.

"You damned fool. They were showing you a shoulder holster," Flintlock said.

Santos shrugged. "I have never seen such a thing, señor. What is a shoulder holster? I thought they meant a man who carried a gun stuck into his pants like you."

"Not many men use a shoulder rig, Sam," Rocheford said. "The Mex probably never saw one."

Santos shook his head. "Never."

"Seems like an honest mistake," Rocheford said. "No harm done."

Irritated, Flintlock said, "No harm done? Look at my arm. I could be dead."

"But you're not, are you?" Rocheford said. "I say we're now even for the bullet you put in me in Denver. I'll concede even more, Sam. Since no town is ever big enough for two bounty hunters, from now on I'll stay out of your way." He stuck out his hand. "Is that fair?"

Flintlock refused the proffered hand. "It's bad luck to shake hands over dead men." Then he said, "Yeah, it's fair."

CHAPTER FIFTY-ONE

Come morning as Flintlock and O'Hara ate tortillas and beans for breakfast, Diego Santos timidly approached the table and said, "Are the gentlemen leaving today?"

"Why?" Flintlock said, his tone hostile. He was still sore at the little man for the shoulder holster mix-up.

"Well, our cemetery is filling up fast and soon there will be no more room."

"Don't worry, we're leaving," Flintlock said.

Santos smiled. "That is very gracious of you, señor. I will tell Mayor Hooper."

"Why didn't he come himself?" Flintlock said.

"The mayor is indisposed. He said so many Americano pistoleros in Nube Blanca has given him the croup."

"Tell him to drink some seltzer water," Flintlock said. "That's the sovereign remedy for the croup."

"I will tell him, señor, but the news that the Americanos are leaving will cure him pretty quick, I think."

Santos made to move away from the table, but O'Hara said, "Good frijoles, compadre. You make them yourself?"

"No, I have a fat lady in the kitchen who cooks the beans," Santos said.

"Well, give her my compliments."

Santos smiled, bowed, and stepped away.

O'Hara looked up and saw Flintlock glaring at him. "Sam, sometimes it's nice to be nice."

Feeling sour, Flintlock said, "I've eaten better beans in better places."

"Nothing will please you this morning."

"I know. I'm sorry. The beans are just fine."

"Two more dead men weighing on you, Sam? Remember, they came after you. You didn't have any choice in the matter."

"That doesn't make it any easier. I had no quarrel with those Polk boys and they had none with me. If it wasn't for the blood money sitting in my room, I wouldn't even have been here."

"And Rocheford would have died," O'Hara said.

"Nate can take care of himself."

O'Hara toyed with his beans and then dropped his spoon onto the plate. "How did you get the drop on them?"

"One of them hit his head on the olla outside my door and cussed. It woke me up."

"The Great Spirit was on your side, Sam. He used the olla to save your life."

"You really think so?"

"Yes, I think so. Sam, you look like hell. Maybe you should shave and trim your mustache. Right now you look like you just came down from a high mountain in winter."

Flintlock rubbed his stubbled chin. "Yeah, I guess I do look a tad rough. I'll shave before we leave."

The laughter of women sounded from the back door of the cantina, then Nate Rocheford walked in with Biddy Sales on one arm, Jane Feehan on the other. "Good morning Sam, O'Hara," he said, grinning. "Isn't it a fine morning, made even finer by two beautiful women?"

Jane laughed and said with practiced flattery, "La, Nate, you are a one with the ladies."

"And so handsome with it," Biddy said.

Rocheford reached down and squeezed butts and the women squealed in delighted indignation. All three laughed as the bounty hunter escorted them to a table.

Flintlock felt a twinge of jealousy, envious of Rocheford's way with women as though the fairer sex was putty in his hands. The deaths of his two enemies last night didn't seem to trouble Rocheford in the least. The matter seemed of little importance and already forgotten.

O'Hara could read Flintlock's emotions because they were always written so clearly on his face. What he understood and his friend didn't was that Nate Rocheford was a hard, unfeeling killer, something Sam Flintlock never was or would ever be.

CHAPTER FIFTY-TWO

Flintlock and O'Hara went outside to ready the packhorse for the trail. They were surprised to see Biddy Sales and Jane Feehan already mounted, their skirts hiked up above their knees.

Biddy answered the question on Flintlock's face. "We're leaving, Sam. It's just too unhealthy around you, and we reckon it's only going to get worse."

Flintlock nodded. "Can't say as I blame you for that. Where are you headed?"

Biddy shook her head. "We don't rightly know. We've still got Morgan Davis's money and since he has no further need for it, Jane and me figure we'll put it to good use."

"We figure we'll find a town somewhere and open our own bawdy house," Jane said. "Maybe up Chloride way. Nate told us the town is booming on account of the silver mines. Hundreds of miners, eight saloons, and no church are good signs for ladies in our line of work."

"I reckon so," Flintlock said. "If I'm ever up that way—"

"Don't look us up, Flintlock. Trouble just seems to follow you, and we've had enough of that to last us a lifetime. Well, so long, tattooed man. I sure hope you find your ma." Biddy kicked her horse into motion and Jane Feehan followed her. They didn't look back.

Flintlock watched them go with an odd sense of loss.

After they left Nube Blanca, Sam Flintlock and O'Hara rode west, crossed the Pecos at the Rustler Breaks, and swung south away from the barrier of the Guadalupe and Delaware mountains.

Once they crossed into Texas they made camp beside a narrow creek sheltered on both banks by cottonwoods and willows. Unwilling to risk a fire that might attract the attention of outlaws and bounty hunters, they ate a cold supper of tortillas, beef, and water and then sought their blankets. The night was clear and cool, the sky ablaze with stars.

Flintlock lay sleepless on his back. "O'Hara?"

"Yeah?"

"Suppose we just leave it, dump the money right here and ride away."

"Finders keepers, Sam. All we'd do is make somebody else rich."

"Whoever was lucky enough to stumble across it?"

"Right. If you're going to do that, you might as well keep the money yourself."

Flintlock watched the blue smoke from his cigarette curl in the air above his head. "I guess the only decent thing is to give the money back to the army."

"Yup, that's the decent thing all right," O'Hara said. "That is, if we can hold on to it long enough. If Rocheford was right, a heap of mighty bad folks want it."

Flintlock got up on an elbow "O'Hara, I'm not going to sacrifice my life to protect the army's money. Too many have died already. The damned payroll became cursed from the minute King Fisher killed the escort and stole it."

"Then we find an army patrol and give them their money," O'Hara said. "Then we head for the Arizona Territory and look for your mother."

After a thinking silence, Flintlock said, "O'Hara, did we dream it, you think? I mean, the whole thing about King Fisher and metal men. Did we camp here beside this creek and just wake up from the same bad dream?"

"No, Sam, it was real. The bullet scar you got on your arm proves it."

Flintlock sighed and lay back on his blanket. "Hell, I didn't think it was a dream anyway."

CHAPTER FIFTY-THREE

A kick in the ribs woke Sam Flintlock. He opened his eyes and looked into the hard face of an Apache with yellow and blue war paint across his cheekbones and bridge of his nose. He carried a Sharps .50 and had a holstered Colt on his hip.

Thinking the man was likely an army scout, Flintlock tried what he hoped came off as a friendly grin. "Well, I'm glad to see you."

The Indian made no answer, and the unwavering muzzle of the Sharps remained pointed at Flintlock's head. The Apache picked up Flintlock's Colt from his blanket and tossed it aside then said something to O'Hara in a language Flintlock did not understand. O'Hara did and tossed away his holstered gun, and in answer to a growl from the Apache, his knife followed.

"Damn it, O'Hara. I thought you never slept," Flintlock said. "You let this feller walk right into our camp."

"Even a half-Injun has to sleep sometime," O'Hara said.

"Couldn't you have done it some other night? This

here Apache could have lifted our hair. I'm surprised he didn't."

"He's army," O'Hara said.

"Figured that," Flintlock said. "But he's still an Apache."

"Mescalero. Only Mescalero scouts wear the soldier blue headband."

Hanging from a leather strap slung over the Apache's shoulder was a brass hunting horn. He raised it to his lips and sounded a single, high-pitched note.

"Now what?" Flintlock said.

"Now we wait for the cavalry to arrive," O'Hara said.

Flintlock tried to rise to his feet, but after a snarl from the Apache, he sat down again. "Friendly cuss, ain't he?"

"Don't do that again, Sam," O'Hara said. "If a Mescalero has any doubt about your intentions, he'll blow a hole through you with the fifty just to be on the safe side. This one won't take any sass."

After a few minutes, the Apache blew his horn again, the same hunting call. He moved backwards to a cottonwood and sat, his back against the trunk, but he never took his eyes or his rifle off Flintlock.

"He doesn't like you, Sam," O'Hara said. "I think it's the thunderbird on your throat. It's bad medicine."

"Not much I can do about that," Flintlock said.

"Every now and then, smile and tip him a nod. That might help."

"I'll try it." After a few moments, he said, "There I

tried it, but all he did was stare at me and finger that cannon on his lap."

"This is one hard-to-please Apache, Sam. Just sit real still until the white men arrive."

"Or his kinfolk," Flintlock said.

"Ravenous wolves of the plains, gentlemen, predators of the prairie. Observe them well. This scum will cut any man, woman, or child in half with a shotgun for fifty dollars. More animal than human, they will surrender to any vice their base, brute natures can devise."

Sam Flintlock, his hands tied behind his back listened in silence as the cavalry major, hands on hips, delivered a lecture to his second lieutenant and sergeant on the kind of human trash that stoops low enough to steal an army payroll.

"Caught red-handed, I'll be bound," the major said. "You'll both hang at Fort Concho, lay to that."

"Major, I told you how we come to have the money," Flintlock said.

"And a tissue of lies it was," the officer said. "A dead man arisen from the grave with a dream of power, metal men, infernal machines. Pah! Even a man of honor like myself could make up a more believable lie than that."

"It's the truth," Flintlock said. "Every word of it. O'Hara, tell him."

"Sam, he won't listen to me," O'Hara said.

"Indeed I will not," the major said. "I refuse to take the word of a ruffian, especially a half-breed cut from the same cloth as his partner in crime."

"What about all the people from Happyville dead from smallpox in the long grass?" Flintlock said. "Do you think I made that up?"

"No, I'm sure you passed that way. The army is aware of that tragic graveyard and its implications," the major said. "Obviously the dead were carried here by the surviving townsfolk in an attempt to end the outbreak with a quarantine. But when even that desperate measure failed, they set fire to the town and fled. God knows where the poor souls are now. Scattered all over creation, I should imagine. Damn you, sir. You even lie about the hurting dead with your wild tale of starting the fire yourself."

Flintlock's anger flared. "Who the hell are you, mister?"

"I dislike hearing my name bandied about by low persons, but I am Major Jonathan Starke." He waved a hand. "This is Lieutenant Uriah Henan and Sergeant Castillo. Both have been ordered to shoot down you and your breed friend like the mad dogs you are should you try to escape." As though he'd instantly dismissed Flintlock and O'Hara from his mind, the major said, "Lieutenant Henan, we'll move out as soon as the money has been transferred to the wagon."

The lieutenant saluted and left to see to his men. Major Starke stepped to the canvas covered wagon that had 7TH CAVALRY REGIMENT stenciled on its side in black paint, a relic of Custer's last campaign and a long way from its native Montana.

Starke had ten buffalo soldiers with him and two guarded Flintlock and O'Hara while the others loaded the money into the wagon.

After a couple of minutes, Major Starke approache
Flintlock again. "I think it's only fair you know th;
the paymaster you murdered when you stole the pa
roll was a very special friend of mine. That is why I'
applaud your hanging at Fort Concho, especially th
moment you drop through the trapdoor and brea
your damned neck."

Still as a bronze statue, the Mescalero stood by th
wagon and stared out into the grassland. He felt th
watcher's presence, the eyes on him and the other
His vision as keen as that of a hawk, he searched fc
movement or a flash of metal in the sunlight but sa
nothing but the ripple of the buffalo grass in th
wind. He was out there, the watcher, but he kept hin
self hidden. The Apache was uneasy.

Then came the major's order to move out, scout t
the point. He mounted his horse and rode through
morning that followed him with a thousand eyes.

CHAPTER FIFTY-FOUR

The day was hot, the climbing sun promising it would be hotter still. Sam Flintlock and O'Hara, their hands tied behind their backs, feet bound under the bellies of their horses, rode at the rear of the column in the dust. Sergeant Castillo, his carbine across his thighs, shared their misery. On all sides, the flat land stretched away to rippling horizons.

They were two days out from Fort Concho, moving through rolling country, when O'Hara turned his dust-streaked face to Flintlock and said, "Do you see them?"

"Yeah, for the last hour. The Apache is riding flank between us and them, a sure sign that he's worried."

"It's hard to tell, but unless those boys are covered in dust, they seem to be wearing tan uniforms. They sure look like some kind of *rurales* to me."

"Hey, Sergeant, do you see those fellers?" Flintlock said.

"I see them," Castillo said.

"Does the major know?" Flintlock said.

"I'm sure he does."

"Why are they pacing us at a distance?"

"Hell, if I know," Castillo said.

"O'Hara says they look like *rurales*," Flintlock said.

"That's what I take them to be." Castillo wiped his sweating face with a large blue bandana. "Either that or some local warlord has himself his own private army."

"They could be after the money," Flintlock said.

"Sure they are," the sergeant said. "Right now they're trying to work up the courage to come get it. Damned greasers."

Flintlock said, "There's a lot of them."

"About a hundred, I reckon—a full-strength troop. If they have the belly for a fight, that's enough."

As Flintlock watched, three of the Mexicans rode out from the others and trotted in the direction of the column. They wore tan colored uniforms, peaked caps, and cartridge belts across their chests. Two of the riders had rifles slung on their backs and the third's uniform glinted in the sun. He had stars on the collars of his shirt and a row of medals glinted on his breast.

"They want to parley," Castillo said, his black eyes amused. "Now the fun begins."

"You think it will come to a fight?" Flintlock said.

"The major isn't going to give them the money, so what do you think?"

"Cut us loose, Sergeant, and give us our guns," Flintlock said. "We'll be sitting ducks trussed up like this."

"You're prisoners," Castillo said. "Prisoners don't fight."

The wagon creaked to a stop as Major Starke halted

e column. Castillo undid his holster flap and then
ulled his horse wide of his two charges to better see
d hear what was happening.

After a while Flintlock said, "Castillo, what are they
ying?"

The sergeant turned a cropped head as big as a nail
eg. "The general calls himself Don Carlos Lopes de
eralta. He's demanding ten thousand in gold and
lver coin for safe passage to Fort Concho. By the
ok on the major's face, he isn't buying it."

"Damn you. Cut us loose," Flintlock said, his voice
iked with urgency.

Castillo ignored that. "Uh-oh, the *generalissimo*
n't look too happy about that. Wait, the major is
alling him out for a bandit and a scoundrel. Well,
at tears it."

The general and his men galloped away and at the
me time Starke yelled the order to dismount and
rm a skirmish line. Sergeant Castillo joined his
oopers, leaving Flintlock and O'Hara alone—
elpless, defenseless, and since their horses were tied
the back of the wagon, immobile.

"We're targets, Sam," O'Hara said, stating the
bvious.

Flintlock nodded but said nothing.

"Here they come."

The first charge was a mounted, probing attack
ade by half the bandits' number to test the firepower
f the buffalo soldiers. The troopers performed well
nd used their Sharps carbines to good effect, emp-
ing six or seven saddles before the Mexicans called
retreat. There was one casualty on the army side.
he Mescalero had been killed early in the fight.

Bullets had split the air close to Flintlock and O'Ha
and it was obvious they'd be among the first to g
hit when the main attack came.

Sergeant Castillo was a good enough soldier to s
the danger and rode to the rear of the wagon an
untied his prisoners' feet. "Get right behind the wago
you two, and stay there. I see you make a run for it, I
shoot you down."

Major Starke watched as his prisoners were made
kneel behind the wagon. "You men stay there. An
attempt to escape will be dealt with severely."

"We've already been told that, Major," Flintlo
said. "For God's sake, untie our hands and give us
chance to fight."

Starke struck a heroic pose and said, "Murdere
and thieves cannot be trusted to bear arms. Prisone
ye are and prisoners ye shall remain."

"And ye can go to hell," Flintlock said.

"They're coming again!" a voice shouted.

Moments later, the firing began again . . .
earnest.

Half the Mexican force had dismounted and a
tacked on foot, taking advantage of every scrap
cover they could find. The remainder of de Peralta
men remained mounted behind the firing line. A
were armed with Winchesters that would take the
toll of the soldiers.

From his position behind the wagon, Flintlock sa
little of the battle. When he saw half a dozen buffa
soldiers fall back and then make an attempt to refor
their line, he feared the fight was going badly f
the army. Lieutenant Henan, bleeding from a hea
wound, joined his troopers and fired his Colt at th

nemy. Moments later he was cut down in a hail of
unfire, several soldiers falling in the same volley.

Flintlock frantically tried to untie O'Hara's wrists,
ut his swollen fingers were unequal to the task and
e gave up as bullets tore through the wagon's canvas
op and forced him to his knees again.

He saw Major Starke fall, killed instantly by a bullet
> his head. Sergeant Castillo downed two bandits
ith his revolver before a mounted Mexican drove a
iber into his chest. The dog soldiers fought to the
ist man, neither giving nor asking for mercy.

The shooting died away. Scowling bandits, angry
ver the high number of their compadres who'd
een killed and wounded, surrounded Flintlock and
'Hara and brandished their weapons. One huge,
carred brute, a knife in his hand, stepped to Flint-
ock. Instead of stabbing him, he turned Flintlock
round and cut the rope that bound his wrists. He did
ie same for O'Hara.

The big man, an officer of some kind, then said
omething in Mexican that Flintlock didn't under-
and.

O'Hara translated. "He wants to know why we were
risoners of the Yankee soldiers."

Flintlock said, "Tell him we stole the army payroll
nd they caught us."

"Are you sure you want to say that?"

"Bandits set store by other bandits," Flintlock said.
Go ahead, tell him."

O'Hara translated what Flintlock had said. This
rew peals of laughter from the surrounding men,
nd the officer slapped Flintlock on the back. "*Eres
emasiado estupido para ser un bandido.*"

"What did he say?" Flintlock said.

"You don't want to know," O'Hara said.

"Yeah, I do. Tell me."

"He says you're too stupid to be a bandit."

Flintlock nodded and grinned at the big ma

"And some day I'll put a bullet in your belly."

O'Hara didn't translate that.

CHAPTER FIFTY-FIVE

"I am your father," General Don Carlos Lopez de Peralta said. "And you are my sons. Welcome to my army."

Sam Flintlock and O'Hara lifted their wineglasses as O'Hara said, "You do us great honor, General."

"You may call me Excellency," de Peralta said. "For it is by that title I am known."

Outside in the courtyard, women wailed for the dozen dead bandits killed in the action against the buffalo soldiers. At the same time, a fiesta was in full swing as de Peralta's men got drunk and celebrated the capture of the army payroll.

His Excellency's headquarters was located a mile south of the Rio Grande, a former Spanish mission that had seen better times. He had converted the chapel for his living quarters and filled it with looted furniture and rugs. Portraits of long-dead Spanish gentlemen and their dark-eyed ladies hung on the walls.

De Peralta was an imposing figure. He stood well over six feet, and his great belly hung between his legs like a sack of grain. His eyes were black, overhung by heavy eyebrows. His unshaven face was jowly, the skin open-pored and greasy. The front of his uniform tunic was covered in medals, all of them French and none of them earned. A slender, pretty señorita sat on the man's massive lap and twirled his lank black hair around her forefinger, pouting at his lack of attention to her.

De Peralta said, "Flintlock and O'Hara, you are the first of my new recruits. With the Yankee money I can now hire more soldiers and make myself the most powerful man in Chihuahua and perhaps, God willing, all of Mexico after I unseat that popinjay Porfirio Díaz."

Flintlock exchanged glances with O'Hara. This crazy man was spouting the same nonsense as King Fisher, chasing the same mad dream of power. It seemed to Flintlock that nothing under the sun ever changes.

De Peralta waved a dismissive hand. "Now out you go, *mis soldados*, and enjoy yourselves." He shrugged. "If you wish, say a prayer for our dead."

Flintlock and O'Hara rose to their feet. The general was nuzzling the señorita's hair, his hand exploring, and they were already forgotten.

If Flintlock thought de Peralta was a trusting man that notion was banished quickly when they left the mission and stepped into the plaza. Two of the general's soldiers were waiting for them, rifles over their shoulders. Around them, people were dancing and getting drunk, the clothes of the women a riot of color, a swirling cascade of blue, yellow, and red as ever changing as a kaleidoscope. The rhythm of guitars provided a pulsing counterpoint to the laughter of the señoritas and the drunken roars of the soldiers.

Their two stone-faced shadows following them, Flintlock and O'Hara stepped through the maelstrom of noise and color and found a table away from the crowded plaza and shaded by a tree. They sat, but their guards remained standing. Almost immediately a smiling woman laid a bottle and two earthenware cups between them.

Flintlock grinned at the guards. "Won't you boys join us?" This drew blank looks and he said to O'Hara, "Good. They don't speak English." He uncorked the bottle and sniffed. "Tequila." He poured a cup for himself and one for O'Hara. "All right. How the hell do we get away from here?"

O'Hara tried his drink, made a face, and pushed the cup away from him. "We have no guns, no horses, and a couple hardcases guarding us, so I can't come up with a plan right at the moment."

Flintlock nodded. "Yeah, those two look trigger happy and they're probably sore as hell that they can't join in the fiesta."

"All the guns they picked up after the fight were thrown into the back of the wagon," O'Hara said. "I saw your Hawken among them."

"I set store by that gun," Flintlock said. His hand strayed to the pocket of his buckskin shirt but he had no makings. "Damn, I need a cigarette." He turned to the guards and made a smoking motion with his fingers.

Staring at him, the man reached into his shirt and threw tobacco and papers onto the table without saying a word.

"Obliged." Flintlock built a smoke, inhaled deeply and said, "O'Hara, don't look now but I see the army wagon. It's behind you between two adobe houses."

"Guards?"

"None that I can see. The general already had the money carried into the mission so there's no need to guard it."

"Guns?"

"Plenty of those around already. I guess they think there's no need to guard some rifles and pistols."

"What's your thinking on this, Sam?"

Flintlock drank, watching O'Hara over the rim of his cup. Without taking the cup away from his mouth, he said, "This crowd will be snoring off a drunk tonight. We can grab our guns and then a couple horses."

"Without being seen?" O'Hara said.

"Look around you," Flintlock said. "Nobody will be awake come midnight."

O'Hara's eyes lifted to the guards. "What about them?"

"We can take care of them when the time comes."

O'Hara was silent and Flintlock said, "Well?"

"It's mighty thin, Sam. A heap of maybes there."

"No maybes. We can do it just like I said, O'Hara. Trust me on this."

O'Hara groaned inwardly but said nothing.

CHAPTER FIFTY-SIX

A crescent moon climbed high in the sky, and Sam Flintlock's prediction that the fiesta would end in drunken snores had come to pass. The only activity was across the deserted plaza, where torches burned in the darkness and old women prayed for the dead soldiers, their bloody bodies washed and laid out under clean white sheets ready for burial. Couples had sought sweaty beds in the adobe houses surrounding the mission and only a few drunks remained. Propped up against walls, they were snoring.

As new recruits, Flintlock and O'Hara had not been assigned living quarters and were expected to sleep where they could. They stretched out under the striped awning of what looked like a commissary where spices in jars, strings of peppers, and bottles of tequila were for sale. The place was shuttered, as it had been during the fiesta when the general had supplied the food and drink, and there was no owner in sight.

One stroke of luck that pleased Flintlock immensely was that their guard had been reduced to one. He suspected that the other one had deserted his post to grab a bottle and court a señorita. The remaining guard, his broad, peasant face bored and unhappy, squatted beside Flintlock and O'Hara, his rifle across his knees.

A moment later, the missing guard staggered drunkenly across the plaza, gave up the struggle, and stretched out on the table where Flintlock and O'Hara had been sitting earlier. Alarmed, they kept their eyes on him. The man had lost his rifle but carried a revolver at his side in a flapped holster. Once on his back he didn't move and seemed to be unconscious.

His face showing his relief when the bandit lay on the table and snored softly, O'Hara nodded to Flintlock. It was time.

Flintlock clutched his belly and groaned, his boot heels gouging the ground. The guard looked at him but didn't move. Groaning louder, Flintlock acted the part of a man with a bad bellyache, a fine performance he hoped would not go to waste. Finally, the guard took the bait. He stood and looked down at Flintlock .

O'Hara said, *"Él ésta enfermo,"* and then in English, "He is sick."

The guard seemed perplexed. He took a knee beside Flintlock and stared into his face.

It was happening just as Flintlock hoped it would. He swung a left hook that slammed into the guard's chin. The man didn't make a sound. He toppled over, sprawled in the dirt, and lay still. Flintlock rose to his feet and looked around him, an alarm bell ringing in his head. Had he been seen?

The moonlit plaza remained quiet, the only sound

the murmur of the old women praying for the dead. A skinny dog walked out of the gloom, stared at Flintlock for a moment, and then slunk away.

Flintlock tossed the unconscious man's rifle to O'Hara, untied his bandana from around his neck, gagged the bandit, and then used the guard's own belt to bind his wrists behind his back. Flintlock dragged the man into the shadows where O'Hara joined him.

"Sam, we have a rifle," O'Hara said. "Should we make a play for the horses?"

Flintlock shook his head. "No, I'm not leaving here without the Hawken."

O'Hara started an urgent whispered protest, but just as urgently Flintlock said, "O'Hara, the Hawken is both wife and child to me. I won't go without it."

O'Hara's exasperation showed, but his tone was even when he said, "All right. Let's go rescue your kinfolk."

The firearms had been thrown haphazardly into the back of the wagon and in the darkness by the dim light of a match it took time for Flintlock to find the Hawken and then his battered Colt. O'Hara's revolver was still in the holster and he picked it out it right away.

Behind the wagon lay vacant ground. Sandy and covered with cactus, it was full of shadows. Clouds brushed across the crescent moon and stars winked out and reappeared as they passed. The horse lines were clear on the other side of the mission. The shortest route was to walk across the plaza and risk being seen. The alternative was to loop wide around, stay to open ground, and come at the horses from behind Neither held much appeal for Flintlock, especially a long circuit in the dark across unknown terrain.

"How do we play this, Sam?"

Flintlock decided to take their chances on the plaza.

"I'll feel like a man walking to the gallows," O'Hara said.

"It will be fine. Just walk slow and easy as though we're going nowhere in a hurry. Nobody will ever notice us."

CHAPTER FIFTY-SEVEN

Flintlock and O'Hara's stroll across the plaza was uneventful except for a drunk who staggered toward them, stopped and stared, blinking like an owl, and then moved on. They passed the guttering torches where the old women knelt and reached the horse lines without incident.

It was dark there, the sliver of moon giving little light. A pole corral, set at a distance, held a single horse, a beautiful palomino stud with a flaxen mane and tail. An ornate silver saddle hung on the corral's top pole.

Flintlock's mischievous nature was immediately aroused. His teeth gleamed in the gloom as he grinned and said, "I bet that's his Excellency's hoss and saddle. I'm going to take him."

"Hell, take what you want, Sam," O'Hara said. "Just do it quick. We're pushing our luck."

O'Hara chose a better paint than the one he rightfully owned as Flintlock stepped into the corral and said soothing words to the restive stud.

It seemed that Don Carlos Lopez de Peralta was a

careful man, always ready for flight or fight, because a saddle and bridle lay on the ground in front of each horse.

O'Hara quickly saddled the paint and led it to the corral where Flintlock approached the palomino, the silver saddle ready in his hands.

He never made it.

The rattle of a dozen rifles thrown to shoulders stopped Flintlock in his tracks.

The palomino glared at him and pawed the ground as he dropped the saddle and slowly turned. He saw O'Hara with both hands raised as though he was trying to grab handfuls of stars. General de Peralta looked mad enough to bite the head off a hammer. A line of soldiers, all of them sober, had their rifle sights on Flintlock and two others he recognized as his former guards. They groveled at the general's booted feet.

De Peralta raised his voice in an outraged roar. "What is the meaning of this? Why did you attack my men"—he kicked the guard nearest to him—"these pig dogs?"

Flintlock thought quick. "Excellency, we thought we heard voices out in the badlands and planned to investigate. We feared for your life."

"And you decided to take my personal mount that no one but me is allowed to ride?"

"We didn't know the horse was yours, Excellency," Flintlock said. "He is indeed a fine animal."

"Do you take me for a fool?" de Peralta said. "You took guns from the wagon and then tried to steal horses. I ask myself why you did these things. And the answer comes to me that you planned to go to the

Americanos and tell them about the money and my whereabouts."

Flintlock said, "But, Your Excellency—"

The general undid his holster flap and drew his Colt. "No, do not lie to me again. I cannot abide liars." He gave a loud shriek, "Pig dogs!"

The sobbing, cringing men at de Peralta's feet immediately threw up their hands and begged for mercy. But there was none. The general shot them both, one after the other, a single bullet to the head.

As gun smoke drifted he said to Flintlock, "For your treachery and betrayal you and your companion will suffer the same fate, but at a time of my choosing. I made you my beloved sons, but you threw that gift back in my face. Now I can't bear to look at you." De Peralta said something in Spanish and two soldiers stepped forward, manacles clanking in their hands.

As the chains were applied to O'Hara's hands and feet he said, "I think it's all up with us, Sam."

Flintlock shook his head. "No, it's not. I'll think of something. Don't worry." He looked at the general and said, "Excellency, can I have my Hawken?"

A rifle butt to the back of his head was his only answer.

Sam Flintlock woke to find himself shackled to the wall in a tiny room with one small window high up the wall. A stone bench was opposite him. He figured it was a bed and that he was in what had been the cell of one of the brother monks who'd manned the mission for Spain. The room was cold and dark and the hard flagstone floor offered no comfort.

As his aching head cleared and his eyes became accustomed to the gloom, he realized he was alone except for a shackled skeleton in the corner, still with shreds of rotting flesh attached to its bones. Whether the poor wretch was male or female he didn't know, but it was obvious that the only way out of this prison was death.

His throat was dry and it took some effort, but he managed to throw back his head and shout, "O'Hara!" His voice sounded loud in the confines of the tiny room.

An answering silence mocked him. The old Spanish men had built their missions to last. The brick walls of his cell could be two feet thick and the door was of sturdy oak reinforced with iron. No sound could penetrate such barriers and Flintlock didn't try again.

The thin light glowing in the window told him the dawn had come. He yanked on his chains. They were securely stapled to the walls and locked with a massive iron padlock. There was no escape from this place. He could only hope for a miracle.

"Hoping for a miracle, ain't you, boy?" Old Barnabas sat by the skeleton, his arm around its bony shoulders. "Well you ain't gonna get one. Miracles are for some pale, puny, prattling preacher, not for the likes of you."

"Leave me alone, Barnabas," Flintlock said. "I've got a damned headache and you'll make it worse."

The old mountain man shook the skeleton until it rattled. "You'll end up like this feller here, just skin and bones. You should have killed all them whores and the redskin and took the money while you had the chance. But no, you had to play the saint and you've ended up here. You-know-who says you're such a dunderhead he doesn't think he wants you in hell. He says all you'll do is cause trouble."

"Well, the feeling is mutual," Flintlock said. "I don't want to go to hell either."

Barnabas rose to his feet. "Just for your information, Sam'l, we still don't have that Jack the Ripper feller that all the folks are talking about. Pity. I look forward to meeting him. Well, I got to go."

"That's it? You're just going to leave me here?"

"Nothing I can do, boy. Helping you would be a good deed and where I come from, we don't do good deeds . . . only bad deeds, if you catch my drift. Say, if you do meet that Ripper feller, though I admit that your present circumstances make it unlikely, give him my regards."

Barnabas vanished in a cloud of yellow, sulfur-smelling smoke.

Sam Flintlock measured time by the change of light through the tiny window and the once-a-day visit of two taciturn soldiers who brought him a meal of tortillas, beans, and water and placed an empty slop bucket in a corner. He asked about O'Hara, but his question was greeted with a stony silence.

On the third day—it may have been the fourth, Flintlock was not sure—his chains were unlocked and he was taken from his cell.

"Where are we going?" he asked one of the guards, a gray-haired man with a kind face.

The soldier understood enough English to reply, "His Excellency will consider your treason and pass judgment on you." He would add nothing more, but his oddly pitying glance convinced Flintlock that his fate had already been decided.

CHAPTER FIFTY-EIGHT

Once again Sam Flintlock found himself facing General de Peralta in the man's luxurious office. There was no girl on the man's knee. She was replaced by a row of stern-faced officers who flanked his ornate desk chair. His Excellency wore his best uniform, all his French medals, and a scowl.

"Samuel Flintlock, you stand accused of high treason," de Peralta said. "How do you answer this charge?"

"Where is O'Hara?" Flintlock said. He knew he wasn't going to get out of this alive and dispensed with calling the lowlife, two-bit bandit *Your Excellency.*

"The savage has already been sentenced to death. He will be shot at dawn tomorrow," the general said. "He knew my heart was hardened toward him and did not beg for clemency."

"Mister, nor will I," Flintlock said. "As far as I'm concerned you can go to hell."

"Then I will meet your defiance with my terrible justice. You will be shot at dawn tomorrow." De Peralta waved a hand. "Take this wretch away. He smells."

Flintlock's guards didn't understand that last, but

their leader's meaning was obvious. Flintlock was bundled out of the office and to make himself look good in front of the boss, one of the guards kicked him hard in the butt. He knew it would do him little good, but on his way to the cell Flintlock studied the man's face. It had a scar over the left eyebrow, just a few teeth and those rotten, and a nose that had been broken more than once. Not that it would do him much good, but it was a face he'd remember.

Flintlock was shackled to the wall again. A few minutes later the cell door creaked open and a monk wearing a heavy brown robe was allowed inside. Middle-aged, with a fine, ascetic Spanish face and bright blue eyes, he kneeled beside Flintlock and said in good English, "My name is Father Alfonso Giron. Are you a Catholic, my son?"

Flintlock shook his head. "I'm not anything, padre. I've never been much of a one for churchgoing."

The priest smiled. "I will say a rosary for you tonight. Do you mind?"

"Not at all. God and me aren't exactly on speaking terms so I need all the help I can get."

"God will always hear you and speak to you, my son. This is a thing I know."

A silence stretched between the two men, each seeking common ground, but then the priest said something unexpected. "If you were a Catholic I could hear your confession and give you the Last Rites, but since I am unable to deliver spiritual solace, perhaps I can cater to your physical needs."

Father Giron reached inside his robe, produced a

pewter flask, and smiled. "Brandy, my son, to ease your suffering."

Flintlock grinned. "I reckon that will do the trick, padre."

The priest held the flask to Flintlock's mouth and let him drink. After fifteen minutes of this, the flask was drained and Flintlock was feeling no pain.

"Thank you, padre," he said as the door opened and Father Giron was ordered to leave. "Are all priests like you?"

"I can only speak for myself, my son. I do what God dictates."

"Thank Him for me, huh?"

Father Giron rose to his feet. "You can thank Him yourself. He'll listen."

Through the warm glow of the brandy working its amber magic, Flintlock said, "And don't forget to say those prayers for me tonight. I don't want to show yellow at dawn tomorrow."

Smiling, the priest said, "I don't think a man who wears a great bird on his throat will show cowardice in the face of death."

"It's a thunderbird," Flintlock said.

"Yes, I know," Father Giron said. "And you must never make it angry." The priest made the sign of the cross over Flintlock and blessed him. "I'll be with you and your companion tomorrow. I hope I can bring you some comfort."

Flintlock hiccupped. "Padre, I reckon you've already done that."

* * *

In due time the effects of the brandy wore off and Flintlock faced the lonely darkness of a night that seemed endless. As his eyes became accustomed to the gloom, he saw the skeleton in the corner grin at him.

"How you doing, feller?" he said. "You look a little peaked, if you don't mind me saying so."

The skull grinned.

"I'm to be shot come dawn," Flintlock said. "But I guess it's better than starving to death. Is that what happened to you, huh?"

There was no answer.

Flintlock nodded. "I'm losing my mind. Talking to old Barnabas is bad enough, but trying to start a conversation with a pile of bones is plumb loco." He rattled his chains. "Well, what do you think? Am I crazy? Ah, you have no opinion on that. I'm supposed to be looking for my ma, you know, but now I guess I'll never find her. Yeah, I'm disappointed all right. Like a bride left at the altar."

The skeleton showed no interest.

"Ah, well, you're not one for conversation, so I'll leave you alone."

Flintlock looked at the window high on the wall where the spiders lived. It was still a rectangle of darkness.

My God, would this night never end?

CHAPTER FIFTY-NINE

Sam Flintlock had fallen into a fitful sleep and missed the changing of the light. He woke to the slamming open of the cell door and the harsh voices of men tasked with the execution of another human being.

As Flintlock's chains were unlocked, Father Giron stood to one side and read prayers from a small black missal. The priest's face was gray as though he was the one facing the firing squad.

"Thank you for showing, padre," Flintlock said as he was pushed and pummeled past. "I appreciate it."

Father Giron nodded and managed a smile.

Despite the early hour, at least a hundred people— soldiers and civilians—had gathered in the plaza. Flintlock had wondered at the reason for the free-standing wall of mud brick built at the edge of an acre of waste ground. Now he knew.

O'Hara was already there, his hands tied behind his back. He had a bruise on his left cheekbone but other-wise seemed unharmed.

Flintlock was dragged to the wall, his hands were

tied, and his back was shoved against the rough mu«
brick.

"Morning, O'Hara," he said. "How did they trea
you?"

"Badly. You?"

"Badly." Flintlock looked at the sky. "Going to be
hot one today."

"Seems like," O'Hara said. "I'm glad. If it was a col«
morning, I might shiver and they'd think it was from
fear."

"Him there with the prayer book is Father Giron
He's a right nice feller. Brought me brandy."

"And me."

Flintlock nodded. "He's a good man."

"Seems like," O'Hara said.

"Not much of a one for talking when you're abou
to get shot, huh?"

"No. It does wear on a man."

"Well, stand firm, O'Hara. We'll show this rabbl«
how Americans die."

"Will they offer us a blindfold? I don't want a blind
fold. I want to look those sons of bitches in the ey«
when they pull the trigger."

"You can refuse it. I know I will." Flintlock smiled
"That's the ticket, O'Hara. Look them in the eye."

A few moments later a file of eight soldiers carrying
rifles trotted to the wall and lined up opposite the
condemned men. An officer with a saber stood t«
the side.

"It's been real good knowing you, Sam," O'Har«
said.

"You too, O'Hara. It's been a pleasure."

The officer raised his saber and barked a command, and his firing squad shouldered their rifles.

Flintlock swallowed hard and counted his life in seconds.

The morning erupted in gunfire.

Blue-coated cavalry charged into the plaza, shooting as they went.

Fighting for his own life, the firing squad officer suddenly lost interest in Flintlock and O'Hara. Surprised, shocked, the eight riflemen of his command were quickly cut down, half of them failing to get off a shot. The officer raised his saber to cut at a passing buffalo soldier and paid for his temerity when the trooper fired his Colt into the man's face and dropped him.

The plaza was filled with cavalrymen drawn from the 9th and 10th regiments out of Fort Concho. The United States had been slow to anger, but once aroused, America was a terrible enemy. The black troopers thirsted to avenge their comrades left dead on the plain and mercy didn't enter into their thinking. Here and there, chivvied by their officers, De Peralta's soldiers tried to make a stand, but they were annihilated and their bloody bodies soon littered the ground.

Flintlock looked to the mission where a dozen Mexicans were still fighting. Through the thick pall of gun smoke he saw General Peralta stick his head out of the door and then quickly duck back inside. Flintlock yelled out to a passing cavalryman to untie his bonds.

The soldier, a huge sergeant with the fire of combat

in his eyes, stared at Flintlock, made up his mind, an
yelled, "Turn around."

The man's saber flashed downward and Flintloc
felt the keen blade slash the rope and pass betwee
his palms like the cold flicker of a serpent's tongue. A
the rope fell to the ground, he looked at his hand
expecting them to be cut and bloody, but the sabe
stroke had been so precise they were unharme
Before he could thank him, the sergeant gallope
away.

Flintlock untied O'Hara and said, "De Peralta."

He didn't need to say more.

Flintlock grabbed the fallen officer's Colt from th
holster and ran into the plaza. He was well aware
the danger. The buffalo soldiers were out for bloo
and anyone not on a horse and wearing a blue co
was a target. As he ran between plunging, rearin
horses he yelled, "American! American!" above th
roar of gunfire and the screams of the dying.

A few soldiers gave him hard looks as he passe
but no one shot at him or aimed a saber blow at h
head. Flintlock thought himself lucky as he cleare
the press and ran for the horse lines. He figure
de Peralta had left the mission already, trying to mak
a run for it.

Jogging past the unlit torches where the old wome
had prayed, Flintlock headed for the palomino . .
and ran headlong into trouble. Two of the general
men stood between him and the corral. Both fire
their rifles but shaken by what was happening in th
plaza they hurried their shots. A bullet cracke
through the air an inch from Flintlock's left ear an
the other kicked up dirt at his feet.

He fired on the run. One of the bandits went down and the second frantically tried to work the lever of his Winchester, but the rifle was jammed. In despair, the man threw the gun at Flintlock then took to his heels, shrieking and waving his hands in the air as he ran.

Flintlock let the man go, but a battle-crazed cavalry trooper galloped past him and ran down the fleeing bandit. The soldier's saber rose and fell and split the Mexican's head from crown to chin. With his saber running blood, the trooper swung his horse around, saw Flintlock, and charged. The horseman aimed a cut at Flintlock's head, but he ducked and the blade sliced air inches over his head. As the trooper controlled his unruly horse and again raised his saber, Flintlock yelled, "I'm an American, damn it!"

The buffalo soldier stayed his hand, but his saber was still raised as he said, "What the hell are you doing here?"

"I was captured," Flintlock said.

Flintlock saw the man's mind working, then the trooper said, "Stay the hell out of the way, you damned fool." He swung his horse around, heard firing from the far side of the plaza, and galloped in that direction.

Two narrow escapes from death within a couple minutes made Flintlock's heart race as he ran for the corral, warily looking around for any sign of berserk horse soldiers.

Then came bitter disappointment. The corral gate was open and the palomino and its silver saddle were gone . . . and so presumably was Don Carlos Lopez de Peralta.

The palomino's tracks led out of the corral an looped around a ruined outbuilding that had onc been the mission's smokehouse. Flintlock guesse that de Peralta was heading east and probably had head start of at least a mile. With no time to saddle horse, Flintlock shoved the Colt in his waistband an picked out a broad-backed steel dust. He bridled th mount and rode it bareback, following de Peralta tracks.

An excellent tracker—it was one of the skills tha old Barnabas and his mountain man cronies ha taught him well—Flintlock kicked the horse into flat-out run. The time had come for a reckoning, an he was willing to kill the steel dust to achieve it.

CHAPTER SIXTY

Sam Flintlock rode across flat, brushy, desert country relieved here and there by patches of juniper and catclaw cactus. A rising plume of dust ahead of him marked Carlos de Peralta's position a mile in hand and the palomino seemed to be running strong.

He kicked the steel dust to greater effort and the horse responded, revealing a willingness to run and plenty of spunk.

The rising sun was hot and he sweated from the effort of riding a galloping horse without a saddle. The cadenced drum of the steel dust's hooves was almost hypnotic as it ate up distance and showed no sign of faltering. Ahead of him, de Peralta's dust blossomed in a yellow cloud—but it was lessening.

Flintlock figured that either the palomino was running across firmer ground or the big horse was almost out of steam. Time would tell.

The steel dust was gaining.

Soon, the distance had closed so much that even through the dust Flintlock saw de Peralta glance over his shoulder and then rake the palomino's flank with his spurs.

The steel dust's head came up and the rhythmic thud of his hooves became ragged and his breathing labored. He was slowing. The horse had shown heart and Flintlock was reluctant to push him further, but push him he must. He kicked his mount's ribs and urged him on.

De Peralta did the unexpected. He swung the palomino around and charged. He let the reins trail and with a revolver in each hand, began shooting. Flintlock roared his anger and drew his Colt. He rode right at the Mexican, firing as he went.

Disaster struck.

Flintlock heard the solid *thwack!* of a bullet as it hit the steel dust.

The brave little horse grunted, ran for a few more yards, then his front legs went out from under him. Flintlock cartwheeled over the horse's head, hitting the ground hard. His gun went flying from his hand. Winded, he tried to rise.

De Peralta stood over him, the muzzle of his Colt just inches from Flintlock's head. The man's grin was evil. "Pig dog! You escaped the firing squad, but you will not escape this time." He thumbed back the hammer of his Colt. "Scum, I will shoot you in the belly and leave you to die, squealing in agony like the pig you are."

Flintlock found his breath. "You go to hell, crazy man."

Keeping his grin in place, De Peralta moved the muzzle of his gun until it pointed at Flintlock's belly. "I will enjoy this very much, I think."

An instant later his head exploded.

A bullet had struck de Peralta's right temple, traveled clean through his head, and burst out the other side of his skull just above his left ear, spraying blood, bone, and brain like a small, scarlet fountain.

A moment later, Flintlock heard the flat statement of a rifle.

He rose to his feet. O'Hara, he and his horse covered in dust, rode toward him at a walk, the butt of a Winchester resting on his thigh.

"Good shot," Flintlock said, grinning.

"Not so great," O'Hara said. "A hundred yards with a Winchester rifle is no great thing."

"You saved my life O'Hara. I won't forget it."

"And I won't let you forget it."

Sam Flintlock rode the palomino back to the mission at a walk with de Peralta's body hanging over the saddle. Unfortunately, unwashed, unshaven, and covered in dust, they were immediately arrested as suspicious characters, possible murderers, and held in a disused wine cellar.

Flintlock had to admit that was a step up from the stinking cell he'd previously occupied. "I'd say the young lieutenant was a real nice feller. Very polite. I bet he went to West Point."

"He still arrested us," O'Hara said. "There was nothing polite about that."

"Do you think he believed me when I told him we were returning the payroll money when we were captured?"

"If you were him, would you?" O'Hara said.

"Not a word of it."

"Then there's your answer." O'Hara looked aroun the cellar. "All the wine is gone."

"I guess they drank it all at the fiesta." Flintloc stared at O'Hara. "Whatever happens, don't mentio King Fisher. If the lieutenant is any guide, the arm isn't going to listen to a story about a metal man wh wanted to be president of the world."

"So what do I say? Make it all clear to me, Sam."

"We say we found the army wagon abandone and like the good citizens we are we decided t return it to the military. We met up with Major Stark and his men and were headed for Fort Concho whe de Peralta attacked us. For some reason he spared ou lives and took us prisoner."

O'Hara considered that and said, "Maybe meta men would be easier to believe."

"No, stick to the story I just gave you. Otherwise w could face a noose for being in cahoots with a bunc of murderous Mexican bandits."

"Have it your way, Sam. I just hope you're right."

Flintlock nodded. "Trust me."

CHAPTER SIXTY-ONE

Like the monk's cell, the wine cellar had a single small window just under the arched timber ceiling, but Flintlock had found a wax candle with a supply of lucifers. As darkness fell, he lit both, filling their dreary surroundings with shifting, shadowed light. Rats scurried noisily in the corners and from outside the solemn back-and-forth tread of a sentry punctuated the night.

A key clanked in the lock and the cellar door creaked open. A soldier flanked by two others holding rifles made his way down steps worn by a hundred years of feet. The man, corporal's stripes on the arms of his faded blue shirt, held a silver tray, one of de Peralta's spoils, and said, "Grub's up, boys."

There were coffee cups on the tray and tin plates of fried bacon and a dollop of some kind of mush. "I pounded the hardtack and fried it in the bacon grease," the soldier said. "Makes for a fair meal."

Flintlock and O'Hara were hungry and raised no objection to the bill of fare. It was a soldier's meal and they were glad to get it.

"I'll pick up the plates in the morning," the ma said and turned to go.

"Hold on a second, Corporal," Flintlock sai "What's going to happen to us?"

"I don't rightly know." The soldier scratched h head and then said, "The colonel is pretty mad at th Mexican prisoners we took. If you threw in with then you should probably hope for the best and expect th worst."

"What's the worst?" O'Hara said.

"A bullet or a noose. That would be my thinking.

"And the best?"

The corporal shook his head and looked sa "Injun, I don't reckon there is a best."

After the soldiers left, Flintlock dropped his for onto his empty plate and said, "Things will work ou fine after I talk to the colonel. Hell, O'Hara, do w look like Mexican bandits?"

"Sam, we look like some kind of bandits. Yo haven't been near a mirror recently."

Colonel James McKenzie, a spare, severe-lookin officer, seemed out of place behind de Peralta's des amid the ornate splendor of the general's office. was dawn—for soldiers, the middle of the day.

McKenzie had listened in silence to Sam Flintlock explanation about why he was in the camp of a not rious brigand who'd killed American soldiers an stolen an army payroll.

The colonel's cold blue eyes moved to O'Har "Carlos de Peralta's body was identified by sever

his soldiers and his . . . ah . . . mistress. You
lled him?"

"Yes, just as Flintlock told you."

"Why did you kill him?"

"He was about to shoot Flintlock in the belly,"
Hara said. "But I done for him first."

"He treated us like animals," Flintlock said. "And
: were facing his firing squad when you attacked the
ission."

"Yes, that is the testimony of"—Colonel McKenzie
ad from a slip of paper on his desk—"Private Judah
atson. He says he freed you from your bonds."

Flintlock nodded. "He put in some fine work with
e saber, Colonel."

"All my troopers are good with the saber," McKenzie
id. "You were there when Major Starke and his
tail were killed."

"Yes, sir," Flintlock said. "Since we were unarmed,
:'d been told to take cover behind the wagon."

"Why were you unarmed?"

Flintlock hesitated and McKenzie said, "Come now,
an, answer the question."

"Major Starke thought we might have been involved
the stealing of the payroll."

"And were you?"

"No, sir. We were not."

"How did Major Starke and his men perform in the
ttle?" the colonel said.

"They fought to the last man and died with their
ce to the enemy," Flintlock said. "They were all
ave."

"Warriors," O'Hara said.

McKenzie stared over his steepled fingers and

Flintlock thought he'd seen friendlier eyes look
him over the barrel of a gun.

Finally the colonel said, "Mr. Flintlock, one of
junior officers told me that you are known on t
frontier as a desperate character who associates wi
known criminals and all kinds of low persons.
bounty hunter, I think he called you. The thunderbi
tattoo on your throat is a mark of Cain, I'll be boun

Flintlock nodded. "Just about sums me up, Colon
But O'Hara here is neither a criminal nor a l
person. He saved my life yesterday."

"The noble savage?"

"You could say that."

"Colonel, we didn't steal the army's money." Fli
lock had reached the end of his tether and was si
and tired of hearing about the damned payroll. "A
that's a natural fact. Now it's up to you. Believe wh
you want."

"Mr. Flintlock, I have no doubt that you shou
have been hanged years ago, but that is a matter f
the civil authorities, not the army," Colonel McKen
said. "However, despite major Starke's opinion, I
not think you were involved in the theft of the payr
Yesterday you had ample time to escape but did n
and you and your companion killed a dangero
enemy of the United States. In all good conscience
cannot find you guilty of treason or any other
fense." He gave Flintlock another of his icy star
"This may come as a disappointment to you, Mr. Fli
lock, but I do not think you deserve the reward for t
return of the payroll. I think it should be shar
among the families of the enlisted men who di
trying to save it. Have you any objections? If you ha
speak up."

"I have no objection, Colonel," Flintlock said. "Seems fair to me."

"And you, O'Hara?"

The Indian shook his head. "Those colored boys deserve it."

"Very well then, but I will make one concession," McKenzie said. "As a reward for visiting on Carlos de Peralta the fate he deserved, you make take his palomino horse as my gift."

"That's very generous, Colonel," Flintlock said. "We sure do appreciate it. The palomino is a fine animal."

The office waved away Flintlock's thanks. "You may go now, but may I suggest something?"

"You sure can, Colonel," Flintlock said. "Suggest away."

"I strongly suggest that you and Mr. O'Hara take a bath at the first available opportunity."

CHAPTER SIXTY-TWO

Sam Flintlock relaxed in the unaccustomed luxury of his Excellency Don Carlos Lopez Peralta's French Imperial bathtub, a massive alabaster edifice resting on four silver-plated claw feet. It was, a soapy Flintlock decided, a tub fit for a king. Located in a whitewashed adobe, it was situated a discreet distance from the rear of the mission.

He'd made a few inquiries to a Mexican peon who'd served the general as a low-ranked factotum and the man had revealed the whereabouts of the bathtub and provided hot water and a large towel. Flintlock had said to O'Hara, the peon was a Mexican, but he played a white man . . . an observation he was later to regret.

As he scrubbed his back, Flintlock was singing the last verse of "O'er the Lea" when the door to the bathhouse opened and a slender young señorita stepped inside. He recognized her as the girl he'd seen on de Peralta's lap. She smiled and stepped toward the tub.

Flintlock was relieved that soap bubbles covered

his nakedness. "Howdy, señorita." Stating what was obvious, he said, "I'm taking a bath."

The girl smiled but said nothing.

Flintlock grinned in return. "Care to join me?"

The señorita smiled an enigmatic Mona Lisa. She stepped closer, her black eyes glittering. Suddenly her arm came from behind her back and the blade in her hand flashed. Narrowly avoiding the first downward slash, Flintlock scrambled to his feet, slipped on the tub's slick bottom, and crashed backwards. Soapy water cascaded around him soaking the stone floor.

The girl was on him like a tigress.

As her knife plunged for his throat, Flintlock managed to fight her off. He grabbed her slim right wrist and twisted. She squealed in pain and her knife dropped into the tub, landing between his thighs. Snarling in frustrated rage, her fingernails clawed for his eyes.

He grabbed both her wrists and pulled her into the tub. With remarkable strength she pushed on Flintlock's shoulders, forcing his head under the water. He came up choking and gasping for air and decided he'd had enough. Making the lacy blob of soap on the point of her chin the target of his fist, he clipped her hard, She went limp and fell on top of him.

Flintlock pushed the unconscious señorita off him, scrambled out of the tub, and covered himself with a towel. The girl lay on her back in the water, her red skirt and flurry of white petticoats soaked. Afraid she'd drown, he pulled her out of the tub and laid her on the floor.

He dressed hurriedly and when the girl began to show signs of recovering, he helped her to her feet.

She stood quietly for a few moments, her clothe dripping, luxuriant black hair falling limp and we over her shoulders. Looking down at her dishevele state, the señorita's pretty face took on an ugly expres sion and she said, "Pig dog!"

"Honey, is that the only English you know?"

She aimed a slap at his face

He grabbed her wrist, said, "Right. I've taken enough from you for one day," and shoved her out the bath house door. "Next time I see you I'll take a stick t you."

"Pig dog!" She flounced away, dripping water wit every step.

"What did you want me to do, shoot her?" Flintloc said.

"I guess not," O'Hara said. "Maybe Colone McKenzie would have shot her for you. She did try t kill you."

"She was mad clean through because she though it was me who killed the general. I can't blame her fo wanting to get even for the death of her feller."

O'Hara looked back at the sandy bush flats. "Wel she isn't following us."

Flintlock nodded. "That's a good thing."

An hour later, they crossed the Rio Grande and i felt good to be back on American soil. The sun wa high in the sky and cast no shadows on the grasslanc around them.

O'Hara cleared his throat. "Before we reach th Arizona Territory there's one thing I got to say, Sam.

"Talk away, O'Hara. I'm listening."

"Only this . . . if we see any women in distress, we leave them strictly alone and ride on. Do you savvy that?"

"Sure do. I'll leave them strictly alone." Flintlock grinned. "Until the next time."

TURN THE PAGE FOR AN EXCITING PREVIEW!

THE GREATEST WESTERN WRITER OF THE 21ST CENTURY

A western hero whose adventures embody the spirit of the American frontier, Smoke Jensen is bestselling author William W. Johnstone's most beloved creation. In his powerful new novel, Johnstone chronicles Smoke's early years. Before he went off in search of his father, long before he became a legend, Kirby Jensen was a young man trying to make a living with the gifts God gave him— courage, cunning, and lightening speed with a gun.

Kirby has just earned his first paying job as a deputy U.S. marshal for the Colorado Territory and is sent to Las Animas, where a band of ruthless outlaws have been robbing trains, cattle, banks, and anything else they can get their hands on. Then the real fight begins.

When Kirby strikes, he's all in. What happens next will become the stuff of legend, as Kirby braves bullets, blood, and treachery to face down the most dangerous outlaw in the Colorado Territory— and earn a reputation for justice and the rule of law on a lawless frontier.

National Bestselling Authors
WILLIAM W. JOHNSTONE
with J. A. Johnstone

THIS VIOLENT LAND
A Smoke Jensen Novel of the West

Coming in October 2016,
wherever Pinnacle Books are sold.

CHAPTER ONE

Northwest Colorado Territory, August 1870

The snowcapped crag known as Zenobia Peak towered above the two men on the small, grassy plain at its base. At some point in the past, a slab of rock in the shape of a crude rectangle had tumbled down into the field from those rugged slopes above. The rock was small enough that one man could move it— if he was a very strong man.

The rock sat up on its end, the passage of time having sunk its base slightly into the earth. That, along with the sheer weight of it, discouraged anyone from tampering with it—which was good because the stone marked a place special to the two men who stood beside it.

A simple legend was chiseled into the rock.

EMMETT JENSEN
BORN 1815 DIED 1869

The few words couldn't sum up the man's life. It took memories to do that.

Smoke Jensen stood at the grave of his father, his hat in his hands, and remembered.

The images that went through his mind seemed to have a red haze over them. *His father and his older brother Luke going off to war. The evil in human form riding up to the hardscrabble Jensen farm in the Missouri Ozarks. His sister being raped, his mother brutally gunned down. And the vengeance he had ultimately taken on the animals responsible for those atrocities, Billy Bartell and Angus Shardeen.*

Red was the color of that vengeance. Red for blood . . .

The memories cascaded faster and faster through his thoughts, out of all order. They were each part of what had made him the man he was. *Hearing about the death of his brother in the great conflict that had split the nation. His father's return after the war, to find nothing left to hold him and his son—the only remaining Jensens—on the farm. His sister Janey leaving. No telling where she was or if she was even still alive. And the day Emmett Jensen and his son, whose given name was Kirby, set off for the frontier, bound for the unknown.*

Battles with the Indians, meeting the old mountain man called Preacher who gave him his current name. "Smoke'll suit you just fine. So Smoke it'll be." His father's killing. The long and so far fruitless search for the men responsible.

Smoke scrubbed a boot in the dirt. *And the reputation building around him as one of the fastest guns the West had ever seen . . .*

Years of memories—long, bloody years—had come back to him in a matter of heartbeats.

He drew a deep breath and looked down at the rock-turned-tombstone, glad that time and the elements had not erased the words he had chiseled there. Preacher stood some distance away, having told Smoke that he needed some private time with his pa.

It was hard to know if Emmett could really hear him, but Smoke spoke to his father anyway, telling him what he had done, how he had settled part of the score for the wrongs done to the Jensen family.

And that he wasn't done yet. Not by a long shot.

He stood there in silence for another moment, then he put his hat on and turned toward Preacher.

"He was real proud of you, boy," the old mountain man said. "I know that for a fact. Same as I am."

The lump in Smoke's throat wouldn't let him reply.

"Where are you goin' now?" Preacher asked as they walked back to their horses.

"I'm heading back to Denver to turn in my badge. I don't reckon I'll be needing it anymore."

Preacher scratched his beard-stubbled jaw. "Oh, I wouldn't be so quick to do that, Smoke. A tin star can come in mighty handy from time to time." He paused, then added, "Most 'specially iffen you're still wantin' to go after them fellers what kilt your pa."

Denver, Colorado Territory

The low-lying building was made of white lime-stone. A United States flag flew from the flagpole out front, flapping gently in the breeze. Chiseled above the doorway were the words *United States Federal Office Building*.

Smoke Jensen, taller than most men, with shoulders someone once described as "wide as an axe handle" walked inside. On his shirt, he wore the star of a deputy U.S. marshal.

"Hello, Deputy Jensen," Annie Wilson greeted him as he hung his hat on the hat rack just inside the door. Middle-aged but still quite attractive, she flashed him a welcoming smile.

"Hello, Miss Wilson. Is the marshal in?"

Uriah B. Holloway was the chief U.S. marshal for the Colorado District. A while back, he had appointed Smoke as a deputy U.S. marshal for the purposes of locating Angus Shardeen, who had once ridden with John Brown and had personally taken part in the Pottawatomie Massacre in which several pro-Southern sympathizers were murdered.

After John Brown's death, Shardeen had started his own group and made his presence known by burning homes and killing innocents in Southwest Missouri. Shardeen had killed Smoke's mother, then stood by and watched as his men had used Smoke's sister Janey.

Smoke would have gone after Shardeen anyway, but the appointment, though temporary and without pay, had made his vendetta legal.

"He's in his office, Deputy. If you wait just a moment, I'll let him know you're here."

Smoke walked over to look through the window as Annie went into the office to announce him. He saw a couple boys sitting on the ground with their legs spread, playing mumblety-peg with a pocketknife.

"Ha! You lose, you lose! You have to root the peg out with your teeth!" one of the boys said triumphantly.

Smoke smiled as he recalled playing that game with his brother, back before the war. They'd played a different variation of the game. The object had been to see who could throw the knife into the ground and stick it the closest to their own foot. When Luke left for the war, he was still carrying a scar on his right foot from where he had thrown the knife too close.

That was a much more innocent time. In fact, as Smoke thought back on it, it was the only innocent time he had ever known in his entire life.

"Deputy Jensen?" Annie said, coming out of Holloway's office. "The marshal will see you now."

"Thank you, Miss Wilson."

Holloway was standing behind his desk when Smoke stepped into his office. "Hello, Smoke," he greeted as he extended his hand.

Smoke took it and shook.

"How's that old horse thief, Preacher?"

"Preacher's doing well," Smoke said, speaking of the man who had become not only his mentor but also the closest thing he had to a father since his own pa had been killed.

He took the badge from his shirt and placed it on the desk in front of Marshal Holloway.

"What's that for?" Holloway asked with a puzzled frown.

"I want to thank you, Marshal, for putting your trust in me and making me your temporary deputy. That helped me take care of my business."

"It wasn't just your business, Smoke. If it had been, I would have never let you put on that star in the first place. There were federal warrants out for Shardeen and his men." Holloway pointed to the star. "There's too much prestige attached to wearing that badge, and too many men have died defending its honor, to give it out to just anyone. I would have never let you wear it if I hadn't thought you deserved it."

"I appreciate the trust, Marshal."

"Do you appreciate it enough to wear that star permanently? With proper compensation, I hasten to add."

"Are you offering me a full-time job, Marshal?" Smoke asked.

"Yes. You do need a job, don't you? I mean, you don't plan to eat off Preacher's table forever, do you?"

Smoke laughed, admitting, "I am getting a little tired of game and wild vegetables." He reached for the star, picked it up, and held it for a long moment, examining it.

He looked up at the man across from him. "Marshal, you do know that I'm after Richards, Potter, and Stratton, don't you?"

"Those are the men who killed your brother?"

"Yes, sir. And as far as I've been able to determine, they aren't wanted anywhere."

"You suspect that they killed your father, too, don't you?"

"I more than suspect. I know they did."

Marshal Holloway held up his finger. "Listen to me carefully, Smoke. You *suspect* they killed your father, don't you?"

Smoke wasn't sure where the marshal was going with that statement, but he picked up on the inference. "Yes, sir, I suspect they did."

"Then as a deputy U.S. marshal, you can always hold them on suspicion of murder."

"You do know, don't you, Marshal, that they aren't going to let me do that?"

Marshal Holloway smiled. "You mean they might resist arrest?"

"Yeah, they might." Smoke smiled, too. "They might even resort to gunplay in resisting."

"Well, as a deputy U.S. marshal, you would be fully and legally authorized to counter force with force."

"All right, Marshal." Smoke pinned the star back onto his shirt. "You've just hired yourself a new deputy."

Holloway shook his hand. "And now you'll be drawing forty dollars a month and expenses."

"Sounds good to me."

"But I'll be expecting you to do more than just look for those three men. Are you ready to start earning your pay?"

That surprised Smoke. "You have a job for me already?"

"Yeah," Holloway said. "I want you to go to Red Cliff over in Summit County. Go see Sheriff Emerson Donovan. He's a friend of mine . . . who was once my deputy, by the way. An outbreak of cattle rustling is so severe it's causing some of the ranchers to go out of business."

"Cattle rustling? Wouldn't that be a state crime?"

Holloway smiled. "It would be, if we were a state. But Colorado is still a territory, therefore any crime that's committed here is a federal crime." He handed Smoke a piece of paper. "Here is an arrest warrant signed by a federal judge. You can put whatever name or names on it that you need."

"What if the names are Stratton, Potter, and Richards?"

"Who knows? Someday, those may be just the names you put on there."

CHAPTER TWO

Bury, Idaho Territory

The town began as a "Hell on Wheels" settlement. As an End of Track location during the building of the Union Pacific, there had been high hopes for the town in the beginning. It had a bank, probably the best school building—a large two-story—in that part of the country, and a weekly newspaper, the *Bury Bulletin.* Businesses included a large mercantile store, several saloons and cafés, a large hotel, a leather shop, and a brothel. It boasted a sheriff, a deputy, and a jail. A handful of ranches and a lot of producing mines lay around the town, as well.

Nearly all of it was owned by three men—Muley Stratton, Wiley Potter, and Josh Richards.

Some citizens resented the presence of the three men, believing that they were bad for the town. Others thought differently.

"You have to admit that the town has grown considerably since they arrived," someone had said.

"Yes, but grown how?" asked another, pointing out that there were more saloons than any other type of business. "Most of the newcomers who work for Potter, Stratton, and Richards are riffraff of the lowest element. Why, I believe most of them are gunfighters and outlaws. How can a town grow, and survive, with such people?"

What was not owned by Stratton, Potter and Richards was the Pink House.

Billing her business as a "Sporting House for Gentlemen," Flora Yancey even advertised her services in the town, hiring boys to tack up handbills.

> *The Pink House*
> *Is a Sporting House for Gentlemen*
> *Where Beautiful and Cultured Ladies*
> *Will provide you with every*
> *Pleasure*

She made no apologies about running a brothel. "Why should I be ashamed of it?" she would reply to anyone who questioned her. "I give my girls a clean place to stay and I insist that the gentlemen callers be on their best behavior. If they are not well-behaved, I don't let them return."

Flora had been in town for more than four years, having arrived as a member of a theater group. The owner of the repertoire company for which she'd worked had lost all the box-office receipts in an after-show poker game. Rather than face his troupe with the disgrace of his betrayal, he'd made an attempt to recover the money at the point of a gun. That attempt

had failed, and he was shot dead. He now lay buried
in the Bury Cemetery under a marker sporting an
epitaph.

> *Here lies McKinley Hall*
> *A thespian of renown*
> *He took his final curtain call*
> *When one slug from a .44 put him down*

Disgruntled and betrayed, the rest of the theater
company had left town, but Flora, seeing potential
business opportunities, had stayed. She was a beautiful woman and her role in the theater had inflamed
the fantasies of many men. She knew that she had
only to play upon those fantasies to become very successful. It was rumored that she had once been the
mistress of Crown Prince Ferdinand of Austria. Another rumor had it as Prince Leopold of Belgium.

Whenever questioned as to whether or not the
rumors were true, and if so, just which crowned head
had she been with, Flora always replied, "A lady never
informs upon the indiscretions of gentlemen of station." She knew that such rumors fed the fantasies of
men who wanted to "do it with a woman who had done
it with a prince," so she did nothing to dispel the rumors.

When Flora had made enough money she'd built
the Pink House and hired only the most attractive
women she could find. She then went into semiretire-
ment, preferring to manage the affairs of "her girls"
over providing her personal services to the customers.

Janey Jensen, who had been calling herself Janey
Garner, sat in the parlor of the Pink House with
Flora, one of her "girls" named Emma—no las

ame available—and Sally Reynolds, the local school-
acher.

Sally had met Janey the day she first arrived in Bury
id found herself in the middle of a shoot-out. Shortly
iereafter, Sally had learned that the Pink House was
 brothel, that Flora was the owner or madam of that
ouse, and that Janey Garner was not only the busi-
ess manager of the PSR Ranch, she was also the
iistress of Josh Richards, who was the majority owner
f the ranch.

Despite what she'd learned, Sally passed no judg-
ient on anyone. On the contrary, Flora and Janey
ad become her closest friends. She'd also become
iends with all the girls who worked at the Pink House.

At the moment, Emma was Sally's partner in a game
f whist. It became obvious that they were losing the
and.

Emma sighed. "Oh dear. I'm afraid I overbid the
eal. I'm such a nincompoop."

"Nonsense, you are just a woman who bids with a
egree of unbridled courage," Sally said, and the
thers laughed.

As the game continued, conversation picked up.

"You being from the Northeast, you more'n likely
idn't see much of the war, did you," Emma asked
ally, making the sentence more a declarative state-
ient than a question.

"I didn't see any of the war, except for what I read
1 the newspapers," Sally replied.

"You were lucky," Emma said. "I lived in Corinth,
lississippi. We had a very big battle real close by."

"Yes, I read about Pittsburg Landing," Sally acknowl-
dged. Emma shook her head. "No, it was Shiloh."

"In the South, you called it Shiloh. In the North, v called it Pittsburg Landing."

"How odd. Well, I remember all those wounde boys being brought into town. I was very young the but I remember it very well. Wounded boys were lyir out on the lawns of people's houses, on their fror porches, even." Emma shook her head again ar sighed at the memory. "It was just awful."

Sally reached across and put her hand on Emma "Oh, you poor dear. I'm sure it must have been ba for you."

"Let's change the subject. I see no reason we shou talk about such horrid things." Janey had her ow terrible memories of the war, memories that sh didn't want to share. "Tell us about New York," she sa to Sally. "I know you once said you had been there."

"Yes, I've been there. I have an aunt who liv there."

"Oh, please do tell us about it," Emma said.

"It is almost indescribable. Trains whiz along c elevated tracks throughout the city. The streets a crowded with carriages and wagons that never see to stop. And at night the entire city uses gaslights, that when you look out your window it is as if you a gazing at a huge, sparkling jewel.

"But it is most impressive at Christmas. All th stores, even the lampposts, are decorated for the hc iday. Swags of green are stretched between lamppos from one side of the street to the other so that whe you travel, you are traveling under a green canopy."

"Did you ever attend the Woods Museum an Metropolitan Theater?" Flora asked.

"Yes. I saw a delightful production there, called
:ion."

Flora laughed. "I was in that production."

"Oh, my!" Sally said. "How wonderful to meet
>meone famous!"

"I wasn't famous, dear. I was just one of the women
earing tights and a bodice that revealed my bosom."

"Oh, I would love to go to New York one of these
ays," Emma said. "But I know I never will."

"Why not?" Sally asked.

"Because I think such a large place would just scare
1e to death," Emma replied breathlessly.

"Besides, I could never let her go," Flora said. "If I
id, I'm afraid all the cowboys who have fallen in love
ith her would riot in protest."

"Yes ma'am, we more'n likely would." Unnoticed, a
owboy had come into the parlor at that precise
1oment. He stood there holding his hat in his hand.

"Do you see what I mean?" Flora asked with a little
huckle.

Janey recognized him as one of the cowboys who
orked at the PSR Ranch, and she knew that he was
robably there for her. "Hello, Cecil, are you looking
>r me?"

"Yes, ma'am, I am. Mr. Richards, he sent me to
 tch you."

"To *fetch* me? Is that what he said?" The inflection
f Janey's voice displayed her irritation at the word.

"Well, uh, no ma'am. He didn't quite put it like
hat. What he said was, would I go to town and find
ou and bring you back."

"What if I don't want to go back?"

"If you don't want to go, I don't reckon there anything I could do about it," Cecil said. "But M Richards would more 'n likely be atakin' it out on m if I was to go back to the ranch without you."

"All right," Janey said, smiling. "I wouldn't want see you get in trouble. Go on back. You may tell hi that I'll be there, shortly."

"Ma'am, if it's all the same to you, I'd just as soc ride alongside your surrey."

Flora set her cards on the table. "You don't have go back, Janey. You don't have to go back ever. Ju tell Richards that you've decided to come work for me

Janey laughed. "Ha, wouldn't he like that?"

"Why do you work for him, anyway? You coul make as much money here as you do working for hir You could make even more money. I know you don have any qualms about our business because someor could say you are doing the same thing for Richards

"That's true," Janey said, making no attempt deny the charge that she was Richards's mistress.

"And, my dear, your position with him is tenuous best. Someone is going to shoot him dead one these days. Richards's enterprises, by your own adm sion, are suspect."

"That's true as well."

Janey had no idea that the men she was workin for were the same men who had killed her father. Sh didn't know, and had no way of knowing, that h father was dead. She had no idea that someon named Smoke was looking for her employers. Even someone had told her that he was, it wouldn't hav meant anything to her. She didn't know anyon

med Smoke. As far as she knew, her brother, if he
s still alive, was named Kirby.

nver

Because there was train service from Denver to Red
iff, Smoke decided to board his horse at a local
ery stable while he was gone.

"Seven?" the hostler asked. "Your horse's name is
ven?"

"Yes."

"Why did you name him that?"

"I didn't. He named himself. Look." Smoke
inted to the white markings on the horse's face.
ie markings formed the perfect numeral seven.

The stable man nodded. "Yeah, I see what you
ean. Well, don't you worry none about Seven while
u're gone. He's in good hands."

Seven looked over at Smoke, who smiled and
atted him on the face. "You be a good horse for this
ce gentleman. Just rest for a while. I'll be back
on."

Leaving the stable, Smoke walked down to the
:pot, where he bought a round-trip train ticket with
voucher that Marshal Holloway had given him. "Is
e train on time?"

"We got a telegram from its last stop," the ticket
;ent said. "It's runnin' no more than fifteen minutes
so late. It won't be too much longer. Just have a
at and make yourself comfortable, Deputy."

"Thanks, I will." He bought a newspaper, then took
seat on one of the padded benches in the waiting
om.

A young mother was sitting just across from him,

and he touched the brim of his hat in greeting. S
nodded her head in reply. Her son was sitting on
floor in front of her, playing with a carved horse a
wagon.

Smoke began carefully reading the newspap
looking, as he always did, for any mention of t
names Richards, Stratton, or Potter. It didn't se
likely that he would find them as easily as seeing th
names in the paper, but he didn't want to leave a
stone unturned. People like those three might wi
up with their names in the paper. If there were
wanted posters out on them, they would have
reason to worry so he was pretty sure they would
vain enough to have their names in the paper for j
about any occasion.

After a long perusal of the paper, he put it asi
writing it off as a fruitless attempt.

"Folks, the train for Golden, Central City, Eag
Glenwood Springs, and points west has arrived
track number three," the ticket agent said, holdin
speaking tube to his mouth. "If you are holding ti
ets for that train, you need to proceed to track numl
three now."

The town of Red Cliff wasn't announced, b
Smoke knew it was between Central City and Eagle

"Mama, that's our train!" the little boy shoute
and started running toward the door.

"Johnny, come back here!" his mother called out
panic.

Getting up quickly, Smoke ran after the boy, swe
him up in his arms, and brought him back to I
mother.

"Oh, thank you, sir," the grateful mother said. "

is so excited about this train trip. I fear he might get too close to the track and get careless."

Smoke tapped the star on his shirt. "You see this badge?" he said to the boy.

The boy nodded.

"I'm a United States marshal, and if you don't want to get into trouble with me, you'll stay close to your mother. Do you understand?"

"Yes, sir," the boy replied in an awed voice.

The mother smiled. "Thank you again. He'll stay close to me now. He doesn't want to go to jail. Do you, Johnny?"

Johnny reached up to take his mother's hand. "No, ma'am. I don't want to go to jail."

"Then you hold my hand, and we'll go outside together to board the train."

"Yes, Mama."

Outside the depot was the smell of smoke under the car shed, though the roof was high enough that the smoke wasn't oppressive. Six tracks could be seen under the shed, with concrete walks extending out between them. Four of the tracks were currently occupied, including track number three.

Smoke glanced toward the faces in the windows of the cars in the train on track number two, which was slowly pulling out of the station. He wondered, in passing, if one of them might be Stratton or Potter or Richards.

He had never seen Richards, but Smoke somehow knew he would recognize the man if he saw him. He couldn't explain exactly how—just something in his gut.

He climbed aboard his train and settled into his seat, then stared out the window as the train departed the station, rolled through the city, and finally into the unsettled countryside.

His assignment had nothing to do with finding the three men he had sworn to bring to justice, but the badge would give him more flexibility in his search.

When he asked questions from behind that star, the response was a little quicker and more detailed. The biggest advantage to the badge was that it gave him the freedom an ordinary citizen wouldn't have when taking the law into his own hands.

He didn't have to worry about that. He *was* the law

CHAPTER THREE

As Janey drove the surrey down the road toward
he PSR Ranch in response to Josh Richards's sum-
ons, the clop of the hoof beats, not only of the horse
ulling the surrey, but also the one Cecil was riding,
uilt a cocoon of sound around her, allowing her to
ink without distraction. She considered Flora's offer
 come work for her, and she knew that the idea
asn't all that far-fetched. She had worked in such a
lace before, for a madam in Dallas known as Chicago
ue. Sue had given her the name she had used for a
hile, Fancy Lil.

It was during that time of her life she had met the
an known as Big Ben Conyers, one of her customers
ho had wanted more than an hour of lust, paid for
d promptly forgotten. He had fallen in love with
ancy Lil," who was touched enough by his devotion
 reveal her real name.

With more between them, Janey had gotten preg-
ant. When she heard the news, Big Ben had been

eager to marry her. He had even taken her to his va
Live Oaks Ranch, north of Fort Worth, and seen to
that she had the best of care until she gave birth
their daughter, beautiful redheaded Rebecca. Jane
had promised Ben that they would be married as soo
as she recovered from giving birth.

Instead, she had cut and run, unwilling to sadd
him with the disgrace of marrying a fallen woma
And she never, ever wanted Rebecca to hear the
cious taunts of other children about her mother bei
a kept woman. She wouldn't doom a child to that so
of life.

It had been easier to leave, knowing that Be
would raise Rebecca with all the love in his gigant
heart. Easier . . . and at the same time, the most dif
cult thing Janey Jensen had ever done in her misa
venture of a life.

"There's Mr. Richards out on the front porch
Cecil said as they approached the house. His com
ment broke her reverie. "I'll put your horse an
surrey away, ma'am."

"Thank you, Cecil." Janey brought the surrey to
halt, then stepped down and handed the reins to th
young cowboy, who led both horses toward the bar
As she approached the porch she could see th
Richards was impatient and irritated.

"Well, I see that ignorant cowhand found you."

Janey climbed the steps to the porch, which e
tended all the way around the big house. "What o
you want, Josh? I told you I was going into town fo
while."

"No doubt to visit with Flora."

"Flora is my friend."

"She is also a madam who runs a brothel," Richards
...id derisively. "If people see you going there enough
...mes, they'll believe you're one of the same."

"What makes you think they don't believe that
...ow?" Janey asked. "They all know what I am. It's just
...at I'm *yours*."

"You don't have to be. You could be my wife, you
...ow."

Janey started to reply that she would rather be what
...e was than be his wife, but she held that response in
...eck and forced a smile. "I know that, Josh. And I ap-
...reciate the offer. But let's leave things as they are for
...ow. I enjoy being the business manager for this
...nch. It gives me a sense of purpose."

"But wouldn't being my wife give you a sense of
...urpose?"

"Not as much. If we were married, I would lose my
...entity as business manager and just be the wife of
...ne of the owners."

"The majority owner," Richards said quickly.

Again, Janey managed a smile. "Yes, you would be
...e majority owner, but I would still be just your wife.
...osh, don't you see that it's better this way? Besides,
...hy do you need to marry me? Don't I share your bed
...om time to time? And don't you know that wives get
...eadaches a lot more often than mistresses?"

Richards laughed. "By damn, you're right. Anyway,
...at's not why I had Cecil come get you. I need a
...aper signed by someone in Denver, and I want you
... take it there in person, get it signed, and bring it
...ack to me."

"I'll need five hundred dollars," Janey said without
...esitating an instant.

"Five hundred dollars?" His eyebrows rose surprise. "Janey, are you telling me that you a going to charge me five hundred dollars to take paper to Denver and bring it back?"

"I'm not going to charge you anything to take paper to Denver. My goodness, if I couldn't do simple thing like that for free, why, I would be t biggest ingrate you ever heard of."

"So you aren't going to charge me for deliveri the paper?"

"Of course not," Janey said. "Why would I do som thing like that? It's like I told you, I'm doing that f free."

"I don't understand. What is the five hundred d lars for?"

"Darling, you don't expect me to go to Denver a not buy several new outfits, do you? That five hundr dollars is just a gift. After all, I know you want me look good. And don't tell me you can't afford it, da ling, because I do your books, remember? I know fu well that you can afford it."

Richards looked at her with narrowed eyes for moment, then abruptly laughed. "You know what? mistress would be a lot cheaper."

"And a wife a lot more expensive," Janey r minded him.

He held up his hands in mock surrender. "All rigl all right. You got me. I'll give you five hundred dolla for the trip. But I expect you to come back lookir more beautiful than ever."

"You are a dear." With a smile that produced dir ples, she kissed the end of her fingers, then touche them to Richards's lips.